PANTS TEAM PINK

SHAMELESS PROMOTIONAL ADVENTURE

(SPACE JUNK BOOK 4)

ANDREW BIXLER

PIP

Books by Andrew Bixler

Space Junk: Beginning no End

Space Junk

More Space Junk

The Deaths of Adam Jones
(Space Junk Book 3)

Pants Team Pink: Shameless Promotional Adventure
(Space Junk Book 4)

For
Alex, Melissa, Abbey, Shannon, Jessie, Meghan,
and Sean

Special thanks to Meghan Lear for cleaning up these
words and to Gary Bixler for providing the interior
illustrations.

ACT 1

Wake Up, Team!
The Adventure Starts Now!!

1

"We return to find our happy-go-lucky heroes trapped inside the ancient, antiseptic halls of academia, surrounded by busted lockers and low on cheer as they battle the evil principal Crotch Licker. Facing a space week's detention for a coordinated effort to protest the cafeteria's institutional grade Z rations, the team is the only thing standing between edible lunches and certain punishment."

"Your plan for school domination will never succeed, Crotch Licker!" Pants cries, her pink pigtails glittering in the gloomy hallway as she holds her fingers up in the Pants sign. "You're not a princi-*pal* at all."

Recoiling at the universal symbol of kiddom, the dastardly disciplinarian says, *"My name is* Kretchler, *and I have no idea what you're talking about. But I want whatever illicit team activities you have planned to stop this instant."*

"Don't play dumb with us, Crotch Licker," Beer retorts, straightening his thick glasses as he backs up their

bubbly leader. *"Your whole thing is knowledge, or learning, or whatever."*

Having kept uncharacteristically tight-lipped, a mischievous smirk suddenly forms on The One's round, mustard-stained face as he reaches into his sweatshirt pocket.

The evil pedagogue immediately recognizes the look and warns the boy, *"Don't even think about it."*

But the insubordination in The One's grin only intensifies as he emerges with a smushed ration cake slathered in pink frosting. *"If there's one thing you should know about me by now,"* he says as he carefully peels back the thin layer of cellophane protecting his after-school treat, *"I never think."*

"Wait!" Horton yells, reaching his pale arm toward the creamy confection.

But by the time he manages to reach the chubby boy, it's already too late. The team looks on with varying degrees of terror and delight as the cupcake soars down the hallway. Crotch Licker is so startled by their total lack of respect for the rules that he doesn't even try to move out of the way.

The cake lands on the principal's starched shirt with a satisfying *THWACK*, followed by the type of silence that can only be found after class, when the ever-present chatter of the school day gives way to the deserted halls of late afternoon.

As the pallor of Crotch Licker's rigid face transforms from a healthy yellow to an outraged orange, The One announces, *"His power is growing!"*

"Pants Team Piiink!" the villain bellows. *"My office, now!"*

Sensing the team's ability to disobey fading, Beer laments, "His authority is too strong. I don't think we can beat him…"

The scene freezes on the team staring down their frosted foe, and as the end theme creeps in, the narrator asks, *"Is there anything that can foil the evil principal's plan for lunchroom domination, or will it be rations for our heroes? Find out next time, on* Pants Team Pink!"

"Aww, right at the good part," Todd moans as the credits begin to roll.

The chaotic scene to which he's greeted when he lifts his sleep visor leaves him wishing he could go on a permanent video vacation. A testament to just how much trash four unattended kids with near-unlimited resources can produce, Todd's room - AKA the ship's communal bridge - is littered with enough moldy ration trays, candy wrappers, and rejected merch to render the floor nearly impassible. The instant he turns off the noise-cancellation on his phone, he's bombarded by the cacophonous racket which has come to serve as the space-hellish soundtrack to his chitty life.

He lets out a miserable whimper, and just as he's ready to let his horrid surroundings consume him once and for all, The One wanders past and questions, "You're watching those old episodes *again?* Don't you ever get sick of them?"

"These old episodes are some of the best in the series," Todd informs the boy. "And they're currently the only thing keeping me from having a psychotic break and murdering all of you in your sleep."

With the bottom of his stomach poking out from under his team t-shirt, The One locates an unopened ration in a disorganized heap on the kitchen counter and glances warily at his merchly friend. "Well, I'll leave you to it."

"Wait!" Todd cries. "Sit, eat…"

"I don't really like eating out here with all the noise," The One says, referring to the relentless pounding, drilling, and braying produced by the seemingly endless renovations being performed on the *Cuddler*.

Calling upon some distant memory of what it was like to feel joy, Todd forces his lips into a tortured grin and shouts, "What noise?"

With a wary shrug, The One throws his tray down on the table, and Todd watches as the boy rips open the expired promotional ration and starts gobbling down its bright pink contents.

When The One finally glances up from his malted meal to find his shipmate staring at him, he asks, "You want some?"

"Fish no," Todd says. "I mean, I think we need to have a team meeting."

"*Brahhh*," The One belches, briefly breaking his feast. "That sounds like… what do you call it? Not fun. Also, the rest of the team is still asleep."

"The space day's already half over!" Todd cries, losing what little brule he had left. "You think *I'm* having fun? While you guys lay around in your soundproof cabins, with your blackout blinds and cushy *beds*, I'm stuck out here on the couch using old ration wrappers to keep out the midnight sun as the never-ending sounds of clanging metal bore into my skull. You know how long the days last out here. These Park donkeys never stop working!"

Spitting out flecks of pink sludge, The One says, "I knew you could hear it!"

"Of course I can hear it!" the merch guy moans, collapsing onto the table. "But that's not the worst part. I'm afraid if we don't do something soon, we're not going to be able to afford to keep up this horrendous lifestyle." Clearly failing to get through to his full-bellied shipmate, Todd decides to put it in words the boy will understand. "That means no more 'studying abroad,' which means back to school for you."

"*What?!*" The One suddenly ceases stuffing his face and lets his chopsticks clatter to the table in outrage. "This injustice will not stand! Wait, you're not talking about the movie, right?"

"No."

"Then this injustice will not stand!" For a brief moment, the kid stands up with his stomach out and his fists on his hips in true heroic fashion. But after a moment, he slumps back down into his seat.

"So, are you going to wake the team?" Todd asks.

"Yes," the boy says, "as soon as I'm done tackling this ration."

When lunch is over, The One spends the better part of the afternoon assembling his teammates and shoving junk off the living room furniture so they have a place to sit.

Once most of the melted candy and hardened gum has been peeled off the cushions, Todd tells them, "You're probably wondering why I asked The One to gather you for this meeting."

"Eh," Beer says, his hair tousled and glasses askew as he taps at the thin sheet of glass in his hand.

"Well, I'm going to tell you anyway," the merch guy says. "Maybe you haven't noticed, but since the Pants Con, the show's ratings have tanked. Fans have begun jumping ship at an alarming rate."

"We still have a lot of fans!" Pants argues from inside her officially licensed *princessfluffypants* pajamas. "The real fans will always stick by us."

"Be that as it may…," Todd grumbles, "pretty—"

"Thank you," Pants cuts him off.

Todd pauses to give the others a chance to interrupt him before he continues, "*Pants Team Pink* is about to go broke. Between the Xenodorks and all the other teams that have formed since the Pants Con, you have more competition for eyeballs than ever. Add to that the failure of *Pants Team Pink: The Movie The Sequel* and the ballooning cost of fixing the *Cuddler*, and you're going to wind up facing a foe unlike anything you've ever encountered – crippling debt. If we don't do something soon, the show is going to lose its top spot in the ratings, and we're going to wind up back on the streets of Earth begging for crits."

When the weight of what Todd is telling the team finally sinks in enough to make them lower their phones, Horton tells the others, "He's right, of course. I've been keeping an eye on the numbers. Viewers are down, merch sales are down, expenses are up. It doesn't look good."

"How could this have happened so soon?" Beer asks. "The con didn't go exactly like we planned, but it's only been a few space days."

"That was a whole space month ago," Todd informs the boy. "That's like a space year in TV time. What's up with you, anyway? You're usually the responsible one. Suddenly you're not getting out of bed until the ack crack of noon."

"Well, you know the old space saying," Beer says. "If you can't beat 'em, fish 'em. Also, look who's talking."

"I prefer *Look Who's Talking Too*," The One interjects.

Ignoring his little brother, Beer tells Todd, "You're supposed to be our fearless merch guy. What the fish happened?"

"Maybe you should ask The One," Todd suggests. "Do you have any idea how many crits we blew on defective black gold replicas?"

"Hey, you know the old space saying," The One argues. "Quantity is number one, or something."

Jumping in with her singular brand of sense, Pants cries, "Would you guys stop fighting and just love each other?!"

"Unfortunately, I think we're going to need more than love to save us this time," Horton assesses, and turning to Todd, he asks, "So, what do you suggest?"

"I've called in a fixer," Todd tells them. "An expert in publicity, he's going to help us get the show back on track. He should be here any space minute."

As if waiting for the right moment to interrupt, the *Cuddler's* doorbell mewls, "*MEOOOW!*"

2

The heavily vandalized elevator doors slide open to reveal the discarded ephemera from a space month worth of Playland sugar binges, along with a strange, yet familiar equine.

"You got a space toilet?" the sweaty mule asks, his floppy ears tied down to keep the construction noise out.

Pointing over his shoulder, The One mouths, "It's in the back."

"How the fish is one of the *Cuddler*'s mechanics gonna help us get our viewers back?" Beer demands.

"That's not him," Todd grumbles, the space months living inside the pink ship evidently having taken its toll. His black mane looks even greasier than usual, and if Beer could remember what day it is, he'd swear the merch guy has been wearing the same limited edition

'Down With XDorksX' t-shirt for the last space week. Smells like it too.

"There he is," Todd says, and as soon as the mule clomps away from the door, a far filthier creature emerges from the back of the flickering box.

Clad in a white Park polo and pleated khakis, his hair parted in such a way as to illicit maximum annoyance from his onetime teammates, The Other One greets them, "Hey, you guys!"

"Uh-uh," Beer says, incredulous. "No way."

"Just give him a chance," Todd pleads.

"He told us he was going to join the Xenodorks!" Pants cries. "What's he doing here?"

"Think of me as an independent contractor," The Other One says. "Pants Team member, Xenodork… I am many things to many fans."

Giving his younger half a skeptical once-over, The One snatches a baggie of celery out of the kid's pocket and tells him, "You sicken me."

"Hear him out," Todd suggests, motioning to the trash pile surrounding them. "It can't be worse than *this*."

"I don't know…," Beer says. "I still don't trust him. What do you think, Horton?"

Scrutinizing their unofficial fifth member's chidiotic grin, Horton rubs his bloodshot eyes and says, "Listening to anything this replicant has to say seems like an astoundingly chidiotic idea. But I've been up all night learning how to program in SCUMM so I can make my own historically accurate point-and-click adventure games, and I'm too tired to think of a better one."

Before any of them can argue, Todd tempts them into the living room with the promise of limited edition candied rations, and the team reluctantly complies, dragging their feet in protest.

As they impatiently wait for their would-be teammate to rummage through his briefcase and hook up his presentation to the *Cuddler*'s projector, Beer tells the kid, "We don't need you to put on a show. Just tell us your plan so we can tell you to fish off."

"Aright, aright." Glancing around for a place to sit amongst the sticky furniture, The Other One finally decides, "I'll just stand."

"I think we've heard enough," The One declares.

Frantically waving his hands, The Other One cries, "Wait, I'm going!" With an awkward smirk, he pulls his shoulders back and clears his throat. "Right about now, you might be asking yourselves, 'Why should we trust this kid with the future of our show? Sure, he may be abnormally brule and a fan favorite character, but what can he do for us?'"

"He's abnormal, all right," The One interjects, reaching over Horton to high-five Beer.

Left hanging, The Other One goes on, "While it's true that the Xenodorks have gained an unprecedented increase in fans following their appearance at the Pants Con, it wasn't enough to outpace Pants Team Pink. It's proof that you guys are the main draw. But even with all those fans, I see the potential for you to grow your audience in a way no show has done before. What I'm proposing is a universe-spanning publicity tour to embiggen your fan base, kicked off by a cromulent new adventure!"

"Wait a space second," Beer says. "Are you suggesting we fly back home and dig through all the replicas and other junk clogging Earth's atmosphere to look for the black gold again? That doesn't sound very fun at all."

A wry smile forms on The Other One's annoying face, revealing the large gap between his two front teeth as he tells them, "What I'm proposing is even more radical – not searching for the black gold."

A confused hush falls over the team as they glance at each other out of the corners of their eyes, wordlessly communicating what they're all thinking – the kid has lost what little brains he had to begin with.

"Before you send me to the ball pits, hear me out," The Other One says. "Interest in the black gold is at an all-time low. It's yesterday's news. Your fans want something new. Plus, there's the not-so-small complication of The Mighty Big Guy declaring a no-fly zone around Earth, shooting down any ship that comes within collecting distance and jamming detectors across the planet. Combine that with the fact that most of the replicas are virtually indistinguishable from the real thing, and the mission becomes unaffordable."

Running the numbers through his phone, Horton grudgingly announces, "He's right."

"You can thank me for designing such high-quality merch," The One says.

"That's real good work," Beer tells his brother. "But if we're not gonna look for the black gold, we're gonna need something even better to lure the fans. So, what's your big idea, Other One?"

"I'm glad you asked," the boy says. "But for marketing purposes, I must ask that you refer to me as *The* Other One."

Rolling his eyes, Beer says, "Anything for the sake of merchandise. Please go on, Duh Other One. I mean, *The* Other One."

Evidently satisfied with this pronunciation, The Other One continues, "I'm sure you've all heard stories about The Dark Side of the Park and the abandoned playground that was built there."

The words pique Horton's interest. "You mean the rumors are true?"

The Other One offers the team a solemn nod and explains, "Deep within the shadows, which for most of the space year blot out half the planet, lies a cursed attraction. Described by ancient advertisements as the scariest destination in The Park, it's said that once you go in, you can never come out."

"Sounds like a bunch of backspace marketing to me," Beer scoffs.

"Legend has it that the fabled attraction is haunted," The Other One announces, prompting Pants to let out a short squeal. "It's just a gimmmick, I'm sure. But it is said that the attraction contains a rare merch item which can be obtained only by those who survive its horrors."

"And I suppose you want us to find this rare collectible," Beer concludes.

"Exactly," The Other One says. "It's the perfect setup for a rebrand. It's got everything – mystery, danger, merch… We'll call it, *The* New *Adventures of Pants Team Pink featuring The Other One.*"

"What about me?" Todd complains.

"And Todd," the kid amends.

"This almost sounds dodgy enough to work," Horton says. "But why would you want to help us? What do you get out of it?"

"That's simple," The Other One tells them. "I get the satisfaction of helping the greatest team in the universe stay on top. And there's the small additional possibility that if I do a good job you might consider making me an official member."

Eagerly looking around at the team, Todd says, "So… what do you think?"

"What I think…," Beer says, pausing for dramatic effect, "is that we'd be better off trying to figure out what the fish all the newly self-aware NPCs in *Immaterial Girl* are up to. I know they're planning something."

"Yeah, this sounds too scary," Pants says. "I'd rather do something like, you know, not this."

Muttering his dissent, Horton adds, "I agree with Beer. The NPCs are definitely up to something. Anyway, even if this haunted playground really exists, which I find highly unlikely, space centuries of neglect have surely left it in a state of hazardous disrepair. I'm scared too, but not so much of ghosts as crumbling infrastructure."

"Oh, come on!" Todd moans. "What about you, The One? Doesn't a haunted adventure sound like fun?"

"Huh?" The One says, the sound of his name suddenly rousing him to attention. "Are we still talking about that?"

"I guess that's that," Beer says. "Thanks but no thanks, there's ration coupons by the elevator, and we'll see you… around."

But as the team moves to disperse, Todd awkwardly jumps up to block their escape, warning them, "Before you leave, remember that this could be your last chance to save the team from irrelevance. Not only that, but without you guys, there won't be anyone left to stop the Xenodorks from filling the programming void."

Biting her shiny lip, Pants decides, "Maybe Todd's right, you guys. It's been a long time since we've been on a real adventure. If the Dorks gain control of the schedule, there's no telling what pranks they might pull. Plus, scary adventures *are* fun!"

"I guess it would be nice to get out of the ship for a change…," Beer says.

"Although I still think it's a bad idea, doing something is usually better than doing nothing," Horton concedes.

When they look to The One for his thoughts, he shrugs.

"Then it's settled," Todd declares. "We've found your next adventure!"

"You've done it again, The Other One," the business boy commends himself. "I have a *shin* this is going to be an incredible adventure. You know… like from *The Simpsons*."

3

The afternoon sun forces the team to shield their eyes as they step outside the comfort of the *Cuddler*. The One already misses his cluttered room and its assortment of rare snacks from every corner of the universe. For the foreseeable future, he'll have to settle for double-frosted ration bars and whatever cheap treats they sell on The Dark Side of The Park.

A group of fans is gathered outside the gate, taking pictures in front of the *Cuddler*'s charred remains, when a magical girl wearing plastic souvenir cat ears notices the team and screams, "There they are! It's Pants Team Pink!"

Jumping up to peak over the fence, a small boy asks, "Is this the start of a new adventure?"

"It sure is!" Pants officially announces, showing her gawking fans the Pants sign. Having replaced her cat pajamas with a travel outfit from her new 'Pantsventure' line, she tells them, "Make sure to stay tuned, because the adventure starts now, you guys!"

But so far, the team is off to a slow start. It being the offseason, the Playland is all but deserted. Aside from a handful of die-hard fans and the occasional Park native, Pants Team Village is a ghost town. The Park mules have set to work repairing the miniature pastel houses surrounding the *Cuddler*, but much of the damage wrought by the Xenodorks still remains. From the scorched plasti-turf lawns to the congealed egg cream rotting on the sidewalk, evidence of the Dorks' treachery can be felt throughout the Playland.

Wiping the sweat from his forehead, the One asks his skinny counterpart, "How are we supposed to get to The Dark Side of the Park, anyway? If you're thinking about making us walk, this is gonna be our shortest adventure yet."

"Don't worry," The Other One assures them. "I've already sent for a Sofa Shuttle. It should be here any space minute. But before you take off, I want to give you these." Opening his briefcase, he reveals a set of what look like old promo items covered in strange symbols. "Souvenirs recovered from the haunted attraction, designed to harness your Park powers and ward off the creatures that roam the grounds."

The team members carefully remove the merch from its case and slip the ancient relics around their wrists. Colorless, like they've spent the last few centuries baking in the sun, each band features a large round face with a unique symbol surrounded by bizarre alien etchings.

Scrutinizing his plastic wristband, The One says, "Feels kind of… cheap."

"Well, I think they're cool!" Pants declares, showing off her new jewelry to the fans in her phone.

"I question how these will protect us from anything," Horton concludes. "But I don't believe in ghosts or curses anyway. So, I guess it doesn't make any difference."

"That's the spirit," The Other One says. "The wristbands should help guide you on your adventure. But try not to break them. I used my Park connections to convince the Historical Society to loan them to me. The curator threatened to revoke my line hopping privileges if I don't return them in the same or better condition."

With his bracelet to his heart, Beer says, "We'll treat them as if they were our own collectibles." As he lowers his arm, he accidentally knocks the fragile souvenir against one of the bright pink trash cans scattered throughout the Playland and grins apologetically. "Oops."

"Here comes the Sofa Shuttle!" Pants announces as the plush brown conveyance rounds the *Cuddler* and floats down through the bright sky.

As soon as the shuttle lands, the team begins hauling their bags onto its sticky, flattened cushions. But once everything is loaded, they discover there's no room left to sit.

Examining their luggage, The One says, "There seems to be an overload of pink bags."

The rest of the team turns toward Pants and she shrugs. "That's my wardrobe."

"How many costume changes do you plan on making?" Beer asks.

"It depends," she says sheepishly.

"On what?"

"The colors, the lighting, the local customs, *everything!*"

Scoffing, The One argues, "Well, we need to do *something.* There's no room for us!"

"Fine," she grumbles, pulling her bags back down in exasperation. "I guess I can leave my winter wardrobe, and my snorkeling gear, and my novelty hat collection. But I'm bringing my officially licensed Pants Team accessories!"

The team cedes this demand, and as Todd drags her excess luggage back inside the ship, they climb aboard the couch and make themselves as comfortable as possible under the circumstances. But before they take off, The One suddenly notices that the instigators of this dubious adventure haven't made any moves to join them.

"Are you coming, or what?" he demands.

Glancing at his business loafers, The Other One says, "I'm flattered that you would invite me. But there are a number of Park duties that require my attention. I'll catch up with you later on."

"I guess that's plausible enough," The One grumbles before turning his attention to their loyal merch guy. "What about you?"

Tugging at his sweat-stained t-shirt, Todd mutters, "Uh, you don't really need me to go, do you? Somebody has to keep an eye on the *Cuddler.* Plus, I thought I'd rent a booth and finally get some sleep."

"No way!" The One protests. "You heard the lesser me. There's gonna be merch on this adventure, and we might need your powers of appraisal. Plus, this whole thing was your idea."

For a moment, Todd looks as if he's about to offer a passionate rebuttal, but instead he just sighs and squeezes onto the end of the couch.

Waving to them spastically as the shuttle takes off, The Other One shouts, "This is gonna be your best adventure yet, you guys! And don't worry, I won't go through your stuff while you're gone!"

As they rocket up through the sky, the couch tells them, *"Thank you for using Sofa Shuttle. Visitors to The Park often wonder which attractions are the most popular. To find out, please insert cash."*

The One's curiosity gets the better of him, and he pulls a stack of Park Bucks out of his shorts pocket. But before he can feed the machine, Beer snatches the wad of play money.

"Don't, you chidiot!" Beer tells his brother. "These Bucks could come in handy."

Scoffing, The One says, "You think ghosts can be paid off? Where we're going, we won't need Park Bucks."

As the couch flies over the shuttered booths surrounding the Playland, Horton asks, "Can we put on some music, or are we just going to listen to you two argue the whole way?" He flips through the channels until he lands on some alien trashcore song and cranks the volume.

But Todd immediately turns the music back down. "What are you trying to do, scare the… ghosts?"

Seizing control of the dial, Pants switches it to Princess Radio, and the rest of them groan, though none of them changes the station.

For the next few space hours, they float across the vast tracts of designer cityscape that surround New Con City, and three payments later, the shuttle begins its descent. They land at the edge of the Old Park, where the first rides were built, their metal skeletons overgrown and rusting in the soft glow of the grinning sun.

Vaguely pondering how the ancient pranksters managed to permanently deface the burning gas ball as he rubs the sleep from his eyes, The One looks out over their crumbling surroundings and says, "What the fish? We're still a long way from The Dark Side of the Park. Why are we landing here?"

"This is as far as the Sofa Shuttles will take us," Todd explains. "We'll have to walk the rest of the way."

"*Aww*," The One moans. "That's the worst thing about adventures – all the walking."

Once they've unloaded the shuttle, Beer tosses the wad of Park Bucks back to his brother and tells him, "Tip the couch."

Grumbling as he stuffs the crumpled bills into the couch's money hole, he briefly considers riding back to the Playland and leaving the others to go on the adventure without him. But before he can make up his mind, the shuttle takes off, stranding them all in no fan's land.

"Are you coming?" Beer calls.

"Hold your rations," The One growls.

Once they figure out a way to lug all of Pants's bags, they start the long journey across the junkyard.

"Check it out, you guys," Pants says, turning her phone so the fans can see. "We're in the Old Park now. The air smells like… used fryer grease and spun sugar."

All around them, Park rats rustle through old fast-food wrappers, and the doors of abandoned passenger cars squeak in the wind.

"They say it's been completely stripped of investment," Horton notes.

"*Ughuhuh*," Todd shivers. "Spooky."

The further they trudge, the darker the world grows, until all that's left of the dim light from the vandalized sun at their backs is a fleeting purple glow. As soon as the last hazy rays are snuffed out, a different kind of light appears on the horizon, and when The One listens closely, he can hear the sound of button mashing wafting on the night air.

4

Carefully navigating the dark ruins of the Old Park, Horton takes out his phone and cranks the backlight to illuminate the littered path in front of them. The raucous noise grows louder as the team and Todd make their way toward the blinking, artificial lights, until they come upon a large tent in the middle of the scrap. Wrapped in strings of multicolored bulbs, a riotous clash of intoxicated cheers and primitive 64-bit sound effects spill from its bright entrance. Between its trashy esthetic and exotic locale, the tent possesses a crude charm unlike anything Horton has found in The Park proper.

"It's an All-Night Barcade," Todd tells them. "Scattered throughout The Dark Side of the Park, they cater to the basest desires of tourists and locals alike. Or, so I've heard…"

The tent being the only sign of lowlife in the area, they step out of the shadows and through the frayed canvas into a world of sensory pleasures. Wall-to-wall arcade cabinets, illicit syrup bars, and a fleet of fruit cocktail waitstaff in skimpy cosplay outfits work overtime to satiate a writhing sea of over-stimulated Park dwellers.

It only takes a few space seconds for Horton's better judgment to be overpowered, and he mutters the only thing he can come up with by way of analysis, "*Whoa…*"

"You said it," The One mumbles through a mouthful of syrup cake.

"Where the fish did you get that?" Beer demands. "We just got here."

Stuffing the remainder of the dripping dessert into his mouth, The One shrugs.

"Listen, you guys!" Pants cries. "Do you hear that?"

"But how?" Even amidst the digital noise, Horton can make out the familiar refrain. He would recognize that theme on this planet or any other. After all, he programmed it. "They're playing our game."

"Come on, you guys!" Pants tells them.

They follow her across the barcade, weaving through the crowd of sweaty, sugar-saturated nerds, until they reach a bright pink machine surrounded by a mob of spectators.

"What the fish is going on…," Horton says as he lays eyes on the game.

Shoving his way to the front of the crowd, he peaks over the edge of the cabinet and stares at the screen, baffled at the sight of the familiar pixelated fighters.

"Hey, back of the line, kid," a gruff Parker in a jean vest and a ratty syrup-stained beard grumbles at Horton, grabbing the sleeve of his fan-gifted black gold t-shirt.

But before either of them can make another move, The One has his phone's stunner pressed under the bulging brute's chin.

"Don't worry," The One tells the hairy Parker. "It's set to 'soil.'"

"If you want to save your ack," Horton says, "you'll tell me where this game came from."

"I-I don't know," the galoot stammers. "I just came to play."

Before The One can zap the truth out of him, an ancient voice announces, "I'll tell yuh how the game got here." His back hunched from leaning over the machine, the crusty Park codger points his crooked finger at the second player controls. "But yuh gotta beat me first. Ant yuh gotta let the big guy go. He's jist an innocent chitiot."

Horton motions to The One to let his attacker crawl to the back of the line and says, "I'll wipe the floor with you, old timer."

"Yuh sure 'bout that?" the codger asks, jutting his gray thumb at the line of challengers restlessly awaiting a turn on the machine.

Suddenly sensing that he's missing something, Horton glances at the screen to discover that the number of wins under the old man's screen name rests at ninety-nine.

"The real number is a lot higher," the coot says. "But—"

"That's as high as the counter goes," Horton finishes, placing his hands on the greasy second player control stick.

Before they begin, the old man points at the cabinet's glowing door. "Yuh gotta pay tuh play."

Pointlessly patting his pockets, Horton searches the room for a token dispenser, when Beer tosses him a dull coin. "I always keep a couple on me, in case of emergency." With the rest of the team watching from the sidelines, he advises, "Now, kick his ack!"

Horton nods, and as soon as the machine confirms payment, Pants's digitized voice cries *"Let's do this, you guys!"*

The codger navigates the character screen with a deftness below his years, quickly moving his cursor over to Pants's smiling avatar. Horton typically plays as himself, but something about the way the old man's gnarly fingers handle the joystick tells him that this isn't going to be as simple as trouncing his teammates. He's never been great with Beer or The One, and the Xenodorks are essentially useless since he nerfed them as payback for rigging the *Cuddler*'s doorbell to play "As Days Go By."

Then it hits him. With the timer ticking down, he performs a series of joystick moves and button presses that to the untrained eye would appear completely random. But someone with knowledge of the game's inner workings would recognize the inputs as a way to unlock its most powerful secret. Created primarily for testing purposes, it's the only character capable of performing every move in the game. Having entered the code more times than he can remember, the pattern is lodged in Horton's muscle memory, and it only takes him a couple tries to get right.

When the hidden avatar appears on the screen, the old man's eyes go wide. "Who the fish is that?"

"You're looking at the architect of your undoing," Horton says, gravely. "The personification of loserdom, he is the destroyer of fun and the end of your winning streak. We call him Todd."

"Hey!" Todd complains from the crowd. "I'm not sure whether to be offended or flattered."

His confidence evidently faltering, the old man snatches his soda off the top of the machine and takes a long swig.

"As temporary reigning champ, you are entitled to choose the stage of your destruction," Horton says.

The old man scoffs. "Please. There's only one stage pink enough to host a battle like this."

Flashing a knowing smile, Horton nods, and the old man makes his selection, transporting their characters onto the furry pink back of the *Cuddler* as it sails through the cartoon sky.

Looking up at the giant screens hanging from the ceiling, the crowd cheers the chosen arena.

As soon as the game's bubbly announcer yells, "*FIGHT, YOU GUYS!,*" the combatants send their Pants and Todd fighters rushing across the *Cuddler*'s back, trading a series of quick blows to test each other's abilities. It's been space months since Horton last played, but after a couple minutes, his fingers start to take over, allowing him to perform attacks he forgot he even knew.

Still, the old man knows his stuff. For every hit the Todd character lands, digital Pants finds a way to answer in kind. The players duke it out as the *Cuddler* carries them up through the atmosphere and out into space. By the time the ship has reached Earth's moon, their avatars are bloodied and panting, having taken enough damage that one strong noogie or a particularly wet willy could send either of them to pixelated purgatory.

"Had enough?" the old man asks as his avatar bounces on the *Cuddler*'s tail, shouting, "*We're all Pants Team Pink!*"

"Maybe this will answer your question." Horton activates his character's special taunt, and his Todd avatar retorts, "*Buy my merch!*" Searching for an opening, he realizes that his power meter is at full capacity, giving him the ability to perform the merch guy's finishing move. "This is the end," he tells the old Parker. "Prepare to be merchandized!"

But as Todd unleashes a mega blast of cheap souvenirs, Horton realizes that Pants has also reached full power and is in the middle of launching a love homing missile, which from where he's currently crouched is unavoidable. The only thing either of them can do is try to outrun the other's attack and hope for a miracle. They dash in opposite directions across the *Cuddler*'s furry back, and the instant their special powers collide, the explosion causes a digital whiteout like nothing the fans have ever seen.

5

As Pants watches the match unfold, she can't decide whether to root for Horton or her computer-generated self.

But it ceases to be a problem once the digital dust settles and the machine announces the one outcome that only she could love: *"IT'S A TIE, YOU GUYS!"*

"Yay!" Pants cries as every other fan in the room boos the results.

"Good game, young man," the old Parker tells Horton. "Yuh might not a won, but yuh put up a heck of a fight."

"You didn't win either," Horton growls. "I want a rematch!"

The mere suggestion sends the crowd into a chant, *"Re-match, re-match, re-match…"*

But the old man balks. "Haven't yuh hat 'nough fightin' fer one night? These olt fingers sure have. Let me buy you and yer frients a drink, and we'll talk games."

The old coot leads them to a table with a direct view of the gaming floor, and he orders a round of pink syrup. While the others wince at the taste, Pants happily slurps down the sugary goo.

"*Ughuhuh*," The One shudders. "Don't they have Ecto Cooler?"

"I thought this it be more appropriate, fer obvious reasons," the old man says. "My name's—"

"Dub," Horton says. "That's the name at the top of the *Pants Fighter Special Ultra Super Warrior* scoreboard."

"Ant yer Pants Team Pink," Dub says.

"How'd you figure it out?" Beer quips, removing his glasses to throw back his syrup.

Laughing, Dub strokes the skin of his sagging chin, which is a shade of gray common to those Parkers who spend the bulk of their days and nights inside the noisy, smoke-filled backrooms of the barcades, and says, "It may come as a su-prise, but not erryone knows Pants Team Pink. We're sort a isolate'it over here on the Dark Site of the Park. Plus the reception's spotty, so it takes a lot longer fer the latest shows tuh reach us. Harter tuh git merch, too."

"I can explain that," Todd interjects, pulling back a strand of stringy hair. "It costs too much to send deliveries all the way out here. Plus, the PFD is very low. The numbers just don't add up."

"PFD?" Dub says.

"Potential Fan Density."

Slamming his empty glass down on the table, Horton says, "Then how the fish did they get that arcade machine? We only made one of them, and it's in the *Cuddler*'s game room. There's something extra fishy going on here." Something causes a ruckus down on the gaming floor, but Horton doesn't take his eyes off the old codger for a space second.

"A-ha…," Dub laughs nervously, choking on his syrup. "Now I hope if I tell yuh the truth, y'all'll go easy on me. Yuh see, I happen tuh be the owner a the biggest arcate machine manufacturer in The Park. Fer tax purposes, I prefer tuh live over here on the Dark Site, but I don't discriminate. Anyway, sometimes if we git hire't tuh built somethin' interstin', we'll built an extra one fer quality control purposes."

"That's a breach of our contract *and* our universal copyright!" Horton cries. "I also blame Todd for not stopping this type of thing from happening."

Waving a stick of fried mystery meat, Todd says, "In my defense… Well, I can't think of a good excuse right now. But I'm sure I'll come up with something."

"Hey!" The One protests. "Where'd you get that meat stick?"

His mouth full, Todd shrugs.

"If it makes yuh feel any bitter, I haven't made a crit off the game," Dub claims.

"What about all the tokens?" Horton demands. "Judging by the crowd, that machine alone is enough to pay for permanent accommodations in a high-scorers booth and unlimited VIP syrup service."

Zoning out from all this business talk, Pants finally whines, "I'm bo-*ored*!"

"As usual, Pants is right," Todd says. "I'd love to drain this crusty Parker of every token he's worth. But that could take space years. Plus, it still wouldn't save the show. We have to keep moving. At this rate, we'll never find the Dark Park."

"I know that!" Horton says. "But we can't just let him get away with stealing my game. I mean, *our* game. I propose we at least smash his gaming fingers. His space days of high scoring will be over."

"What? *No!*" Dub yelps, shoving his ancient hands underneath the table. "What if I kin git yuh where yer tryin' a go?"

In an attempt to inject some excitement into the episode, Pants leans in close to the codger and delivers her next line with exaggerated urgency. "*You mean you know how to find the Dark Park?*"

"Uh, yeah," Dub says, backing away slowly, as if to avoid startling her. "I kin show yuh how tuh git there. But yuh gotta promise tuh let me keep my fingers."

"Fine," Horton says, angrily crossing his arms. "But I don't like it."

"Yay!" Pants squeals. "Can you feel it, you guys? It's the start of a new adventure, finally! We'll call it… 'The Tale of the Haunted Attraction.'"

Shaking his shaggy head, Beer turns his spectacles toward her and says, "That's no good."

"What about 'The Haunted Park Saga'?" she offers.

"Better…," Beer says.

"You should call it, 'The Haunting of Pants Team Pink," Dub suggests.

"All right, that's pretty good," Beer concedes. "Now, can we get the fish out of this tent? My sweat is starting to smell sweet."

Deferring to Dub's extensive knowledge of the tent's floor plan, the team follows his leisurely lead through the maze of games, pausing every few space seconds to schmooze with the old Parkers. When they finally reach the back flap, the exit has been cordoned off due to declining revenue. But Dub instructs The One to slip the security monster a few Park Bucks, and the beast lets them pass.

Outside, underneath the blinking lights of the barcade, Dub tells them, "Holt out yer hants." Digging down in the pockets of his Park shorts, he presents each of them with a roll of tokens. "It's the currency this site a The Park. May they help yuh on yer aventure and compensate yuh fer the unauthorize't use a yer game and likenesses."

With tokens in tow, they head back into the dense shadows blanketing this side of the planet. Dub seems to have a Park sense for avoiding the scrap that litters the dark grounds. As they approach the remains of a giant Ferris wheel, he suddenly stops in his tracks and anxiously ushers them toward an abandoned carnival dog booth at the edge of the path.

Before long, a group of dark figures approaches, passing around a bottle of something dark and speaking in a dialect that Pants can't understand. Laughing maliciously, the one in front suddenly sends the bottle hurtling toward the booth, and it takes all her power not to cry out as the glass shatters over her head.

Once the gang has moved on, Dub dabs his finger in the dark goop dripping down the side of the booth and touches it to his tongue. "Park Punks, drunk on fairyshine. Have tuh be careful. We don't want them tuh mistake us fer a rival team."

"I'm s-scared, you g-guys," Pants stutters to her fans.

As they head deeper into the abandoned playland, Dub tells them, "Don't worry. I'll git yuh where yer goin'." Possibly to take their minds off the danger all around them, he points to a looming shadow up ahead. "Yuh see that hunk a junk? That there use't tuh be my fav-o-rite rite - Shoot the Moon. My frient's call't it 'Puke the Moon,' fer reasons yuh kin probly surmise. Anyway, this is where all the olt rites ent up, once they notch their hunerth fatality."

"You know a lot about this place," Beer says, stumbling along in the dark. "But what can you tell us about the Dark Park?"

Dub turns quiet for a moment and finally says, "One thing I kin tell yuh is it's hauntit."

"So we've heard," Horton's voice says from somewhere amongst the shadows.

Taking a grave tone, Dub continues, "Hunerts a space years ago, in the early days a The Park, a shadowy group of investors decite'it tuh built a brant new attraction tuh lure tourists to The Dark Site durin' the offseason. But soon as construction began, weirt things startit tuh happen. Tools 'it go missin', ant rites 'it start all by 'emselves. Turns out, they built the place over an olt mascot burial grount. Worst a all fer the investors, the crowts never show't up. The park was only open fer a single season afer they shut it down. The only ones what visit now are the ghosts of retire't mascots and insolvent executives hopin' to make a quick crit."

Unswayed, Horton says, "I'll believe it when it reaches into my wallet and steals my Park Bucks."

"Oh, yer Park Bucks are no good in there," Dub says. "Anyway, that's not far off from what I set first time one a the olt-timers tolt me the story a the Dark Park. But win I went tuh check out the rites fer myself, I hurt the sound of ghost tokens clatterin', ant I never went back."

"What do you mean, 'rites'?" The One asks. "Like some sort of ritual mascot sacrifice?"

"He's saying 'ride,'" Beer clarifies.

"Ohhh," The One says. "I get it."

As they continue to trek across the dark scrap yard, Pants hears a strange tune playing somewhere in the distance and asks, "What's that sound?"

They all stop to listen, and a shadowy smile stretches over Dub's withered face. "That's yer rite."

6

Huddled inside the decomposing walls of the ancient station, forced to endure its repetitive tune while they await the arrival of their haunted transport, Todd starts to second guess this whole adventure.

"Are you sure it's coming?" Pants asks as she sticks her head out into the inky shadows surrounding them.

Checking the time on his cruddy phone, Dub says, "Never been more sure a anythin' in my life. It's on a strict schetule. Been runnin' nonstop since it was first hook't up tuh The Park's power grit. It's more reg'lar 'an I am."

"*Ughuhuh*," Beer shudders for all of them.

When the old Parker extracts a snack stick from his shorts pocket, The One growls, "What the fish is that?"

"It's a new type a meat stick," Dub says. "Somethin' call't Soylent Pete. Yuh want a bite?"

The codger offers the stick to The One, but upon sniffing it up close, the boy says, "Uh, never mind."

The One refusing a free snack is more than enough to convince the rest of them to pass.

"Suit yerselfs," the old-timer says, pointing toward the tracks as he bites off a hunk of dehydrated flesh. "There it is, jist like I set."

Todd suddenly hears the clacking of metal wheels bearing down on the platform, accompanied by a ghostly glow flickering in the distance. For a moment, he fears the team is about to be met by an actual apparition. But he breathes a sigh of relief when the 'Ghost Train' pulls into the station, revealing itself as nothing more than a repurposed Park coaster with a googly-eyed spirit painted on the front.

Flinging his snack wrapper onto the tracks, Dub says, "Tolt yuh. Welp, I'll see yuh win yuh git back. Speaking of, I feel I shit warn yuh, the last kits who took this train never return't. Or maybe I jist miss't 'em. Anyway, I'm off."

"Wait a space second!" Todd yelps, tripping after the old man. "You're not coming with us?"

"Fish no," Dub says, visibly shaken by the suggestion. "I tolt yuh, I ain't never steppin' foot near the Dark Park again."

"This adventure just keeps getting better," Todd says. "If we get out of this with our souls intact, I'm going to give The Other One such a firing."

As the team debates whether or not to continue the adventure, the Ghost Train looses a spooky moan, and Beer shouts, "What the fish is that?"

"The train's leavin'," Dub says. "If yer goin', yuh bitter git. It won't be back 'rount till t'morrow. But if yuh wanna sleep on it, yuh kit crash at my place."

"We gotta get the fish outta here!" Todd announces as the train begins to roll away from the station.

"What about my bags?!" Pants wails.

They hurl as much of the pink luggage aboard as they can, and as the train begins to pick up speed, the merch guy tells her, "We have to leave the rest."

"What?!" she cries. "No! I need it."

"We'll pick it up on the way back," he assures her as the rest of them awkwardly climb aboard one of the dark passenger cars. "Come on!"

Before she can argue any further, he grabs her hand and drags her into the car just as the train pulls away from the platform.

Waving to them from the station as the moaning locomotive ushers them into the dark, Dub shouts, "Don't worry, I won't go through yer stuff or try on any a yer costumes while yer gone!"

The compartment is like something out of an old cartoon, its black and white interior dimly and sporadically lit by a single flickering bulb powered by the train's juddering momentum. Outside is total darkness. If it wasn't for the extreme turbulence, Todd decides, it would be impossible to tell whether they were rolling down the track or plummeting into a black hole.

"I don't like this, you guys," Pants whimpers into her phone.

"Everything would be fine if we could figure out a way to shut off this dam muzak," Beer says, referring to the terrible tune spilling from the car's speakers.

Listening more closely, Todd says, "Sounds like 'Night Moves.' It's one of those songs people thought was brule a long time ago."

Scoffing, Beer says, "I refuse to believe this was ever brule."

As the train barrels through the dark, the team climbs onto the black benches lining the cabin walls, and they try to get some rest. After a short while, the movement of the car combined with the soothing sounds of Seger lulls Todd into a dark trance, and he dozes off.

He wakes an instant later to The One yelling, "Hey!"

"What?!" Todd asks, jumping to his feet, only to tumble back onto the seat as the train makes a sharp turn. "What is it?"

"I found an old ration cake under the seat!" the boy announces.

"*Well...*," Beer demands. "How is it?"

The crinkling that occurs as The One wrestles with the package wakes Pants and Horton, and they all watch with mild interest as the boy bites into the ancient snack cake.

Chewing carefully, he says, "It's hard as a rock and tastes like chalk – so pretty good!"

"Then the rumors are true," Horton says. "They never go bad..."

Fearing he might lose his syrup as the train car blindly careens through the dark, Todd leans out the door for some fresh air. The cool night breeze is a welcome distraction from the team's endless shenanigans. As the wind whips through his hair, he's met by a familiar buttery scent, and his mind flashes back to late-night TV marathons on Earth. Even after all the restless nights he's spent on the *Cuddler*'s couch, this is the first time since he got to The Park that he's felt homesick.

Pulling his head back inside, he asks the others, "Do you smell that?"

"Yeah," Beer says, sniffing. "What is it? It's so familiar."

The One thrusts his head out for a better whiff, and in a moment, he decides, "It smells like… stale candy."

"Then we must be getting close," Todd says, gravely.

Startled by the train's warning moan, the reluctant passengers look ahead to find that they're fast-approaching the glowing remains of an old welcome station. But when their dark conveyance finally rolls to a stop, the only welcome they receive comes in the form of another deteriorating platform echoing the smooth sounds of Seger.

"Do you really need all this stuff?" Horton complains to Pants as he helps unload her bags. "It's not like we're spending the night. Oh Space God, please tell me we're not going to be here all night!"

"You'll thank me when you see the new Pants Team head warmers that The One designed," she assures him.

"You mean hats?"

Standing beneath a grinning skeleton covered in faded glow paint, the five of them glance at each other uncertainly, hesitant to begin an adventure that's beginning to look more and more like a nightmare.

"Well, that's… ominous,' Beer says. "Or is it cheezy? I can't tell."

"We can always turn back," Todd suggests, hopefully. But before the team has a chance to argue about it, the train moans and starts rolling down the track. "Well, not anymore."

Watching their only means of escape disappear into the shadows, The One shivers and says, "It's cold on this side of The Park."

"Then it's a good thing…," Pants says as she rummages inside one of her duffel bags, "I brought these!"

"Aww, do we have to dress up in your stupid costumes?" The One asks as she passes out the pink apparel. But as he scrutinizes the gift more closely, he quickly changes his tune. "You got us new team jackets? I take back all the things I ever said about you."

"I also got us camera pins so we won't always have to have our phones out, unless we want to get a better shot," she says. "Wait a space second, what did you say about me?"

"Uh, nothing…," he tells her, slipping the jacket around his shoulders.

She even got one for Todd, emblazoned with his official title – Merch Guy.

When the team is finished adjusting to their new wardrobe, Beer asks, "So, now what do we do?"

Swimming in his pink uniform, Horton motions to the glowing skeleton on the wall, and they follow its bony pointer finger to a line of arrows painted on the floor. "We go that way."

The team follows the glowing arrows out across a vast parking lot strewn with the abandoned junkers of failed vacations past. As they approach the gate of the shadow park, the remains of its crumbling entrance obscured in darkness, Beer can almost hear the tortured sounds of ancient space shanties drifting on the wind. But before they reach their haunted destination, Todd abruptly stops in his tracks, and they all crash into each other.

"What is it now?" The One asks. "If we stop every time someone hears a Park rat, we're never gonna make it. Anyway, this place isn't even scary."

"Yes it is!" Pants says.

Pointing to the cracked walkway in front of them, Todd says, "Look. The arrows stop here."

"Well, the turnstiles are right there," The One grumbles.

"Wait, we have to be careful about this," Beer yells as the chidiot waddles toward the entrance.

Defiantly jutting out his thumb, The One scoffs at his brother's warning. But when he reaches the gate, a horrifying cackle emerges from the grounds, and he cries out in terror.

"Now look what you did!" Beer shouts. "Who knows what type of evil spirit you just disturbed."

The lights surrounding the entrance suddenly flash to life, revealing the words on the decaying sign – 'Scared_la_d.' A white mist spills out of the gate, swirling up into the air, and through some type of dark magic, it solidifies into a giant skeleton torso floating between The One and the turnstiles.

Shaking in his sneakers, The One whimpers, "I was kidding. The sign is right. I'm just a scared lad. *Please* don't kill me!"

"Run, you chidiot!" Beer tells him.

Grinning down at its sniveling prey, the skeleton snarls, "*Welcome to Scaredyland, the park where all your fears come true. Enter if you dare! But be warned – the only way inside is through me.*"

"I'm sorry to disturb you," The One cries. "I just want to go home!"

"*Home?*" the skeleton bellows, erupting in vicious laughter. "*Scaredyland is your home now. Once you enter, you can never leave.*"

"But I haven't entered yet," The One argues.

Ignoring his pleas, the skeleton reaches out and wraps its bony fingers around the boy's comparatively tiny torso as he screams out in agony. A moment later, his screams cease, and Beer peers at the grisly scene with his mouth open, wondering how he'll ever explain this to Mom. When the skeleton opens its fingers, The One is lying in a ball on the pavement.

The team runs to The One's aide, but as they look down in horror at his twitching body, his eyes suddenly blink open, and he asks, "What the fish just happened?"

"You're alive!" Beer cries, and before he knows what he's doing, he wraps his arms around his brother.

"Get off me," The One grumbles, shaking himself loose.

Scrutinizing the floating monster, Horton steps toward the turnstiles and the skeleton announces, *"Welcome to Scaredyland, where all your fears come true! Enter if you—"*

"Must be on a motion sensor," he says. "People in the Old Park days really used to make an effort."

"O-kay…," The One tells them, still shaking from the fake scare as he gets back on his feet. "*Now* can we go in?"

"Are you serious?" Beer cries. "Look what just happened! We have to be more careful."

But even after such a horrific experience, his brother remains irritatingly undeterred. "Everything about this place is fake. There's nothing to be scared of."

"Then why were you just curled up on the ground like a newborn Star Child?" Beer asks.

"Uh, I thought I saw a token," The One lies, turning to face the giant skeleton hovering over the Scaredyland entrance.

As The One makes his way toward the gate, the monster reaches out for him, but this time the hologram's fleshless fingers pass right through the boy's portly body. "I told you guys," he taunts as he hops the turnstile. "We've got free reign of this place. We can do whatever we—" But before he can utter the last patronizing syllable, something shoves him back onto his big ack.

Once again putting aside their fears for the sake of their teammate, the rest of them race past the holographic skeleton to The One's rescue. But when they find him laid out on the rubber pavement for what appears to be no good reason, they reflexively burst out laughing.

"Hey, this is bringing in a lot of viewers," Pants announces. "Do something else dumb, The One!"

"Chut up, you guys," The One grumbles, rubbing his backside as he clambers to his feet.

Once it's clear that the bulk of the damage is localized to The One's ego, Horton cautiously inspects the entryway, and knocking against the air in front of them, determines, "It's some sort of primitive energy field. It must be hooked into the ticketing system to deter park-crashers."

"*MWAHAHAHAHA,*" the skeleton out front howls. "*No one gets in without a pass!*"

"What the fish do we do now, *TheOneReallyNotScaredKid?*" Beer gripes at his brother.

"*Ha,*" The One scoffs. "Like I would ever choose such a wordy screen name."

"How are we going to get in without passes, you guys?" Pants asks the fans, ominously. "Could this already be the end of *The New Adventures of Pants Team Pink?*"

"That would mean my job here is over," Todd says, rolling up the sleeves of his honorary team jacket. "I won't let that happen." Either out of incredible bravery or pure stupidity, he hurls his fist at the air in front of him, and it instantly crumples against the invisible force field.

As their merch guy nurses his hand, Horton wanders back toward the turnstiles and fiddles with the scanners.

Just as Beer is about to nail The One with a finishing zing, Horton says, "We have a problem, you guys. This tech is so old I don't have the tools to crack it. Even if I did, I'd probably fish something up."

"So, what do we do now?" Pants cries.

"Well, I've got one idea," Horton says. "But it's not very good."

At his command, the team works together to beat up on the turnstiles.

As Beer smashes his sneaker against the metal box, he asks Todd, "Is it working?"

"Yes!" Todd declares, leaning against the barrier. "I mean, no."

"Come on, you guys," Pants tells the fans. "Give us your strength. With our powers combined, nothing can stop us from beating the chit out of these things."

Raising her arm into the air, she brings her fist down on the scanner in one glittery motion, and the box cackles cordially. At the same instant, Todd tumbles through the force field and rolls onto the ground.

"How did you do that?" Horton asks.

"I just hit it," she says.

But when the rest of them try to duplicate the effect, it doesn't work. Again, she brings her fist down on the scanner, causing the machine to cackle, and this time Beer spots the secret of her power.

"It's the bracelet!" he tells them.

The rest of them slide their ancient merch over the scanners, and the machine ghosts howl, granting them access to the Dark Park. As they drag their bags inside, Beer gazes upon the shadowy ruins with a combination of awe and terror. The bright booths, abandoned snack carts, and haunted rides of the unexplored attraction promise fun and games. But underneath the sugary façade, he senses something far more sinister at play.

"We made it, you guys," Pants whispers into her phone, panning across their spooky surroundings so the fans can get a better look. "We're the first kids to step inside Scaredyland in probably a jillion space years. Look! There's the haunted fountain over there, and the haunted restrooms, and that's the haunted information center."

"How do you know they're haunted?" Beer asks as he peeks over the edge of the motionless fountain into a pool of thick black sludge.

"Because everything here is haunted," she explains. "Or cursed."

"Aww, it's gonna take us forever to search this place," The One moans. "Maybe that's how it got haunted in the first place, from all the kids who got lost hunting for merch and never found their way back out."

"Stop it!" Pants cries. "You're scaring the fans."

"Look at that," Horton says, pointing his ghostly finger toward a faint glow further down the path.

When they reach the glowing artifact, The One looks up at it curiously and asks, "What is it?"

"What do you think, yuh dumbskull?" Beer says. "It's a map."

"*Hey!*" The One cries out in protest. "I think you're right… for a change."

"Looks like there's five different 'Ghost Towns,'" Horton observes. "I wonder which one we should visit first."

"*I can help you with that,*" a disembodied voice interjects.

As the team and Todd freeze in their sneakers, Beer slowly turns his head to search the unhallowed grounds for the source of the voice and asks, "Who said that?"

"*I did.*"

Before they can run from whatever horror awaits them, a smiling spirit materializes in the middle of the rubber walkway, and everyone screams.

8

The cartoon apparition, its mouth stretched well beyond mortal limits, is more grotesque than anything The One has ever encountered. Gazing into the bottomless black depths of its eyeholes, he can feel himself surrendering to fright. But as the ghost screams along with the rest of them, he quickly loses his will to wail.

Shedding his fear, he asks the dopey spirit, "Why are *you* screaming?"

"*Everyone was doing it,*" the ghost says, with a shrug of its spectral shoulders.

Upon hearing its animated voice, the team and Todd's howls subside, until they're all staring at the creature in quiet confusion.

"So, uh, what the fish are you?" The One finally asks.

With a twirl of its nebulous body, the ghost announces, *"My name is Ghosty, and I'll be your guide to Scaredyland!"*

"Oh great," The One groans. "Just when I thought this adventure couldn't get any more annoying."

"Have all of you visited Scaredyland before?" Ghosty asks.

"This is our first time here," Pants unhelpfully answers.

"Don't tell it that!" Beer warns her.

But it's too late. Before they have a chance to escape, the ghost's translucent body morphs into a safety screen depicting all the dos and don'ts of the Dark Park. *"At Scaredlyand, we want everyone to have a terrifying but safe time. To make sure things never get too scary, we have a few dozen rules for you to follow. Rule number one: tokens are good for anything and everything at Scaredyland. Remember, you have to spend tokens to make fun! Rule number two: wear your wristbands at all times."* As soon as the rule is uttered, the artifacts around the teammates' wrists tighten. *"This way, if you ever get lost, we'll know exactly where to find you. Rule three: contrary to popular belief, there is such a thing as too much fun—"*

"Aww," The One moans, hanging his head. "Thanks a lot, Pants. Now we have to listen to the whole thing."

"If we don't listen, how are we supposed to know the rules?" she argues.

"Gahh!" The One says as he reaches into his pocket for a conciliatory ration bar. Tearing the wrapper open with his teeth, he gnaws on the frosting-covered snack while the ghost drones on.

"Rule eight," Ghosty continues. *"No hitting the mascots. We know it's tempting, but—"*

Examining the ghost more closely, Horton suggests, "There has to be a way to speed this up. Give me your ration bar, The One."

"What?!" The One cries. "Fish no. You can have it when you rip it out of my—"

But before he can finish his threat, Beer is on top of him yanking the bar out of his hand. "Just give it to him. The sooner this fish head ghost stops talking, the sooner we can get on with the adventure."

Finally wresting the bar away, Beer tosses it to Horton, who promptly throws it down on the rubber road.

"*Rule fifteen: the value of tokens is determined by—*" Ghosty cuts itself off, shifting back to its original form as it hovers over the discarded snack. "*Rule thirty-three: trash belongs in designated receptacles.*"

The One tenderly retrieves his treat and tells Horton, "You know, you could have just thrown out the wrapper." Examining the half-eaten snack, he blows off the dirt and stuffs the rest of it in his mouth.

When he drops the wrapper, Ghosty scolds, "*Rule thirty-three: trash belongs—*"

"Yeah, yeah, I know," The One says, snatching the wrapper off the ground. "There, are you happy?"

"*Rule ninety-four: at Scaredyland, happiness is mandatory.*"

"Enough already!" The One commands, glaring into the ghost's lifeless eyeholes. "We're never going to remember all these rules. If it weren't already dead, I'd kill this chidiot ghost."

"It's not dead," Horton says. "It's obviously some sort of virtual host."

"To make sure you're not doing anything you shouldn't be, take this complimentary rulebook," Ghosty says, and with a wave of its arm, a thick pamphlet slides out of a dispenser underneath the park map.

Snatching the guide, Horton anxiously flips through its fragile pages.

"So, where do we go from here?" Beer asks, adjusting the clarity of his glasses.

Upon hearing the question, Ghosty tells them, *"If you're having trouble deciding which section of the park to visit first, I can help."* With another wave of its formless arm, the map's screen glows to offer them a better view of the grounds. *"Each Ghost Town in Scaredyland has been meticulously designed to deliver maximum fright."* When the ghost guide points at the bottom corner of the map, the first Ghost Town lights up. *"In the Ghoulish Game Gallery, you'll find Scaredyland twists on all the classic Park games, along with more than a few exclusives designed to test the limits of your sanity. Collect enough tickets and you could win terrible merch from our Petrifying Prize Center!"*

Smacking himself across the face to make sure he's not stuck in some alliterative nightmare, The One asks, "Does everything in this place have some stupid gimmicky name?"

Ignoring the comment, Ghosty says, *"When you're finished testing your skills, head across Maim Street to hitch a ride on the Creep Coaster. Do you dare take the plunge down the tallest, fastest, and scariest ride in The Park?"*

"It's no longer the tallest," Horton interjects, wrenching his eyes away from his rulebook. "Or the fastest. I guess it could be the scariest, even though that title currently belongs to the Scaremonger."

Highlighting the next attraction, the ghost continues, *"If you survive that, you'll find more spills and chills over at the Haunted Raceway. Strap into one of our Monster Wagons and challenge your friends in a race around our cursed track to find out which one of you possesses the most death-defying driving skills."*

"Probably me," The One says. "I mean, right? Everybody knows I'm the fastest."

"I'll beat your ack on the track any day," Beer insists. I don't want to brag, but I've seen every episode of *Groovie Goolies."*

Lighting the next area of the map, the ghost tells them, *"Gluttons for punishment can continue their jarring journey by getting lost in the Gruesome Graveyard. Populated by the ghosts of all the guests who never found their way back out, it just might be your last stop."*

"That sounds like spooky fun!" Pants says, garnering contemptuous glares from her teammates. "Well, it does!"

"Finally, if you're still alive, you'll get the chance to unlock the most horrifying location in Scaredyland." The ghost waves its stubby arm over the map to reveal an oversized haunted house located at the back of the park. *"It is rumored that those guests who make it out of Mascot Manor will earn a prize so exclusive that even I don't know what it is."*

Pointing at the drawing of the Manor, The One tells the others, "That's obviously where the final merch is hidden. We should just go straight there."

"I almost forgot," Ghosty says. *"Don't tell anyone, but each Ghost Town contains a hidden token which is granted only to the most fearless guests. Collect all four to gain access to the decaying mansion and a chance to explore its scareifying secrets."*

"Oh…," The One says. "Great."

"But be warned. The creatures that dwell within the Manor's walls don't like company. It is said that once you enter–"

"You can never leave," The One concludes. "Yeah, we get it. It's all very scary. But how are we supposed to find our way around this place. All the lights are out, and everything is shut down. Even if the tokens are still there, the Ghost Towns don't have any power."

Butting in, Ghosty says, *"It's true that the streets of Scaredyland remain hidden in shadow. But allow me to illuminate things for you."*

Their holographic guide floats up above Maim Street, flailing its arms as if casting an evil spell, and after a few space seconds, the dusty streetlamps flicker to life, lighting the empty Parkway. For the first time in space centuries, Scaredyland is filled with the sounds of ancient rides grinding along their tracks. Even the dark fountain near the park's entrance begins spewing black sludge.

Marveling at the old-universe craftsmanship present in every bloody street sign and plastic monster decorating the Dark Park, Horton says, "They *really* don't make haunted parks like they used to."

"You know, I think Pants is right," Beer says. "This might be fun after all."

"Now aren't you glad I forced you to go on another adventure?" Todd asks as he slathers his arms with white goop.

"Why are you putting on sunblock?" The One complains. "It's semi-permanent night on this side of The Park."

Shrugging, the merch guy says, "You never know…"

With the rest of them falling prey to the park's charms, The One is left with no choice but to surrender to fun. "Well, let's get this over with."

"Wait a space second!" Pants cries. "What about all my stuff? We have to bring it with us."

"Eh, just leave it," Beer advises her, motioning at the empty park. "Who's gonna take it?"

"Fine," she says, pouting. "I'll just come back whenever I need a costume change."

Grumbling at the grinning hologram, The One impatiently instructs, "Lead the way, I guess."

9

"*Choose the location of your entertainment,*" Ghosty requests.

The rest of the team defers to Horton, and he analyzes the map until he finally determines, "I think our safest bet is to start at the Ghoulish Game Gallery. I'm already warmed up, and it seems like the least terrifying of the Ghost Towns. Plus, it's the closest."

"*In the Ghoulish Game Gallery, you'll find Scaredyland twists on all the classic Park games—*"

"We know!" The One grumbles. "But that's boring. I say we hit the Creep Coaster first and see if it can outscare the Scaremonger."

The others shrug in mild agreement, and Ghosty tells them, "*Across Maim Street, you'll find the Creep Coaster. Do you dare take the plunge—*"

"We dare, we dare," Beer says. "Just take us there already."

Annoying as their guide is, Horton can't help but be impressed by the tech utilized to bring the ghost to afterlife. Although the hologram's appearance is somewhat crude, its implementation is space centuries ahead of its time and far more ambitious than anything found in today's Park.

The black rubber squeaks beneath their sneakers as the ghost guides them down the central Parkway, lit by the dim glow of the Park-gothic street lamps and lined with unattended game booths, snack shacks, and souvenir stands. The thick blanket of real cobwebs and space dust that have accumulated over such an extended period of disuse makes it all the spookier.

"Who knows what brule stuff we'll find, you guys," Pants tells the fans as she picks a piece of trash off the ground. "I found something already! It's an ancient ration wrapper from back when Scaredyland first opened. This one was 'spooky space franks and moon beans.'"

"Let me see that." Rudely snatching the wrapper from her hand, The One says, "I used to eat that one all the time. They haven't changed the recipe in a thousand space years!"

"I knew my rations weren't just disappearing!" Beer gripes as he struggles to wipe his glasses on the inside of his team jacket.

"Speaking of, that was my last ration bar back there," The One notes, glaring in Horton's direction. "Did anybody bring anything else to eat?"

"I did," Pants says.

"Thank Space God!" The One tells her. "What is it?"

Beaming, she hands him a small pink box and says, "Candy hearts!"

"A boy cannot survive on candy alone," The One laments, even as he dumps the chalky contents into his mouth. "But I'll give it a shot."

Suddenly skidding to a stop in sight of the Game Gallery, Todd shouts, "No way!" The merch guy awkwardly skitters down the street toward a tall box stationed between two shuttered shops. Using the sleeve of his honorary team jacket, he wipes the dust off the glass and peers inside. "I can't believe it. I've had a couple knock-offs come into the shop over the space years, but I never thought I'd see a real, honest-to-Space-God Misfortune Teller."

When they catch up, Horton looks through the glass to find a lifelike mannequin of a cosmic space monster wearing a novelty fez.

Shoving his way in front to get a look for himself, The One says, "Looks sort of… dumb."

"Well this dumb machine is worth a not small fortune," Todd tells them, practically salivating as he runs his hands along the box's edges in an overly familiar manner. "They only made a million of these babies. The Scrapper's Almanac lists the few machines known to have survived the Novelty Wars as 'lost.' It's very likely that this is the last one in the whole universe. Chit, we could cover the rest of the repairs on the *Cuddler* with this machine alone."

The One throws his hands up and says, "What are we waiting for? Everybody grab a corner and let's get the fish out of here."

"We can't leave," Pants cries. "We just started the adventure!"

"She's right," Horton says. "Maybe it would fix the *Cuddler*, but it won't fix our ratings. Also, it's clearly way too heavy for us to lift."

The One presses his shoulder against the machine, and when it fails to move even the slightest bit, he capitulates, "*Fine.* What does the stupid chitty thing do, anyway?"

Waggling his finger, Todd says, "Allow me to demonstrate." He eagerly stuffs his hand in his shorts pocket and emerges with a pair of tarnished pyrite tokens. "I hope it still works." As if performing a sacred ritual, he rubs the tokens between his fingers, and with the utmost care slips them into the slot.

At first, it appears that the machine is out of order, but after a few space seconds, the plastic four-star crystal ball behind the glass lights up, and the alien mannequin springs to simulated life.

The squid monster's mouth tentacles wiggle up and down as it tells them, "*You have awakened Fishtar, and now you must face your fate. With my cosmic powers, I will reveal what future horrors you have in store.*" Fishtar's eyes glow bright red as he clumsily rubs his ball, and a small card pops out the front of the machine. "*The future is now yours. Don't fish it up. Remember, the only way to change your destiny is to feed Fishtar more tokens.*"

As the monster returns to its cosmic slumber, Todd gently plucks the card out of the slot and reads, "It says, 'Your future... it doesn't look so good. Advice: The future is now. Unlucky Number: 97.'"

"What the fish kind of fortune is that?" Beer asks.

"It's a *mis*fortune," Todd clarifies.

Evidently unconvinced, Pants demands, "But why would you want that?"

"For fun, of course!" the merch guy says. "I would think you of all teams would understand that. Do not underestimate the power of Fishtar. Rumor has it this machine really can tell the future."

"*Pfff*," The One demurs.

"I'm inclined to agree with The One," Horton concludes, inspecting the monster through its glass enclosure. "I doubt Fishtar possesses any more ability to predict the future than that failed secret UE project to predict the future."

Slipping the card safely into his jacket pocket, Todd says, "Well, if you don't believe in Fishtar's powers, why not get a misfortune of your own?"

"I'm not afraid, if that's what you're suggesting," Horton says. "It's a waste of tokens. Although, I suppose it's no *less* capable of prognostication than any of the other plastic fortune tellers. In that sense, it's as good a predictor of the future as any." He ponders this for a long moment and finally decides, "Fishtar may have much to teach us after all."

Presumably detecting a lull in spending, Ghosty suddenly announces, "*Standing in one place is bad for your health. There are still plenty of scares to be had. If you're hungry, why not stop at a snack shack for a double-fried Boo Bar or a steaming plate of Gray Matter?*"

A loud groan arises from The One's stomach, and he tells the ghost, "Oh, how I wish it could be. I'd get a Boo Bar, and a Franken-Fleshwich, and some Rotten Candy, and—"

"This has been fun, but viewers have leveled off," Todd warns them as he checks the show's current stats. "We'd better get over to the Creep Coaster before they start tuning out."

"Aright, aright," The One says. "But I gotta take a number two before we go on any rides."

Upon hearing these words, Ghosty notifies them, *"Whenever you need to excrete bodily waste, just make a wish and I'll lead you to the nearest restroom or trash receptacle, depending on the orifice!"*

With his bladder growing anxious, and sensing that this may be his last chance for a while, Horton chases The One and the digital spirit across Maim Street to a bank of public poop closets decorated in plastic bones and fake blood. But when they try to enter the Boils Room, the door won't open.

"What gives?" The One shouts, tugging at the handle.

Spotting their problem, Horton points to a token slot much like the one found on the Fishtar machine.

"It costs two tokens just to use the toilet?" The One moans.

"Restroom maintenance is an essential part of Scaredyland," Ghosty informs them. *"We're sure you'll be happy to know that you're contributing to the safety and cleanliness of the park facilities. Alternatively, you can gain one free restroom pass by answering a short, thirty space minute survey about your experience—"*

"Guts to that!" The One says. "I paid for toilet privileges with the price of admission. Or I would have if we had paid to get in." Glancing up and down the street, he tells Horton, "Keep a lookout."

"Why?" Horton asks. "What are you going to do?"

With a mischievous grin, The One tiptoes to a fake dead plant outside the empty souvenir shop next door and proceeds to squat.

Wildly waving its arms, Ghosty cries, *"Rule number fifty-three: no pooping in the plants!"*

10.

"It was the only reasonable course of action," The One argues as the team tumbles out of the Scaredyland photo booth to make their way toward the towering shadow looming in the distance. "Any of you would have and will sooner or later be forced to doo-doo the same thing."

"He's right…," Horton says, wringing his hands together, his face as pink as his team jacket.

Before Pants can finish showing off their team pictures, and best ugly faces, to the fans, she suddenly lifts her head and cries out in horror, "You mean, you pooped *outside*? That's easy for you guys, but what am I supposed to do?"

"Go in one of the Poison Teacups," The One unhelpfully suggests.

"Or you could just pay the two tokens," Beer points out.

Pants would happily wheedle the tokens out of them, but she's got scarier things to worry about. Watching the giant coaster's skeletal frame rise higher into the night sky with each reluctant step, her stomach twists. As brave as she is when it comes to flying around the universe in the ship *princessfluffypants*, she's always been too afraid to ride any of the coasters in The Park.

Apparently sensing her fear, Ghosty says, *"Don't worry. Along with being the tallest and fastest ride in The Park, it's also the safest."*

"Okay," she says, nervously tugging at the sleeves of her team jacket. "That sounds pretty… safe, I guess."

"*Pfff,*" The One scoffs. "That might have been true back when Scaredyland first opened. But now it's probably the least safe ride in The Park, outside of the Jungle Gym, of course."

"Chut up," Beer tells his brother. "Don't listen to him, Pants. He's just trying to scare you."

"Park rule number one hundred twenty: fear means you're having fun!"

"Maybe you're right," she tells Ghosty, in an attempt to convince herself. "What do you think, Horton?"

Crossing the arms of his pink jacket, her light-deprived friend says, "It should be safe enough, probably."

Somehow his endorsement fails to instill her with confidence, and as they leave Maim Street for a dusty path toward the outer reaches of the park, her fear only intensifies. The remnants of old rides litter the shadowy grounds like a bunch of giant abandoned toys forever waiting to be brought back to life.

Before long, they come to the Ghost Town's dark entrance, and a cold wind sends a chill down Pants's spine.

"*Welcome to the Gorewalk!*" the ghost guide shrieks. "*Unfortunately for you, the first stop in your journey through Scaredyland is likely to be your last. The twisted horrors inside these walls are enough to make a grown humanoid spew. So, be sure to bring your barf bags as you make your way from the Brain Scrambler to the Spin Psycho. But that's only for startlers.*" Saving the worst for last, the ghost-like hologram stretches its incorporeal body big enough to swallow the team whole as it introduces the main attraction. "*Voted the ride most likely to scare you to death, its frame was constructed from the remains of the most evil rides ever to be torn down. At an excruciating twelve minutes and twenty-seven space seconds, and featuring four different track combinations, the Creep Coaster has been specially designed to test the limits of your sanity. But be warned – once you get on, you might never get off.*" The ghost cackles, and the Coaster is revealed in a glowing haze of artificial dark light as the animatronic monsters decorating its entrance howl in anticipation of their next victims. "*Before you risk your souls, remember Rule one hundred thirty-two: keep your hands and feet inside the murder cart at all times.*"

The ghost shrinks down to size, and for a long moment they gawk at the towering death trap – a knotted mesh of mangled Parkwood tall enough to blot out the moons. Pants can't tell whether the horrible structure, with its bent beams and rotting track, is going to collapse at any moment or if it was just designed that way. She nervously follows the others toward the empty line winding underneath the monstrosity, when her fear finally gets the best of her.

"I'm sorry, you guys," she tells the fans as she backs away from the Coaster's shadow. "But I can't do it."

"What?!" The One shouts. "Why the fish not?"

"It's too scary," she says. "You have to go without me."

"You're supposed to be our fearless leader," he says. "Does anyone else want to back out? Beer?"

"Yeah," Beer tells his brother. "I'm sure you'd like that. But there's no way I'm letting you get the first token."

For a space second, Pants fears she's going to be left to wander the Ghost Town all by herself. But as the others run toward the entrance, she notices that Todd's face has gone pale, and he's started shaking in his officially licensed limited edition Pants Team Chucks.

"You guys go ahead," the merch guy says. "We'll catch up with you."

"Aww, not you too," The One moans. "What's *your* problem?"

"Look at the sign!" Todd insists.

Turning toward an ancient warning posted in front of the entrance, The One reads, "'Estimated Wait Time is 97 Space Minutes.' Uh, I'm pretty sure that's no longer accurate."

"Don't you get it?" Digging in his jacket pocket, Todd pulls out his misfortune and shows it to them. "My unlucky number is 97, just like on the sign."

"So, what does that mean?" The One persists.

"It means I'm not going on the ride," Todd says. "I'll stay out here with Pants. We can ride the Scream Catcher. Plus, I have some calls to make."

"You're being irrational," Horton notes. "Then again, it is quite a coincidence."

Throwing his hands up, The One tells them, "Fine, stay here. We'll be back in 12 and a half space minutes, or 97, or whatever."

The boys take off down the tunnel, and once their howls of excitement fade, Pants and Todd are officially on their own.

Shivering in his vacation shorts, Todd says, "It really is sort of spooky out here. It almost feels like we're being watched."

"We are," Pants reminds him, holding up her phone.

"I don't mean the fans," he says. "Although, it could be all the monsters staring at me – their eyes follow you. So, you want to head over to the Scream Catcher?"

"May I suggest the Mind Melter?" Ghosty offers.

"I've got a better idea," Pants says, taking off toward a dark and twisty ride at the other end of the Gorewalk.

When she reaches the back of the line, she holds up her phone so her fans can see the giant black cat spinning its arms in the night air. Displayed above its angry green eyes and mouthful of pointy teeth is a flashing sign that reads "The Purrdalizer."

Todd eventually catches up to her and hunches over to catch his breath. "You're too scared to go on the Creep Coaster, but you'll get on this thing? The ration I ate earlier is still settling in my stomach. Maybe I'll just stay here and—"

But before he can talk his way out of it, Pants drags him through cat's jagged chompers and up to the front of the empty queue.

"Come on!" she whines impatiently as the ride whirls above them.

When they reach the gate, the cat's giant paws slowly lower to the platform and Pants jumps into one of the seats.

Laughing nervously as he straps in next to her, Todd says, "I haven't been on this sort of ride since I was a kid."

"*The Purrdalizer is one of the most popular rides in Scaredyland,*" Ghosty informs them. "*Hold on tight and see if you can escape this black cat's claws!*"

The ghost dematerializes, and Pants can hear Todd whimpering next to her as they wait for the ride to start.

It takes so long that she worries something might be wrong, until Todd says, "Maybe it's brok—"

Before he can utter another syllable, the cat's paws suddenly launch the two of them into the night sky. Pants cackles with glee and Todd screams like a little boy as the cat's arms flail through the air, their view alternating between the star-speckled sky and the Gorewalk below. After a few dozen spins, the cat's frenzy peters out, and the two of them are lowered back to Park level.

As Pants jumps down from her seat and skips out the exit, she tells her fans, "That was so scary, you guys!" Glancing back at Todd as he wobbles through the gate behind her, she asks him, "What do you want to go on next?"

He lifts a finger like he has an idea, but before he can spit it out, he rushes to the nearest glowing trash can and loses whatever was left of his lunch.

When he's finished emptying the contents of his stomach, he tells Pants, "Sorry, but I don't think I can handle any more rides. Plus, I really do have some calls to make."

"So, *you're* leaving me, too?" Pants moans.

"The rest of the team will be done riding the Creep Coaster any space minute," he tells her, wiping his mouth on his pink sleeve as he stumbles off toward the rest area. "I'm sure you'll have a scarier time without me."

Pouting into her phone, Pants says, "I guess it's just you and me, you guys."

"*And me!*" Ghosty reminds her, floating toward the camera.

"Oh yeah…"

11

Clutching his stomach, Todd wanders toward the Wretched Rest Area and sits on one of the weather-beaten benches that overlook the black swamp surrounding the Ghost Town. He stays there, with his head between his knees, until his nausea subsides. When he's finally able to sit up, he wearily searches his pockets for a pack of candy cigarettes and empties the carton into his mouth. From this vantage, what had seemed like a random jumble of rides has transformed into a pack of bloodthirsty monsters standing guard over the Creep Coaster, their twisted faces and spinning limbs taking on a whole new dimension of terror.

The night air is cool and bright under the glow of The Park's moons. But much as Todd would like to spend the rest of the adventure lounging in its lazy luminescence, he's got bigger fish heads to fry.

Chomping down the last of his cigarettes, he takes out his cracked phone and pulls up Park Mule Contracting. A few moments later, the head of the operation answers, an annoyed look on his long, tired face.

"Hey Mr. Honker, I'm just checking to see how things are coming along on the *Cuddler*," Todd says, ignoring the tumult taking place in the background. "I mean, Mr. *Smackers*…"

This slip of the tongue only further irritates the overworked, underpaid equine. *"The damage is worse than we thought. We're going to have to tear apart the entire left ear and rebuild it from scratch before she's spaceworthy."*

Afraid to ask, Todd bleats, "What's that gonna cost?"

"As the old space saying goes," Mr. Smackers says, *"if you have to ask…"*

"Aright, aright," Todd relents. "Just get it done."

But the mule brays. *"There's still the not-so-little matter of compensation. You're already a space month behind on payments. We're all big fans of the team, and we want to trust them, but if we don't see some credits soon, I'm going to have to take my drove elsewhere."*

"I know," Todd says. "Don't worry, I'll get you your crits."

"This may go without saying, but we don't accept Park Bucks," Mr. Smackers adds, in one final insult.

"I got it!" Squeezing his phone, Todd hangs up before he says something the whole team will regret.

Everything is riding on this adventure. If it doesn't pay off in a big way, it could mean the end of Pants

Team Pink as they know it. But no matter how many times he warns them, they refuse to listen.

"Once again, it's up to you, Todd," he tells himself. "The fate of the universe is resting on your shoulders."

To that end, he figures he better put a call in to The Other One to make sure the new episodes are getting maximum universal exposure.

When the kid finally answers, he looks flustered and his breathing is heavy. "*Oh hey, how's the adventure going?*"

"Uh, it's going fine…," Todd says, taking note of the familiar dank walls surrounding The One's sneakier half. "You're still on the ship?"

"*What?!*" The Other One cries. "*No, of course not.*"

"That's the closet I lock myself in whenever I need some time away from the team," Todd says. "I recognize the pink mop behind you – I've used it enough. So, what are you still doing there? You should be out promoting the show, or at least risking your life with us over here at Scaredyland."

Clearly grasping to fabricate an explanation, the kid says, "*I wanted it to be a surprise. I'm filming a promo for the show right here in the* Cuddler."

"O-kay…," Todd says, intrigued but skeptical as muffled chatter seeps in through the door. "Hey, what's that noise? Are you throwing a *party*?!"

"*No, no,*" The Other One claims. "*I would never take advantage of the team's trust like that. That's just the TV. I'm watching 'Last Exit to Springfield.'*"

"Oh…," Todd says. "Well, I guess that's okay. But we're not paying you to watch educational television. If you can promote the show from there, you should be able to do it from out here with us. This is your chance to prove yourself as an official honorary member of the team."

"*Aye aye*," the kid says, saluting overzealously. "*Mission accepted and—*"

The Other One suddenly reaches back and struggles to hold the closet door shut as someone pulls from the other side, and Todd hears a voice call, "*We set up the water slide, but we accidentally soaked somebody's Pants Team Comics collection.*"

"What the fish did he say?" Todd demands.

"*Nobody*," The Other One says. "*I mean, nothing. It's just one of the Park mules.*"

"Wait a space second. Is that…" Holding the hologram up to his face, Todd zooms in on a bright blob of pink gunk stuck in the kid's hair. "*Frosting?!*"

"*A-ha*," The Other One laughs nervously. "*I have to go. My crab juice is getting cold. I mean, warm. I'll catch up with you guys later!*"

Before he can be virtually eviscerated, The Other One ends the call, and when Todd calls back, it goes straight to vidmail.

"I'm gonna make that little chit wish he never came aboard!" Todd howls, pitifully. "Whatever happens, I have to make sure that this is the best adventure the team has ever been on, even if it costs me the rest of my comic book collection. Thank Space God all my really good stuff is locked up safe and sound back on Earth. That reminds me, I better call the store and check if I have any messages. It's all I have left in case worse comes to blurst."

After a few too many rings, a familiar yet conspicuously cheerful face appears on the screen. *"Todd, my favorite son, it's so nice to see you!"*

"O-kay…," he says, searching her wrinkles for any signs of funny business. "What are you doing in the store at this hour?"

"Your store is fine," she assures him, fluffing her blue curls. *"You always worry so much. Relax and enjoy your vacation."*

"I'm not on vacation," he informs her. "It's a serious work adventure!"

"Aright, aright," she says. *"I believe you, kind of."*

Somewhere off camera, Todd hears a loud *smash* and asks, "What the fish was that?"

"Language!" she scolds.

"Uh, Penzy…" A familiar old man in a toga wanders into the frame holding the remains of a priceless golden relic. *"I think I broke whatever this is."*

"Mr. Johaxen?" Whimpering, Todd asks, "Is that my… Chachapoyan Fertility Idol?"

"No problem," the old man says. *"A little of the ol' Elmer's and it'll be good as new."*

"Hey Penzy," a woman's voice calls from off-screen. *"We're out of nachos!"*

Struggling to wrap his head around every outrageous thing that's happening, Todd says, "Are you having a party?! I told you, your friends aren't allowed in the store when I'm not there!"

"What are you, crazy?" his mom says. *"All that time out in space is making you paranoid. You're not coming down with space madness, are you?"*

"Of course not!" Todd cries.

"*Good,*" she says. "*Then I'll see you when you get back.*" But before she can figure out how to hang up, he hears her call out, "*Nah, he won't be home for space weeks. I'm going on a beer run. Whoever pays gets their choice of merch. Don't worry about it. We'll fix that stuff late—*"

In a daze, Todd reaches for his candy cigarettes and mashes the empty box. With the waking nightmare of a lifetime's worth of priceless collectibles shattering in his head, he pushes himself up from the bench and wobbles back toward the Creep Coaster.

The Moon Mummy taunts him with its mad grin, stifling laughter when he steps past its gauzy gate. For a brief moment, as he approaches the Watery Werewolf, he spots what looks like a glowing skeletal mascot riding down the silver flume. Unbelieving, he rubs his eyes, and when he opens them, the creature is gone.

"You're seeing things, fish head," he tells himself.

As he nears the Coaster, a sudden burst of laughter rings out over the Ghost Town, and he starts to think the place really is haunted – until he spots Beer, The One, and Horton running down the exit ramp.

"That's the best ride in the whole Park," Beer declares. "I didn't think we were gonna make it out alive."

"When I saw that ghost sitting next to me, I almost jumped out of my cart," Horton adds. "And I don't even believe in ghosts."

"You know," Beer says, "the track switches around after every ride…"

Bounding along beside them, The One says, "What are we waiting for?"

As they run back around to the entrance, Todd yells after them, "Hold on a space second, you guys!" Panting as he jogs across the Gorewalk, he asks, "So, did you find the token?"

"Oh yeah…," The One says. "I forgot about that. We better ride the Coaster again to look for it."

But before they can go anywhere, a gleeful voice shouts, "Hey, you guys!" Skipping toward them across the Gorewalk, with Ghosty floating close behind, Pants holds up a plastic, coaster-sized souvenir and announces, "I found it!"

12

The moment the team steps out of the Ghost Town, their holographic companion cries, *"Congratulations on collecting your first token! You only need three more to unlock the entrance to Mascot Manor. But in order to find them, you're going to have to face your fears. Plahahaha…"*

As they head toward their next haunted destination, Beer asks Pants, "Where'd you find it, anyway?"

"It was in the Witch's Cauldron," she explains. "You won't believe what I had to go through to get it. It was down at the bottom of the bubbling potion pot, so I—"

"I mean, good job and all," The One says, swiping the token from her hand. "But you just got lucky. Any of us could have found it."

While he's admiring the token, Pants taps him on the shoulder, and when he turns his head, she snatches the prize back from him. "Then why didn't you?"

"Whatever," he says. "It doesn't matter. I'm gonna find the rest of them before any of you has a chance, starting with the Haunted Raceway. I say we go over there next, unless you're space chicken."

Before the others can argue, Ghosty reminds them, *"At the Haunted Raceway, you'll strap into one of our Monster Wagons and challenge your friends to a race around the cursed track."*

Moaning with excitement, The One says, "This is gonna be so sweet."

"If you're looking for sweets," Ghosty suggests, *"why not spend a few tokens on a Scaredyland exclusive Black Ration Cake?"*

"Stop taunting me!" The One tells the ghost.

Aside from the team, the Dark Park is completely devoid of life, but as they make their way down Maim Street, Beer can't shake the feeling that they're being watched by someone other than the fans. Unable to pinpoint the source of his fear, he finally shrugs it off as another one of the park's scare tactics.

Reaching the entrance to the Haunted Raceway requires passing under a frozen collision of giant, hyper-stylized monster mascots competing to see which one can cause the most damage. The monster racers, tongues lolling out of their twisted dragsters, are trailed by artificial flames and big billowy clouds of cartoon exhaust.

"Neat!" Pants exclaims, panning over the sculptures with her phone.

"I can't wait to wipe the track with you," Beer tells The One as they follow Ghosty through the front gate.

"In my nightmares, maybe," The One says.

But as they make their way toward the track, their guide floats into their path and says, "*Before you start your engines, all racers must learn and promise to follow the rules of the Raceway.*"

The ghost's body morphs into the shape of a holo-tube, and when the ancient instructional video begins to play, The One moans, "*Awww…*"

After fifteen space minutes of mascots demonstrating all the things they're not allowed to do, Beer says, "Well, that was mind-numbingly adorable."

"I liked it," Pants says. "But I wonder what happened to the mascots?"

"*Missed something?*" Ghosty asks. "*Watch the video again.*"

But before the title screen reappears, the boys cry out, "*No!*"

Mercifully, the ghost obeys their demand and ends its demonstration in order to lead them down to the track. Stepping around to the starting line, Beer gazes out over the perilous racecourse in search of anything that might give him an advantage. But when he and The One catch each other looking ahead, they get into a spirited shoving match that ends only when they realize Pants and Horton have already begun scoping out the karts.

Lined up inside the pit are a dozen mini, horror-themed jalopies in various states of disrepair. Beer is unsure which qualities are most important in a monster machine, but if there's one thing he's learned from his space days riding around The Park's miniature racetracks, it's not to get stuck with the slow kart.

"*Each Monster Wagon comes with its own unique strengths and weaknesses,*" Ghosty tells them. "*What the* Frankenkart *lacks in acceleration, it more than makes up for with its wide, heavy chassis, used to pulverize smaller vehicles. Or consider the* Bone Crusher. *While its spare frame leaves it vulnerable to collision, its special booster gives it a leg bone up on the competition.*"

"I'm gonna drive the *She-Machine,*" Pants squeals, climbing into a pink mutant of a kart with bulging eyes and a grin full of crooked teeth.

Before Beer can decide which kart to pick, Horton scurries around to the back of the line and says, "I've got a good feeling about the *Black Bat.* It can probably fly, or something."

"I call the *Zombie Zoomer,*" The One yells, sprinting toward a mangled kart made of what looks like rotting flesh.

"Chit!" Beer cries. "This is all happening so fast." Anxiously searching the track, he spots a chrome disc stashed inside a nearby garage, and he asks the ghost, "What about that kart?"

"*The karts in the service bay are in need of repairs and are not fit to race. Please select one of the karts in the pit. May I suggest the* Bug Zapper…"

Desperate to outdo his brother, Beer finally decides, "I guess I'll take the *Monster Masher.*"

With its vampire fangs, fish creature fins, and shaggy werewolf upholstery, the kart is all the best monsters squished into one. Or so Beer figures as he climbs behind the monstrosity's bandaged steering wheel.

Noticing that Todd isn't trying very hard to select his kart, Beer asks, "Aren't you coming?"

"Eh, I think I'll sit this one out," the merch guy says. "I get kart sick."

"A-right…," Beer says, reminding himself never to get old.

As he slips his mummified helmet on, Ghosty says, *"Inside your helmets you'll find a digital display of your kart's vitals, including your current rank and a map of the track. They will also allow you to communicate with your fellow racers as you compete in a death-defying race around Scaredyland. The first racer to complete a lap will be rewarded with the Haunted Raceway token. Once all racers are in position behind the starting line, the countdown will begin."*

Beer presses the ignition switch on the *Monster Masher*'s dash, and the kart's engine coughs to afterlife. Rolling toward the starting line, he pulls up next to The One's *Zoomer*, their engines growling, and rests his foot against the *Masher's* pedal. Pants's pink *Machine* and Horton's *Bat* get into position, and the instant the melted timer flashes 'GO', Beer pushes his sneaker to the floor.

The *Zombie Zoomer* immediately takes off into the lead, skidding and swerving down the track, with the *She-Machine* following close behind. Working to get the *Monster Masher* up to speed, Beer comes to realize that he might not have chosen the fastest kart on the track. But it's not the slowest either. That dishonor belongs to the *Black Bat*, puttering along in a distant last.

As Horton lags behind the rest of them, he shouts through his helmet, *"Aww man, I got the dud!"*

Forced to make a sudden sharp turn, Beer yanks the *Masher's* wheel around and is pleasantly surprised by the kart's response. Between its sturdy frame, slick handling, and horrifying appearance, the *Masher* is a well-balanced amalgamation of monster parts.

By the time Beer rounds the first corner, he's zipping along at full speed. He soon sets his sights on Pants's pink mutant, but uncertain what powers her kart might possess, he takes a cautious approach. When they hit a straightaway, he attempts to get in front of the *She-Machine*, but Pants spots him at the last space second, and her mutant mobile stretches out a pair of hairy, misshapen arms to block him from passing.

Falling back, Beer looks for an opening, but the *Machine* is taking up the entire width of the track. Judging by the airtime she gets whenever she hits a pothole, her kart is definitely lighter than his, but he's not confident that the difference is enough to knock her aside without causing his own kart to spin out. As they zip around the Ghoulish Game Gallery, they approach a narrow ghost tunnel, and Pants is forced to retract her arms. Seeing his opening, Beer speeds up, and as they exit the tunnel, their karts clash.

"*Hey!*" Pants wails.

Glaring at him from inside her mutated helmet, she tries to bring the *She-Machine*'s arm down onto the *Masher's* gilled grille. But before the gnarly appendage can make contact with Beer's kart, he manages to slip ahead of her and into second place.

A torrent of angry pink syllables spills into his helmet, and he answers with a fiendish cackle, "*Grahahaha…* I'm coming for you next, zombie boy."

"*Eat my lifeless dust,*" The One responds.

Beer spots the *Zombie Zoomer* just up ahead, struggling to maneuver along the twisty path leading to the Scaredyland gate, and by the time they bounce over the park's bright entrance, he's almost caught up to the undead kart. To close the gap, he figures now is as good a time as any to try out his kart's special ability. Holding tight to its bandaged steering wheel, he presses the red button in the center of the dash, and the *Monster Masher* produces the peculiar sound of four very different beasts all howling at the same time.

"That's the special power?" Beer moans. "A taunt?"

"*Brahahaha,*" The One cackles as his kart expels a thick cloud of green exhaust.

"Is that supposed to slow me down?" Beer scoffs. "I could catch you with my eyes closed." But as soon as the smoke reaches him, he gets a whiff of the *Zombie Zoomer's* power. "*Ulchh,* you are so dead! Again."

Holding his breath through the rotten cloud, Beer rams the *Masher* into The One's rotting bumper, and they both wipe out screaming.

13

The One glances back just in time to see the *Monster Masher*'s amphibioid grille ram the *Zombie Zoomer*'s rotting back end. He spins his kart's fleshy wheel to compensate for the resulting skid, but it's not enough to keep him on the track. His kart swerves off into the overgrown weeds, shedding putrid body parts until it comes to a final hard splash in the thick bog surrounding this side of Scaredyland.

Stunned from the crash, The One drags himself out of the black muck and up onto the bog's bank, where a white haze materializes to warn him, *"You've gone off course. Your kart is swamped."*

"Don't you think I know that?" the boy growls.

"Please return your kart to the track."

"Fish off!" he says, swiping at the ghost's holographic body.

With his feet planted infirmly in the mushy marsh, he grabs the back of the *Zooomer* and tries to drag it back out, but the busted bumper comes loose, and he slips into the muck. As he struggles to climb back out, the recovered *Monster Masher* drives past, taunting him with its stupid multi-monster howl.

"Grahh!" The One cries, and grabbing his kart's rotten frame, he gradually hauls the mangled machine out of the ancient sludge.

While he's piecing his kart back together, Pants zips past in her *She-Machine*, and he begins to sense his chances of victory slipping through his slimy fingers.

"I'm coming for you!" he warns the others as he straightens his decomposing helmet. But when he attempts to get the *Zoomer* started, the ancient engine is flooded and refuses to return to life. "Come on, you stupid flesh bag!"

Smashing his fists against the dead dash, The One suddenly hears the approach of a familiar rattling sound, and he desperately tries to get his kart moving. But it's too late. Puttering along the track at the speed of a brisk jog, Horton gives The One the thumb as the *Black Bat* rolls into third place.

"You're falling behind!" Ghosty warns.

Ignoring the stupid ghost, The One jams his finger into the starter button again, and by some haunted miracle, the kart explodes to life, expelling a stream of thick black gunk as it takes off down the track. To make up for lost time, he pushes the freakish fusion of putrefied flesh and machine to its limit, and it's not long before he catches up to the *Bat*.

When Horton spots the *Zoomer* making its approach on the wide turn around the Creep Coaster, he shouts, "Bat wings, fly me to the finish!" Deploying the *Black Bat*'s special ability, a couple of flimsy black kite-wings pop out of the sides of his kart. While they flutter wildly in the wind, they fail to lift him off the track. "Dam it, I knew I should've taken the *Ooze Mobile!*"

The One crashes through the *Bat*'s left wing, cackling with his thumb held high as he reclaims third place. When he loops back across the Gorewalk, a dense mist descends over the track, and the map in his helmet shows that he's entered the Gruesome Graveyard.

Although visibility is limited, it's not long before he spots the pink hue of Pants's mutated kart in the fog up ahead. Sticking to the outside of the track, he tries to pass her undetected. But as he putters along the cloudy Raceway, a glowing blue ghost suddenly appears in his path, and he wrenches his kart's wheel.

In his attempt to avoid the apparition, he swerves into Pants's kart and she cries, *"Hey, I'm driving here!"*

Once they come out of the fog, she rams him back, but he somehow manages to maintain control of his wretched vehicle while the *She-Machine* skids off the track.

"You play too rough," Pants wails as her kart crashes into the barrier.

With only one racer left between The One and the Raceway token, he finally reaches the haunted house at the end of Scaredyland – Mascot Manor. The *Zoomer* bounces up a steep incline as the track wraps around the crumbling mansion's faded façade. But as the course takes him up through the topmost floor, its dark walls decorated with disintegrating Space Halloween decorations, there's still no sign of his brother.

Running out of track, he fears he won't be able to catch up. But as he takes the winding plunge back toward the Ghost Town below, he finally lays eyes on the *Monster Masher.* There's still a lot of track between them, but The One figures if he takes to the treacherous slope without braking, he might just be able to out-mash that monster.

Utilizing its wrapped tires to stick to the rubber pavement, the *Masher* was created for the sharp, twisting turns that guard the finish line. But all that extra traction limits its speed. Having finally gotten the hang of the *Zombie Zoomer*'s uniquely loose handling, The One careens down the hill with a complete lack of regard for the rules of the Raceway. The moment he hits the first curve, he spins the wheel of his rotten racekart, sending it skidding out along the edge of the rubber road. Just before the track cuts back, he wrenches the wheel in the opposite direction, guiding the *Zoomer* along the twisting course with unconscious precision. Despite his superior racing abilities, there are moments when he doesn't know how he's staying on the track.

"I got you!" The One warns his brother as he closes in on the *Masher*'s scaly bumper.

When Beer glances back to find the *Zoomer* hurtling down the hill behind him, he yelps and swerves out of the way, allowing the undead kart to bounce through the gap. The One hits the final straightaway cackling as Beer hurls obscenities.

The only thing left between the *Zoomer* and certain victory is empty track. But The One just can't help himself. In one final act of antagonism, he lets Beer catch up and then slams the brakes, causing the *Monster Masher* to collide with the *Zombie Zoomer* and propel it across the finish line.

Holographic confetti falls out of thin air as The One skids to a halt and jumps out of his kart to gloat. But the *Masher* never makes it over the finish line. Instead, it rolls to a stop along the edge of the track, its engine billowing black smoke.

As Beer climbs out of the driver's seat, he yells, "You ackle, you busted my kart!"

Running around behind it, he quickly tries to shove the *Masher* across the finish line. But before he can get it rolling, the *She-Machine* comes zipping down the track to take second.

"I can still beat Horton!" Beer grumbles as he presses his shoulder into the kart.

But soon the *Black Bat* putters down the last leg of the winding course, and despite Beer's best effort, Horton manages to squeak into third place.

"Dam it!" Beer cries, throwing off his helmet as he storms toward The One. "If my kart was still working, I'd run you off the track."

"Hey, I came in third!" Horton announces. "I'm not the worst!"

"That's why they call me Mr. Onederful," The One says.

Smacking the side of his brother's helmet, Beer says, "No one calls you that!"

The One shoves Beer in retaliation, and soon they're wrestling each other to the ground, shouting increasingly dumb declarations of kart supremacy.

As Pants climbs out of her mutated vehicle, she says, "That was fun, you guys! Let's go around again."

Accidentally in agreement, the brothers shout back, "No!"

But that only makes them more determined to throttle each other. If it wasn't for Horton pointing out how stupid they look, there's no telling how long they'd be rolling around the track.

"*Rule seventeen!*" Ghosty says, hovering over them. "*There's no fighting in Scaredyland!*" Once the ghost has stolen their attention, it announces, "*Congratulations on reaching the end of the Haunted Raceway. You all had a great race!*"

"Except Beer," The One quips, narrowly avoiding his brother's retaliatory fist.

"*But only one of you can take home the plastic. The first place racer can collect their trophy from the prize machine near the exit. For even more scares, come back and try your luck against the track ghosts!*"

Once they've calmed down, the team throw off their helmets and wander back toward the Raceway gate, where they find Todd in his honorary jacket leaning against a large prize machine.

"So, who won?" the merch guy asks.

"Does this answer your question?" The One asks as he sticks his wrist under the prize scanner. After a few space seconds, the machine spits out a Haunted Raceway token, and he proudly holds it up for all the team to see.

Observing the shiny souvenir alongside the annoyed looks on the other racers' faces, Todd says, "Oh…"

From the moment Horton lays eyes on The Ghoulish Game Gallery, he can tell he's found his Ghost Town. From the glowing skeletons adorning its dark walls to the scrapcore blaring out of the entrance, the arcade is unlike anything else in The Park. Stepping inside the dim room is like a breath of stale air. The maze of ancient glowing cabinets reaches beyond sight, and the tingle of ungrounded electricity dances across his skin.

As Horton closes his eyes to soak in the extinct aromas and primitive two-dimensional sounds, Beer comments, "It smells like burnt plastic and coagulated pizza grease."

"Ho-ly fried space fritters…," Todd says, ogling the Gallery. "This has gotta be the most valuable room I've ever been in. We're sitting on a digital gold mine!"

"Please," Horton says. "There are many Parkgoers, myself included, who would consider this a sacred place. Show a little class, for Space God's sake."

"Space hell yes!" The One squeals. "I hope they have *Escape From Grandma's House*."

Pushing him out of the way, Beer says, "First, I'm gonna beat your ack in *Kill Racer*."

"We just finished racing," Pants argues, her sneaker boots flashing intrusively.

"Yeah, but this is less real," Beer says.

Before they can explore the place any further, Ghosty materializes to haunt them. *"Inside the Goulish Game Gallery, you'll get to test your virtual skills amongst the largest selection of arcade machines in the universe. Collect enough tickets and you could live to earn a reward from our ghastly Prize Keeper. But be careful or it will be Game Over for you and your friends."* In one final disclaimer, the ghost adds, *"Please keep in mind that all Scaredyland rules you've come to know and respect remain in full effect inside the Game Gallery."*

As soon as the ghost is done blabbering, the team and their trusty merch guy race to the counter to check out the prizes. A mannequin corpse covered in scraps of fake flesh, the Prize Keeper stares out at them from its dusty glass enclosure with a lunatic grin. Horton moves to the other side of the case to escape the Keeper's lidless gaze, but not matter where he goes, its plastic eyes follow.

All the classics are represented – spider rings, finger traps, sticky hands.

"It's the same chit they have in The Park arcades," The One complains.

"Except the whoopee cushions are black," Beer notes. "That's… something."

"I want that big dust goblin!" Pants says.

Taking a closer look at the decaying card in front of the stuffed creature, Horton says, "That thing costs 2,000 tickets! Plus, it's been sitting back there so long it'll probably fall apart the space second you touch it." As he examines the rest of the prizes, he finally spots the souvenir they came for. "There it is – the Ghoulish Game Gallery token."

But when Beer peers at the plastic prize, partially hidden under a thick layer of dust and cobwebs, he moans, "*Awww*, 10,000 tickets? We'll be well into our afterlives before we can collect that many!"

"It's a lot," Horton concedes. "But I think it's doable. We just have to play the right games. And *win*, of course."

"So, which games are the right ones?" Beer asks.

But Horton just shrugs. "We'll have to play to find out. It looks like everything in here has been modified to dispense tickets. We just have to figure out which games give the most tickets for the least effort."

"What about that thing?" The One suggests, pointing to a faded electricity generator designed to look like a bald humanoid biting an old-fashioned light bulb. "It must be easy —
there's only two control sticks."

"Whoa…," Todd says as he approaches the ancient game. "I've heard of these. But I didn't think they were real." Slipping a token into the slot, he selects the 'High' setting and wraps his hands around the metal sticks. His face twists as the wattage gradually increases, until he starts screaming, *"Wahhh!"*

"Should we do something?" Beer cries, his face turning as white as the monster in the machine.

Casually assessing the situation, The One decides, "Nah."

The monster wails in pain, its ears smoking as the wattage tops out at 3,000. But the damage to the merch guy is already done, and he collapses to the synthetic carpeting, twitching from the electricity presumably still flowing through his body.

"Are you okay?" Pants asks.

But before she can reach out to him, Horton pulls her arm away and warns, "Don't touch him. He could still be live."

As they bow their heads to mourn their fallen friend, Todd suddenly reaches up and zaps The One's hand with a bolt of static electricity.

"Yow!" The One wails. "What the fish! You're okay?"

"Sure," the merch guy says, climbing to his feet. "I was just kidding around. There's always some kind of trick to these machines."

"That's dumb," The One says, sucking his fingertips. "Lemme try!" But before he can insert his token, the smoke coming out of the monster's ears turns to fire, and its pale head begins melting like a plastic candle. *"Aww…"*

"Rule 187!" Ghosty scolds. *"Don't break the machines!"*

"Hey, I only know one way to score," Todd tells the ghost.

Waiting impatiently, Beer finally says, "And that would be…"

"High."

"It doesn't matter," Horton says as Todd reaches down to collect his winnings. "How many tickets did you get?"

Slowly adding them up, the merch guy announces, "Five."

"Those cheap bass turds!" Beer whines in disgust.

"Hmm…," Horton muses. "Maybe it was the most effort for the most tickets. Anyway, like Todd said, there's always a trick. Everybody, play some games so we can figure out which ones have the highest payouts."

As his teammates run off to different sections of the Gallery, Horton wanders the blinking aisles of arcade cabinets, searching for a game he can beat. Given enough time, he's sure he could master any machine in the building. But that's a luxury he can't afford. Most of the games have been rendered one-of-a-kinds by now, and so he has no knowledge of their gameplay. But he doesn't want to go in blind. He only has a limited number of tokens, and he can't afford to waste a single one.

Just as he's about to give up and go play Whack-A-Troll, he sees it. Stuffed in a particularly dusty corner of the Gallery, between *Tuna Diver* and *Butt Fighter,* rests a worn game machine with which Horton is all too familiar. One of the few games to escape the physical media purge of the Post-Digital Age, *Meteor Chit* has been a popular pastime for bored kids pretending to do their homework ever since its clandestine creation.

Running his hands over the fake moss covering the ancient cabinet, Horton says, "This is going to be a piece of ration cake."

He digs a token out of his pocket and slips it into the slot, but nothing happens. Futilely smacking the start button a few dozen times, he pulls his leg back to start kicking, when he notices the problem.

"*Two* tokens? That's double what it costs in The Park!"

Grumbling, Horton feeds the machine another one of his precious coins, and the title screen appears. He immediately sets his infected farmer to work mowing the overgrown lawn outside his Earth shack. But his character quickly gets stuck in the weeds, causing him to be transformed into a permanent lawn ornament.

Mentally threatening the ghost of the game's creator, Horton pumps two more tokens into the machine, and this time he gets half the lawn mowed before succumbing to his phytoid affliction.

"I'm coming to get you...," he says, glancing at the scoreboard, "HDJ."

By his fifth attempt, he almost manages to survive the whole night, utilizing the shotgun to blast apart the flesh-eating plants while successfully collecting enough Ripple to hold his condition at bay. But before he can reach the pitcher of screwdriver to buy himself a little more time, his digital farmer gets tangled up and turns the shotgun on himself.

"Dam it!" Horton shouts. "I almost had it that time."

Cracking his fingers, he decides to employ a different strategy this time – and it pays off. His next game, he gets all the way to the final level before accidentally mowing into a bottomless puddle. It was a good run, but his score is still a long way from the top. The gap is so big, in fact, that he begins to wonder if he's missing something.

"I feel like there was a secret lever or power-up or… something," he muses, thinking back to the games of his youth.

This time, he leaves no corner unmowed. He hits every patch of tall grass and collects every payout from the college. But even after all that, the top score is still hopelessly out of reach. He thinks about giving up, but the weight of the remaining tokens in his pocket convinces him to give it one last half-acked attempt.

Randomly positioning the joystick, Horton weaves his farmer back and forth across the yard, hardly bothering to avoid the deadly obstacles in his path. When he swerves toward the shack to avoid a treacherous patch of crab grass, he accidentally steers the farmer's mower through the front door, where he discovers a hidden item in the form of his father's ghost.

When the farmer collects the floating spirit, the game cabinet flashes and cries out, "Meteor chit!"

"I got *you*!" Horton says as he watches his score climb. Glancing around the empty arcade, he suddenly remembers his friends and wonders how they're scoring. But before he goes to look for them, he decides, "Just a couple more games…"

At first glance, the digital toy factory appears abandoned, its colorful machines having fallen into permanent disrepair. But Pants knows better. Peering through the scope of the plastic bazooka resting on her shoulder, she cautiously steps down a dark aisle strewn with stuffing. A mountain of partially melted baby dolls blocks the way, and when she leans down to move them, she hears a muffled patter coming toward her.

She quickly whips her head around, pointing her barrel down the dark corridor, and the sound stops. For a few long space seconds, she stares into the darkness, and just as she's about to lower her weapon, a neon blue puffball leaps out of the shadows.

"*Yah!*" she yelps as the stuffed bear rushes at her from across the aisle.

Muscle memory kicking in, Pants presses a button on top of her bazooka to launch an anti-plush missile, and an instant later, the bear bursts apart at the seams. But before she can relax, she hears a soft rumbling in the distance. She blindly fires into the passageway in front of her, but it's not enough to stop the horde of ravenous plush animals that bursts forth out of the darkness.

Balls of stuffing rain down as the neon beasts explode one after another, until Pants is pushed back against the baby doll barricade. Smashing her finger down on the bazooka's trigger, she frantically fires at the fluffy man-eaters until there's nothing left to blow up.

Low on ammo and covered in fuzz balls, Pants digs through the pile of melted dolls blocking her path, until there's enough space to squeeze through. As she limps into the final arena, a large warehouse full of old toy machines, a soft whimper echoes out over the factory floor. In a moment, the sound transforms into a petulant wail, and from out of the shadows stomps a sobbing baby doll as tall as a spacescraper.

Wiping the tears from its plastic eyes, the doll spots Pants down below and tells her, "You're going to be my new dolly!"

But as the monster reaches down to snatch its living toy, Pants rolls through its grasping fingers and takes off running. Sliding between its wobbly legs, Pants takes aim and her missiles explode against the doll's ankles. The giant toy spins around, an evil plastic grin forming on its adorable face as it starts stomping.

Ducking out of the monster's path, Pants narrowly avoids being caught underfoot, and with the last of her ammunition, she fires at the enemy's weak spot. As if guided by some invisible virtual force, the missile slams against the battery pack hidden under the doll's curly locks, and its plastic torso erupts in a ball of black fire. The doll shrieks and bats at the flames, flailing around the arena until its arms finally drop, and its giant body begins to tip. Hurling herself out of the way as the monster crashes to the arena floor, Pants takes one last look at the melted face of her vanquished foe and pulls off her game goggles.

Waking from her virtual daydream, it takes her a moment to come back down to actual reality inside the musty arcade. But soon her game fog lifts, and she returns to the real adventure with just enough time to enter her name on the *Toy House of the Undead* scoreboard. Seeing her initials at the top of the ranks is nice, but her real reward is the giant stack of tickets piled up next to the machine.

Gathering her winnings, she heads back to the prize counter to meet up with her friends. But when she gets there, none of the others have shown up yet. With a happy shrug, she feeds her tickets into the machine and waits for the Prize Keeper to count them. There's a bunch of brule merch inside the monster's cage, but what she really wants is the stuffed dust goblin, with its hideous slobbery jaws and bloodshot eyes. When the Keeper is finished counting, she winds up with 2,651 tickets.

"Wow, that's a lot," she tells the rotting ghoul. "It's way more than I need for the dust goblin." Glancing around the counter she adds, "And if the rest of those guys win as many tickets as me, we'll have enough to get the token plus a bunch of other prizes. Right?" She takes the Keeper's dead grin as confirmation. "Right."

When the rest of the team finally shows up, Horton points his spindly finger at the pile of rotting stuffing in front of the prize door and asks Pants, "What's that?"

"Uh, I don't know," she tells him, trying not to sound suspicious. "It was there when I got here."

"Hmph, weird...," Horton says. "So, how many tickets did you win?"

Pointing to the total above the Keeper's corpse, Pants says, "651." She forces herself to smile, and when the boy turns around, she tells her fans, "Shhh..."

"Well, I finally got the high score in *Meteor Chit*," Horton announces. Reaching into his team jacket pocket, Horton pulls out a small wad of tickets and says, "I haven't counted them, but it feels like it's around 500."

"That's all?!" The One cries.

"So, how the fish many did you guys get?" Horton demands.

Rubbing his fingers, Beer reluctantly tells them, "We got sort of caught up playing hover hockey. He kept hitting the puck at my fingers. I had no choice but to beat his ack. Anyway, we figured you guys would win more than enough to get the token."

"Hey, if you touch the table, your fingers are gonna get smacked," The One argues. "It's in the rules."

As they drag each other down onto the sticky floor, Todd steps around the fighting siblings and feeds his tickets into the machine. "I have 783."

"That means we have a total of 1,934 tickets," Horton reads off the ticker.

"But we need 10,000!" Beer cries. "What the fish are we gonna do now? How many tokens do you guys have left?"

They all dig into their pockets and hold out their hands to reveal fewer than a dozen of the counterfeit coins left between them.

Desperately counting and recounting the pitiful handful of change, Horton tells them, "We're never going to make it…"

"Don't say that!" Pants scolds, holding up the team symbol. "There's always a chance."

But despite her show of team spirit, the rest of them appear defeated.

"Face it," Beer says. "No machine in the whole Game Gallery pays out enough to make up the difference."

But just as it seems like all hope is lost, Todd raises his stout button-mashing finger and informs them, "That's not strictly true."

Waving for them to follow, their fearless merch guy takes them on a winding path through the ancient arcade toward a collection of games relegated to the furthest corner of the Gallery. A primitive place, dedicated to machines without screens, the blaring analog sound effects and burnt out flash bulbs give Pants the creeps. She sticks close to her teammates as Todd leads them to a row of long machines that look old enough to predate fun.

"No… not that," Beer moans. "Anything but Skee-Ball!"

"They call it Scream-Ball here," Todd says, motioning to a faded sign above the lanes. "But it's basically the same thing."

Starting at the merch guy like he's an alien from a dumb planet, The One says, "This isn't going to work. I've played this game before, and I never won more than a few tickets."

"You must not have been any good," Todd breaks it to the boy. "No offense. But if you spent any real time in The Parkades, you would know that this is one of the few games to offer a progressive jackpot. Every time someone plays a token, the pot grows, and the longer it's been since anyone has won, the more tickets there are in the pot. The next person who gets a perfect score wins the whole thing," Pointing to a ticker above the game, he adds, "Fortunately, these machines happen to be hooked into The Parkwide Skee-Ball network. And it's been a *looong* time since anyone has rolled a perfect game."

A terrible mechanical sound suddenly shrieks out, and Pants spins around to find *Big Bertha* laughing at them.

"Whoa," Beer says, adjusting his glasses to read the number. "With 22,348 tickets, we could win the token and have enough left over to get any prizes we want."

"This is just the chance we needed!" Pants says.

Slipping his last token into the closest slot, Todd says, "Let's find out which one of you has the best chance of pulling it off. You'll each get two balls to decide who's going to roll for the team. There are nine total, so I'll save the last one in case you're all terrible."

"Why don't we just climb up there and put the balls straight into the hole?" The One suggests.

Scoffing, Todd says, "You can try."

Ball in hand, The One stomps down the lane, but when he tries to shove the ball under the metal net protecting the holes, the machine delivers a strong *zap*. "Ouch."

"*Rules number nine and fifteen!*" Ghosty suddenly scolds from the sidelines. "*No climbing on the machines, and* no cheating*!*"

"I'll go last," Horton tells them. "I haven't played this game since we were kids. Plus, you know how I feel about sports."

Since The One is already standing in front of the lane, he throws first, releasing a torrent of space profanity as soon as he gutters out. Beer rolls next, landing one ball in the 30-point hole while the other bounces off the hump at the end of the lane and drops into the gutter. Not bad but not nearly good enough to win them the jackpot.

As Pants steps up to the machine, she tells herself, "Okay, you can do this. All you need is a perfect game."

By sheer luck, her first throw lands in the 20 hole, and she takes a step back to compose herself. Hoping to outscore Beer, she aims for 30 this time. But her hand is so sweaty that the ball slips through her fingers, bounces over the bumper, and rolls into the 50-point hole on the next machine over.

"Does that count?" she asks, hopefully.

"We did our best," Horton says, as he shuffles up to the lane. "But there's no way we're going to get a perfect game." Hardly bothering to aim, the pale kid tosses his first ball, and as if carried by some dark magic, it effortlessly glides down the lane and into the 100-point hole, beating the rest of their scores in a single roll.

"I guess I don't need to throw," Todd whispers, handing over his ball. "He is the roller of legend, the one the old gamers speak of – the Skeemaster."

But even this performance isn't enough to impress The One, who tells his friend, "Eh, lucky throw. I'll bet you the rest of my tokens you can't do it again."

16

As The One hands over his tokens, he grumbles, "Lucky… throws."

Horton's Scream-Ball skills are unlike anything Todd has ever seen. It only took the kid three games to hit the jackpot.

Hauling the tickets up to the prize counter, the merch guy tells the kid, "You should really think about joining The Park Leagues. You'd make a killing in endorsements alone. Plus, you'd gain a ton of new fans."

"Not interested," Horton says. "If I wanted to be a professional gamer, I'd play something a lot more fun."

Fulfilling his merchly duty, Todd smoothes out all the tickets and feeds them to the Prize Keeper. When he's finished, Horton has the honor of selecting the Ghoulish Game Gallery token, and the animatronic skeleton points its boney finger toward the plastic disc, releasing it into the prize slot.

Reverentially reaching into the machine to pluck out the precious prize, Todd drops onto his knee and announces, "I present this token to Horton for getting us this far. To the Skeemaster, long may he roll!"

"Would you stop calling me that!" Horton demands as he snatches the token.

"*Wow*," Ghosty says, waving its translucent paws. "*You guys are doing great! You only need one more Ghost Town token to gain entry to Mascot Manor. But first, why not stop by a Scaredyland gift shop? You'll find one on every corner of Maim Street!*"

As the team heads for the exit, Todd yells after them, "Wait a space second! We still have a bunch of tickets to spend. What else should we get?"

The team spends half the night selecting their prizes, and when they finally get back out onto the Parkway, they drag their feet toward the only Ghost Town they haven't visited, all the way on the other side of Scaredyland.

Rummaging through a pocketful of long-expired candy, The One says, "Welp, it looks like Beer is the only one who hasn't won a token. I mean, besides Todd. But he doesn't count."

"If you keep sucking on that old sweetmeat, you're gonna end up with candy poisoning," Beer warns his brother as he attempts to untangle his new old Scaredyland yo-yo. "Anyway, the next token is mine, or Pants's, or Horton's. Or even Todd's. But one thing's for sure. I'm never gonna let you get your sticky hands on it. I don't know how you can eat that chit, anyway."

Loudly sucking on a candy ring manufactured centuries before he was born, The One says, "I eat my candy the way only a token-winner can – the best."

Pants, usually one for prizes of the cute stuffed variety, opted for a bunch of plastic jewelry, which clacks loudly as she bounces along the rubber blacktop, reminding them, "Peace and love, you guys! Don't worry, Beer. You'll get the next one, probably."

"It doesn't matter which one of us gets the token," Horton reminds them as he's dragged along by his ghost leash. "No matter who finds it, we all win."

"Easy for the Skeemaster to say," Beer mumbles.

Glaring back at his teammate, Horton growls, "That's not my screen name, and you know it!"

All this arguing and candy talk is giving Todd a headache. But he supposes it's a small price to pay for a new adventure. When this is all over, the whole universe will have new episodes to watch, even if they're not quite the same as the old ones. Plus, when he considers the alternative, stuck on Earth sleeping in the back of his scrap shop, he's reminded of how lucky he's been to be an honorary part of the team.

Reaching for another candy, The One says, "I hate these weird yellow ones. I mean, what's with them, anyway?"

"I'll take it," Beer offers.

But before he can grab the candy, The One deftly pinches it out of its wrapper and holds it over his tongue. "I'd rather eat it than let you have it."

"Gimme that!" Beer cries, grabbing The One's arm.

But before Beer can wrench the yellow candy away from his brother, The One tosses it down the street, and the ghost leash drags Horton down the Parkway after it.

"All the same," Todd comments to himself. "I could use an actual vacation."

Predictably, as the sugar starts wearing off, The One starts whining. "All this candy is making me thirsty. I'm gonna check if the drinking fountains still work."

"Not if I check first!" Beer cries.

While the two of them run off in search of hydration, Pants goes looking for the restroom, and suddenly the merch guy receives a short respite from the team's antics. It may not be a real vacation, but it's the most time he's had to himself in space weeks. He had almost forgotten how nice the quiet can be.

Strolling down Maim Street under the soft glow of the parklights, he passes a "haunted" bakery, a children's tattoo parlor, and half a dozen souvenir shops. A few of them have been boarded up for real, but most for effect.

When he approaches the Fishtar machine, he searches his pockets for tokens and comes up empty. But as he turns away to resume his twilight ramble, his merch sense starts tingling, and he checks the token return to discover two shiny Scaredyland coins. He figures they must have been there for space centuries just waiting for him to come along and find them.

"Fishtar, you did it again!" Todd tells the cosmic squid. For a long moment, he hesitates to ponder whether the tokens are worth more than his misfortune. But in the spirit of the adventure, he finally decides, "Fish it," and slips the coins into the slot.

"*You have awoken Fishtar, and now you must face your fate*," the monster says. After it's done rubbing its plastic ball, a card pops out, and the squid concludes, "*The future is now yours…*"

Plucking the card from the slot, Todd reads, "'The future is complicated. Advice: Join the Scaredyland Fun Club today! Unlucky Number: 4.'" Presently unable to decipher the misfortune, he slips it into his pocket next to the first one and gently pats the machine. "That's all the misfortune I can afford, I'm afraid. I'm out of tokens. But I'll be back. Something tells me my future is in the cards – I mean, besides the slogan on your box."

With his future in-pocket, Todd takes back to the street. It's not long before he runs into Beer and The One fighting over a drinking fountain covered in faded green slime. But the dark liquid streaming out of the bubbler doesn't look like water.

As soon as Beer spots Todd walking toward them, he yells, "It's soda! There's three flavors – brown, orange, and green."

Curious, Todd tries some of the green and says, "That's the sweetest, flattest thing I've ever tasted."

"It's Ecto Cooler!" The One says, sipping from his old promotional canteen.

After they've had their fill, they find Pants watching Horton try to drag his ghost leash out of a toppled Scaredyland trashcan. His jacket ruffled and dark hair askew, he looks like he's been chasing his pet all over the grounds.

"How do those things work, anyway?" Beer asks.

But Horton just shakes his head as he struggles to hold the invisible creature at bay. "I have no idea."

"Let me try," Pants says, taking hold of the novelty leash. As soon as she has custody of the pet, it calms down, settling at her sneakers.

"Fine, stay with her," Horton growls. "I'll just play with my glow-in-the-dark bouncy ball." But when he throws it down against the pavement, he fails to account for the double bounceback caused by the rubber cement, and the ball soars into the night sky. "Well, that was fun, briefly."

As they watch the glowing ball bounce away down the street, Ghosty materializes and screams, "*Rule thirty-three!*"

"Which one is that, again?" The One eggs the digital ghost on.

"*Trash belongs in designated receptacles!*"

"Come on," Beer says. "We're wasting precious dark. Let's get over to the next Ghost Town while we're still awake. What's it called again?"

"The Gruesome Graveyard," Todd reminds them.

"So dumb," The One says. "So, how do we get there?"

"*Making your way to the Gruesome Graveyard is simple, if you know where to look,*" Ghosty tells them. "*Just follow your ghost!*"

The annoying apparition leads them on the path of most shopping, winding down the street until they're almost to the shadowy house looming in the shadows. But before they reach the slipshod attraction, their ghostly guide takes them down a dark alleyway between a couple shuttered souvenir shops and out toward a wide hilly play area covered in plastic turf.

"Are you sure we're still in Scaredyland?" Todd asks the ghost.

"*That depends,*" Ghosty says. "*When you're in a space cemetery, are you still in the mortal world?*"

Thinking over the question, Todd finally answers, "Yes."

"This is scary, you guys," Pants's voice quavers as they approach the twisted metal gate. "Maybe I'll just—" But before she can space chicken out again, she notices a strange machine near the entrance and cries, "Hey, they got a token smusher!"

Huddled outside the Graveyard gate, the team hands over more than half their combined wealth, and Beer comments, "I can't believe it costs five tokens for this stupid thing. What do you even want it for, anyway?"

"To remember our time here," Pants says, posing for the fans. "It's not like we're going to need them anymore. We already beat the Game Gallery. I mean, right?"

"She's not wrong," Horton assesses. "But it seems like a good idea to save them, just in case."

Pouting dramatically, Pants whines, "But we might never come back here!"

"The cost is relatively cheap, as far as souvenirs go," Todd notes, unhelpfully.

"Aright, aright," Beer relents. "All I can say is this better be worth it."

Carefully placing the tokens into the slots, Pants shoves the tray into the machine, and the team anxiously waits for it to work its archaic magic.

But after a few space seconds, The One, sucking on a rock-hard stick of watermelon taffy, determines, "I think it's busted."

"Oh great," Beer says, throwing his hands up with an angry flourish. "We just lost those tokens for nothing! Maybe I wanted Fishtar to read *my* misfortune. Did you ever think of that?"

"Well, no," Pants admits. "But we still have some tokens left, and if you wanted a misfortune, why didn't you get one while you had the chance?"

Desperately searching his brain for a winning argument, Beer finally says, "It's not that I *wanted* one. But I *might* want one, later."

"Uh, you guys," Horton interrupts. "I think you have to crank it."

"You mean, using elbow grease?" The One says, incredulous.

Bunching up the shiny pink sleeves of her team jacket, Pants grabs the lever and starts turning. After a few hard cranks, something clatters into the slot below, and she plucks out their shiny souvenir.

"It says, 'Ghoulish Game Gallery, Scaredyland,'" she announces. "And there's a picture of a cute ghost!"

"Let me see!" Beer tells her as the team gathers around the defaced coin. "Okay, so it was worth it, this time."

Checking his phone, Todd warns them, "This has been an amusing detour, but we should probably get back to the main adventure."

"Right," Beer says, turning to gaze up at the bent bars surrounding the Graveyard.

Beyond, lies a fake-haunted play place populated by plastic headstones and virtual ghosts. Shrouded in thick fog, its dimensions are as vague as the artificial dread that pervades it.

Poking his pudgy finger into Beer's shoulder, The One asks, "Scared?"

"What?" Beer cries, his muscles tensing. "The only thing I'm scared of is your chidiot face."

But that's a lie. No matter how hard he tries to pretend, the truth is that he's terrified of being humiliated in front of the fans. If he doesn't win whatever horrendous challenge awaits them, he'll be the only member of the team without a token – not counting Todd of course, but why would he?

When Pants tries to drag Horton's invisible pet through the gate, the ghost leash pulls away from her and takes off flapping down the Parkway.

The moment they step over the threshold, Ghosty materializes to deliver the rules. *"Welcome, young ghouls, to the Gruesome Graveyard! Behind me, you'll find a haunted playground full of wacky headstones, goofy ghosts, and other spooky surprises. But if you want to win the token buried beyond, you won't just have to contend with the resident spirits – you'll also have to survive each other. All living souls who enter the Graveyard will have their heart rates monitored. If your pulse gets too high, you will be declared one of the living dead. The last one to get out alive will receive the Gruesome Graveyard token."*

Eagerly rubbing his hands together, The One glances at his fellow team members and says, "This is gonna be like scaring a baby."

"Why would you scare a baby?" Pants says. "I don't like this. Can't we just stick together?"

But The One just shakes his head and tells her, "I wish it was that easy."

"But it is!" she argues.

"If you look at your wristbands, you'll find a number indicating your current heart rate. If at any time during play it exceeds 110 beats per space minute, you will be rendered 'scared stupid.'"

Beer nervously looks down at his wristband to find a blinking blue display showing that his pulse is already creeping up toward 90 beats per space minute. Just discovering this information pushes it up to 92.

Patting his pockets, The One suddenly cries, "Oh no, I lost the Raceway token!" Beer's heart rate briefly spikes before his brother says, "Just kidding."

"Aww fish!" Todd says, holding up his bandless wrist. "I guess I'll have to sit this one out, too. Dam it. Oh well."

"While the kids roam the Graveyard, parents and assorted guardians can relax their bones inside the Maniac Mausoleum," Ghosty tells the merch guy. *"Featuring soundproof walls and a full syrup bar, it's the best place to unwind this side of the afterlife."*

With that, Todd flashes them the Pants sign and wanders off toward the marble-like rest building.

Staring into the fake fog, Beer doesn't need to consult the merch on his wrist to know that his heart rate is getting dangerously high. He starts to ask their guide one last question, "What if we—" But when he turns back, the ghost is already gone.

The kids glance dubiously at one another, huddled between the dark gravestones, and before Pants can start lecturing them about the importance of working together, the rest of the team takes off running into the fog. Weaving around the disorderly headstones, Beer quickly loses sight of the others, along with anything else that might give him some hint as to his current whereabouts. Blindly feeling his way forward, he crashes into one of the plastic headstones and tumbles over it onto the fake grass.

Laid out on his back, he calls out for the others, "You guys?" But his words are drowned out in the mist.

Once he catches his breath, he drags himself around the front of the plastic monument and reads, "Ol' Man Corcoran – 'Git off my lawn.'" Realizing his transgression, he rolls off the fake grave and apologizes to its imaginary inhabitant, "Sorry."

His wristband reads 99 beats per space minute and climbing as he gets to his feet and stumbles through the gray cloud toward a static shadow looming in the distance. Deep within the sea of fog, he finds a small toolshed, presumably the quarters of some long-deceased caretaker and as good a place to hide as any. He fumbles the knob, but the little building is locked.

"Chit!" Beer shouts, pounding against the faux wood door.

As he searches for another way in, he hears what sounds like the rattling of ghost chains slowly moving toward him. Afraid to stray too far lest he run into something really scary, he ducks back into the fog behind a nearby headstone.

As the rattling gets closer, he watches his heart rate slowly climb – 101, 102, 103…

He tries to convince himself that the sound is just another Scaredyland trick, but the fear has already taken root inside his mind, in the form of vague monsters more terrifying than anything that could actually exist. Leaning against the plastic tablet, he hears the creature jiggle the knob of the shed door – 104, 105…

Turning back, it shuffles across the fake grass in the direction of his headstone – 106, 107, 108…

But just as Beer is about to start whimpering for mercy, the monster slinks past him, and he peeks over the plastic plaque to find a creature of the sparkly pink variety – 102, 101, 99…

Her plastic ghoulry clacking as she moves around the side of the cottage, Beer decides that this is his chance. He takes his sneakers off to deaden the sound of his footfalls, and as soon as she's out of earshot, he slips out from behind the headstone. Calling upon years of brotherly scare tactics, he quietly sneaks after her, keeping his distance so that she doesn't spot him through the haze. As she makes her way back across the Graveyard, he knocks against one of the headstones, just to put the fright into her, and she lets out a short shriek.

Trembling as she stares into the thick fog, he sneaks up close enough to grab her, and when she turns back around, he says, "Boo…"

"Wahhh!" Pants wails before crumpling to the turf.

"Stop screaming," Beer tells her. "It's just me."

Having been scared badly enough to be knocked out of the game, her wristband starts flashing gray, indicating her new status as one of the living dead.

"You jerkhead!" Pants tells him as fear tears stream down her cheeks.

In a clear violation of Scaredyland rules, she shoves him, and he takes a step back. But where Beer expects to land on fake grass, his foot only finds fog, and he tumbles down into the soft dark.

18

As The One searches the dense fog, a horrible, girlish howl suddenly rises out of the Graveyard, and he looks at his wristband to see one of his friends' status lights change from living to undead.

"That didn't take long," he notes to himself. "I guess Pants is out."

But she scares easy. Beer and Horton are the ones he really needs to worry about. Even so, it's his game to lose.

As he creeps along the Graveyard's edge, he hears a soft rustle and ducks behind one of the novelty headstones. After a few space seconds, he peeks back and spots a large black bird with a rotting head wandering the fake grass.

"What the fish is that thing?" he asks, popping a musty peppermint.

"The bird you're looking at is called a Scaredyland vulture!" Ghosty wails, appearing out of thick fog.

Nearly spitting out his candy, The One whispers, "What the fish?! Are you trying to fake kill me?" He checks his wristband to find that his heart rate has spiked to 105 beats per space minute.

"The Scaredyland vulture is a native species specially engineered to survive on ghost grubs and snack crumbs."

"What are ghost grubs?" The One finds himself asking. But before the holographic spirit can answer, he tells it, "On second thought, just chut up and get the fish out of here before you get me caught."

"Rule five: cursing in Scaredyland is strictly forbidden."

"Chut the fish up!"

"Rule five…"

"Aright, aright," he says, swiping at the annoying guide. "Just get outta here."

Once the ghost is gone, The One nervously searches the graveyard but finds no sign of life, virtual or otherwise. He pops another flavorless candy into his mouth as he tries to decide on the best strategy for scaring the rest of the team, when he hears the familiar sound of Pants's ghoulry jangling nearby. Squinting through the haze, he spots the glow of her plastic necklace bouncing in the fog.

"She's never gonna scare anyone with all that clacking," he whispers to himself, holding his hand over his mouth to keep from laughing as she aimlessly stumbles around the gravestones.

As fun as it would be to scare her to fake death all over again, he suddenly gets an even more devilish idea. While she skips on in search of living flesh, he creeps along behind her, doing his best to avoid detection. He can feel his fear rising as he steps out into the open fog, and while his heart rate has come down significantly, his wristband shows that it's resting at an elevated 95 beats per space minute.

Weaving around the headstones, he notices a soft rumbling in the distance. A warning moan suddenly erupts from some hidden speaker, but it's not until the flashing gate drops in front of him that he realizes he's wandered onto the Raceway track. Boxed in, he turns to find a ghost kart speeding toward him, and the only thing he can think to do is brace himself for a sliming. But at the last space second, the phantom racer swerves, honking and jutting out its translucent thumb as it putters past.

"Wow...," The One says as he watches the ghost drive away down the track. "It seemed like we were moving a lot faster than that."

He checks his wristband to find that his heart rate has topped out at 108, just inside the safe zone, and he figures if he can survive a ghost crash, there's nothing that can scare him out of the game. By the time the gate lifts, he assumes he's lost Pants. But when he listens close, he can still make out the ghostly sound of plastic clacking in the fog. Feeling his way through the thick haze, he follows the sound across the nebulous burial ground toward a shadowy structure in the distance.

In his haste, he slams into one of the fake headstones, and as he pulls his leg back to give the plastic monument a good kicking, he spots another figure drifting through the gray vapor. He follows the shadow up toward the little building, where he finds Horton peeking in the window.

The One creeps up through the headstones, snickering at the scare he's about to put into his friend, when he notices Pants sneaking around the other side of the cottage. Before she sees him, he ducks behind one of the plastic slabs and watches as she makes her way around the side of the little building. He had been looking forward to spooking them himself, but seeing them scare each other to fake death is even better. He can hardly contain himself as they move toward the corner of the shack, and when they come around to meet each other, Pants lets out a fog-piercing shriek. If she wasn't undead already, she would be now.

As soon as she calms down, she asks Horton, "Why aren't you scared?"

"I knew you were there," he tells her. "I could hear your ghoulry clacking from across the Graveyard."

The whole thing turns out to be less satisfying than The One had hoped, so while their guards are down, he slips from behind the grave and leaps out of the fog, howling, "*Blrha-rrr!*"

They both scream this time, and Horton backs into the side of the cottage, bonking his head against the plasti-wood siding.

"You ackle!" he shouts, holding up his wristband. "You just killed me!"

"Me too!" Pants moans. "I mean, you know, you would have…"

Throwing his hands up and dancing around them the way only the living can, The One announces, "I am The One! I am the best character on the show."

"You still have to kill Beer," Horton notes, stupidly. "He's out there somewhere, waiting to scare the digital life out of you. And I'm going to love every space second of it."

Momentarily ceasing his selfebration, The One says, "Like he could ever scare me. If you're listening, Beer, you might as well come out now and take your scare like a boy."

"Hey!" Pants cries.

"Don't worry, I'll go easy on you," he fake promises. "But if I have to come find you, you're gonna wish you were already undead. *Brahaha—*"

The One is cut off mid-laugh when he feels something cold latch onto his ankles, and he slowly twists his head around to find a pair of dirt-caked hands reaching out of the open grave behind him. Instinctively kicking free, his sneaker slips on the plastic grass, and his arms pinwheel as he stumbles backward into the hole.

Darkness envelopes him, and he crash-lands on the hard dirt. The fall knocks the wind out of him, and he gasps for air as he claws at the sides of the grave. Just as he starts to pull himself up, the dirty hands of the undead latch onto his team jacket, and he screams like he's never screamed before.

Pointing to the flashing souvenir around The One's wrist, the zombie moans, "I got *you!*"

When Beer's face emerges from the shadows, the only thing The One can bring himself to do is gawk in disbelief. "But wha— no…"

"You're the worst, and I'm the best!" Beer gloats, pointing his dirty finger in his brother's face. "I knew this would be the perfect scaring spot."

After this hard of a fall, The One can't even bring himself to argue. "I don't believe it. Is this real life?"

"I guess that depends on your definition of 'real,'" Beer says.

Once Pants and Horton help the battling brothers climb out of the empty grave, the team heads back across the Graveyard toward the front gate, where they find Ghosty waiting for them.

Spinning and flipping in the night air, the Ghost tells Beer, *"Congratulations, you've killed all your friends! As the sole survivor of the Gruesome Graveyard, you are entitled to claim your prize."*

Beer walks to the prize machine stationed inside the Ghost Town's gate and waves his wristband under the reader to collect his token.

"You now possess all four Ghost Town tokens," Ghosty informs them. *"With all the tokens combined, you have gained admittance to Mascot Manor.* Plahahaha!"

"We did it, you guys," Pants tells the fans. "We finally made it to the end of the adventure. Who knows what scary fun we have in store?"

"Let's get over there and find out!" Beer says.

But as they race toward the exit, Horton impatiently reminds them, "What about Todd?"

"Oh, right…," Beer says, deflating.

They find the merch guy in the Maniac Mausoleum, napping amongst the vacation caskets of Scaredyland's most esteemed record holders. Locating the cushy crypt by the sound of his guttural snores, they haul the plush massage casket once belonging to Zeb Pefry, owner of the universe's largest collection of plastic prizes, out of the wall, and Todd mumbles, "Just gimme fourteen more space hours."

19

Looming large behind its reinforced fence, Mascot Manor is a deliberately dilapidated mansion in the style of the old Park Lords. Its dark paneling, crooked architecture, and dopey gargoyles combine to give the structure a distinctly eerie, yet chidiotic quality.

"We finally made it, you guys!" Pants squeals as she pans over the grounds with her phone.

Still recovering from his nap, Todd yawns and asks, "So, how do we get inside?"

"We must have to use our tokens to open the fence," Horton decides, pointing to the large token-shaped slot next to the metal barrier.

Patting his pink team jacket, The One says, "Oh no, I can't find my token!"

The others look at him stone-faced, and Beer reminds his brother, "You already made that joke."

"Oh yeah…," The One says, plucking the Haunted Raceway token from his pocket.

As Beer prepares to insert the Gruesome Graveyard token into the slot, Todd says, "Wait a space second! Are you sure you want to do this? Those tokens are probably worth more than all of us combined."

"We can't quit the adventure now," Pants argues. "We're finally at the last… whatever."

"Yeah," The One backs her up. "Even I want to see what's inside the stupid haunted house."

Horton nods and Todd whimpers as Beer slips the first token into the wall, only for it to roll back out into the token return.

"Oh well," Todd says. "We'll just have to take them home and add them to my collection for safe keeping."

Wiping the giant coin on his jacket, Beer tries inserting it again, and this time the gate emits an evil cackle as the first bolt unlocks. The One uses the Haunted Raceway token to unlock the second bolt, followed by Pants with the token she found by the Creep Coaster. When Horton inserts his prize from the Ghoulish Game Gallery, the last bolt unlatches and the gate begins to slide open.

"We did it, you guys!" Pants announces. "We—"

But her excitement is short-lived as the gate grinds to a halt, leaving only a sliver of space for them to fit between its rotting bars.

"Oh great," Todd says, frantically pressing the coin return. "Now we lost the tokens *and* we're stuck out here."

"Please," Horton tells The One as the boy slams his sneaker against the bars. "No amount of kicking is going to solve this." With panic gripping the rest of the team, he gets to work examining the ancient gears that operate the gate, when he suddenly finds himself standing on the other side. "Hey, there's enough space to slip through!"

Pants goes next, and when she stops onto the lawn beyond, she cries, "Yay, we did it again, you guys!"

Beer follows, then The One, who even with his gut sucked in just barely manages to squeeze through the bars.

When Todd's turn comes, he gets about halfway through before he starts flailing. "I'm stuck!"

Inspecting the situation more closely, Horton confirms, "Yep, he's stuck all right."

"So, do we leave him here or…?" The One asks.

"We can't leave him!" Pants scolds. "Come on, everybody. With our powers combined, we can pull him out!"

Grabbing hold of Todd's arm, Pants gives the signal, and the team tugs. But after a couple space seconds the merch guy starts screaming, and they let him go.

"I'm never going to make it," he says. "Just go on and let me die with dignity."

"Okay," The One says.

"No!" Pants wails.

"We almost had him," Horton says, eyeing the merch guy's substantial stomach. "We have to pull harder, but not so hard that we tear his arm out of the socket."

Frantically waving said arm, Todd tells them, "Wait! I can just live here. A life stuck in this gate could be okay, so long as you guys bring me candy three times a space day and clean up my poop."

"One more time!" The One cries for dear social life.

All together, they latch onto the sweaty nerd and yank with everything they've got, ignoring his frantic pleas for mercy.

"Just a little more," Horton yells over the agonized howls.

Just as it starts to feel like they're about to rip Todd's arm off, there's a loud crack, and he tumbles through the bars. Unfortunately, the team is there to break his fall.

"Get… off!" Beer chokes as the merch guy wobbles to his feet.

"I think I'm okay," Todd says, testing his arm. "Aww, except I ripped my team jacket."

Gasping for air, The One tells him, "Well, that's the only one you're going to get!"

It takes the team a few space minutes to recover after being crushed alive. But once they pick themselves up out of the weeds, there's nothing left between them and the haunted house of their nightmares.

Once Horton's head stops spinning, he examines the gate and determines, "It's broken."

"Then our work here is done!" The One declares.

The Manor looks even more inhospitable up close. Although Horton still doubts its haunted reputation, he can't help feeling a little spooked. By all appearances, the towering house was built by hand, and what he assumed would be more plasti-plank siding is actual petrified Parkwood. Glaring down at them through broken shutters, the place almost feels alive.

As they make their way across the dead lawn, Beer and The One suddenly cease their bickering, and Todd hardly mentions all the valuable lost souvenirs poking out of the weeds. The only one who doesn't seem to be affected by their creepy surroundings is Pants. The rest of them freeze at the bottom of the porch, and before they have a chance to argue over who should go first, she happily hops past them up the staircase and knocks on the giant door.

Beaming back at them, she asks, "Are you guys coming or what?"

While they mumble amongst themselves, the big Parkwood slab slowly swings open, and a familiar ghost materializes in the darkness behind Pants. When she turns back, she yelps at the sight of their holographic guide floating in the doorway.

"Welcome to Mascot Manor!" Ghosty says, laughing ominously. *"The horrors that await you inside these walls are so terrifying that visitors under ten or over a hundred and fifty space years old should consult a Scaredyland physician before entering. There are only two ways out — find the hidden treasure room and defeat the evil that guards it, or run scared. This is your last stop before your* last *stop. Reveal the Manor's secrets and you could walk away with an exclusive piece of Scaredyland merch. Enter if you dare, but I advise you to* watch your step. *Plahahaha!"*

The ghost disappears in a puff of digital smoke, and they all gather around the doorway to peer inside the ancient attraction.

"So?" Beer asks. "Who's going in first?"

"We have a volunteer," The One says.

Nervously adjusting his glasses, Beer tells his brother, "Yeah, okay. You don't have the guts anyway."

"Oh yeah?" The One says, forcefully zipping up his team jacket. "We'll see who has the guts. Move aside." Wavering for just a moment, he tentatively steps inside the house and laughs. "See, there's nothing to—" But before he can finish boasting, he trips into the dark and crashes face-first onto the hard Parkwood floor.

Stepping over him to inspect, Horton warns them, "Be careful. There's a small stair."

As the rest of them trample over their teammate and into the dark entryway, Beer asks, "Is it safe?"

"Probably," Horton decides, gazing up at the tangle of black staircases snaking down from the upper floors. "The house is sturdy enough. I don't think it's going to fall apart. But I'm a little worried about the gags. They've gone unused for so long, they might not work like they're supposed to."

"*The safety of our guests is our second priority*," Ghosty says, startling the whole team, and Todd, as it rematerializes on the porch behind them.

"Yeah, but what do you know?" Beer asks.

"*One more thing*," the ghost tells them. "*Did I mention that the Manor is haunted?*"

"Not exactly," The One says, swiping floor crud off his jacket. "But big surprise."

"*The rooms are infested with the spirits of The Park's retired mascots. If there's one thing they don't like, it's the living. And they'll do everything in their power to scare you off. If one of them spots you, try to stay calm, and remember — they can sense your fear. Manage to sneak past them and you might just make it out alive. That's all the advice I can give you, for now. See you on the other side!"*

"Wait a space second!" Horton shouts.

But before they can ask any questions, their grinning ghost guide waves its illusory paw, and the door slams shut behind them.

20

"This house really is alive!" Pants shrieks as she peers into the dark corridors surrounding them.

Retreating to the door, Horton jiggles the knob and tells them, "It's locked. It must be on some sort of primitive automatic timer."

"The mascots are going to get us!" Pants cries.

Leaning in close, The One tells her, "They say if you're not careful, Mac Tonight will come for you."

"Not Mac Tonight!" she moans.

But Beer tells her, "Don't listen to him. Everybody knows there's no such thing as Mac Tonight."

"Don't listen to him," The One says. "Mac Tonight is as real as you or–*Whaaa!* What the fish is that hideous thing?"

Briefly glancing up from his phone, Todd says, "Uh, it's called a mirror."

Walking toward his reflection in the antique glass, The One says, "But it's one of those wacky mirrors that make you look all distorted and weird, right?"

"Uh, no…," Todd breaks it to him.

"Space God…," The One says as he wipes the candy crust from his cheeks. "I've really let myself go since last adventure. Why didn't anybody tell me?"

Shrugging, the merch guy says, "It just seemed like there was nothing to gain. Plus, you get cranky when you're on a sugar binge."

"*I do not!*"

"Anyway," Todd tells them. "We've hit peak viewership. We gotta keep the adventure moving."

"Wait, I want to see what I look like," Pants says, pushing in front of The One. Confirming the cuteness of her reflection, she holds up the Pants sign at herself and winks. But after a few space seconds, her sparkly image begins to bubble and swirl, transforming into a crusty witch with oozing boils and ratty pink hair.

Deferring to Todd, The One says, "Okay, *that's* weird, right?"

"Yes," the merch guy confirms.

"I don't like this place," Pants decides.

With that settled, the team advances toward the center of the shadowy room, where an ancient chandelier made of genuine plastic bones hangs above a vertical maze of winding staircases and twisting hallways. As soon as the novelty wears off, the kids look at each other for a long moment, and as if communicating by some dark, wordless magic, they all suddenly take off in pursuit of the treasure.

"Wait, what's happening?" Todd shouts after them.

The sound of slamming doors soon fills the musty air as the team begins searching the countless rooms of the labyrinthine house. Scurrying up one of the ancient staircases, Pants runs to the first door she can find. But when she yanks it open, she's met by a brick wall. Angrily throwing the door shut, she moves on to the next one, where she finds an oversized alien baby doll sitting in the center of a bare, windowless room.

"Aww, what are you doing in here?" she asks.

But when she steps inside, the plastic toddler spins its curly head and expels a torrent of green vomit. Slipping and sliding her way back to the hallway, she slams the door just as a wave of bile crashes against the other side.

She backs away as the green sludge leaks into the hall, when she notices a smudge on her new jacket. "My team jacket! Aww, this puke will never come out."

Determined to play through the stain, she moves on to the next room, where she's greeted by a homicidal humanoid hologram wielding a digital axe, and she quickly shuts the door before she winds up murdalized. Over the next couple space hours, she encounters a cartoon cannibal, half a dozen different varieties of bottomless pits, and more evil toys than she cares to count. But she still hasn't found any exclusive merch or other prizes.

When she passes The One wobbling down one of the warped hallways, covered in pink slime, she asks, "What happened to you?"

But he just shakes his gloppy head and says, "Don't ask."

By the time Pants reaches the top floor of the Manor, her sugar high has worn off, and she begins to fear that the team might never find the secret merch.

"Which door should I try next, you guys?" she asks her fans, sending them a quick insta-poll. A few space seconds later, she gets the results. "You picked the one all the way at the end of what looks like the longest, darkest hallway in the whole haunted house. Perfect."

The light from her phone as she creeps down the dim hall causes the spiders and Park bugs to scurry back to wherever they came from. When she reaches the door, she braces herself for whatever new horror awaits her on the other side.

"Here we go, you guys."

Taking a deep breath, she turns the knob and pulls it back to find herself staring into deep space. Gawking out at the stars in hushed fear, she leans in to get a better look inside the infinite room, when her foot slips. Teetering on the edge of oblivion, arms spinning, she blindly reaches back and by the grace of Fishtar manages to wrap the tips of her fingers around the door frame. Summoning strength she didn't know she had, she drags herself back from the edge and hugs the floor.

Still shaking from fright, she turns her phone to give the fans a better look, and the thin piece of glass that is her only connection to the outside world slips from her fingers. For an instant, the universe freezes as she watches her phone tumble out into the darkness. But then the passage of time returns to normal, and the glass communicator lightly clatters down onto the tabletop of infinity. At first, she doesn't believe her eyes. But when she reaches for the phone, she touches her finger to the 'bottomless' floor and discovers that it's all just a trick.

Stepping inside, her sneaker boots squeaking on the very fabric of reality, she tells the fans, "I don't think this is the prize room. But it's still sort of neat." She shows them around while she catches her breath. But when she hears a ghostly moan coming from the hall behind her, she stops breathing altogether. "If that's you, The One, it's not funny."

She slowly turns around, expecting to experience the jump scare of her life. But instead of her candy-munching teammate, she finds a Manor ghost lazily floating down the dark passage. The color and shape of a wad of chewed bubblegum, it doesn't seem to notice her. Doing her best to avoid any sudden movements, she cautiously makes her way down the hall with her phone pointed at the pink spirit for all the fans to see.

When she's almost close enough to reach out and grab the little monster, she whispers, "It's a ghost, you guys."

As soon as the words leave her lips, the apparition spins around to face her. For a long moment, they stare at each other, unmoving. Peering into the dark pits of its undead eyes, Pants gets the impression that she's looking at the end of the universe.

A twisted smile begins to form on the ghost's face, and when it raises its stubby paws to go in for the scare, Pants cries, "You're just so cute!"

Lunging forward, she tries to wrap her arms around the pink phantom, but it dodges her first attempt at cuddling and floats back toward the main hall. She chases it along the corridor and down the staircase, where they run into Todd. While she gets tangled up with the merch guy, the ghost floats right through him and into one of the nearby rooms.

"Hey, you slimed me!" Todd moans. "I mean, it's holographic slime, but still…"

Chasing after the cuddly apparition, Pants opens the door and becomes paralyzed by the sight of an oncoming ghost train, while the pink ghost floats back out and up the crooked stairs. When she finally catches up to the slippery spirit, she corners it at the end of a short hallway with nowhere to hide but a small linen closet.

"There's no place to go," she tells it. "I'm gonna hug the life back into you, even if it's against the rules."

As she lurches down the hall, arms outstretched, the ghost frantically searches for an escape. With nowhere left for it to go, Pants pounces. But as soon as she leaps at the pink hologram, it slips out of sight, and she crashes into the wall.

Rubbing her head, she glances around and asks, "Where'd it go?" Just to be sure, she checks the linen closet and confirms, "It's not in there."

She's almost ready to give up the pursuit, when she notices a strange glow dripping down the wall. Recalling what Ghosty said about the Manor's secrets, she feels along its surface until she discovers a small indent, invisible in the shadowy hallway. When she pulls on it, the entire back wall slides open to reveal a hidden staircase rising into the dark unknown.

Peering up into the shadowy shadows, Pants calls behind her, "Todd, are you still there?"

A few space seconds later, from out in the main hall, he answers, "Yeah…"

"And are you still covered in slime?" she asks.

"Yeah…"

Holding in her laughter, she tells him, "I think I found a secret passage. Tell the others to come up here."

"O-kay…"

Swallowing her fear, Pants holds up her phone-light and steps onto the bottom stair. "So far so good, you guys."

After a few space seconds, she takes another step, and another, until she's at the top of the staircase. As she pans her phone around the dark passage, the light suddenly times out, and the room goes black. From what she could make out during the few space seconds that she could see her surroundings, it looked like she might have stumbled into some old storage room.

As she fumbles with her phone, she spots a familiar pink glow in the corner of the room. Tripping forward over invisible priceless promotional materials, she lunges at the little ghost. But her arms slip through its holographic body, leaving her covered in digital slime.

"Oh, right…"

When she hears her friends arguing about which one of them is going to come up first, she calls, "I'm already up here."

"Pants?" Todd says as he reaches the top of the stairs. "I can't see anything."

"I'll get my phone," Beer announces.

"No, I'll get *my* phone," The One proclaims.

It takes so long that Horton finally says, "*I'll* do it."

But before any of them gets the chance, the lights in the ancient attic crackle to dim life, and Pants lets out a slime-neutralizing scream as the team finds themselves face-to-hideous-soulless-face with the evil spirit haunting the Dark Park.

ACT 11

A Living Dead Nightmare!!
The Secret of Scaredyland Revealed?

21

"Why are *you* screaming?" Todd asks the wailing girl.

"I don't know," Pants says. "I guess I was expecting something… scary."

They all were. But the evil inhabiting the Manor isn't so much scary as it is irritating, floating smugly at the other end of the dusty prize attic.

"What the fish are you doing here?" Beer asks the grinning ghost. "Don't tell us…"

"*Congratulations,*" Ghosty announces. "*You've uncovered the terrible secret of Mascot Manor. For you see, I am the evil that lurks the park.*"

The One interjects with a loud raspberry and blurts, "Lame."

Evidently programmed to ignore such gibes, Ghosty tells them, "*Now that you've caught me, I'm forced to reveal my dark backstory.*"

"Aww, can't we skip this part?" Beer asks.

Processing his request, Ghosty finally says, "*No.*"

After all this adventuring, Todd's stomach is starting to feel like it's eating itself and he asks, "Don't you at least have any snacks?"

"*Of course,*" the ghost says, waving its paw toward the snackless remains of an ancient candy counter stuffed into the back of the dark room. "*The story you are about to hear is so terrifying that even I can hardly believe it. It all started on a night much like this one, at the end of the longest day of the Park year. I ran a small booth selling maps and plastic sun globes, and in order to afford the fryer crumbs I was living on, I had to think of a way to drum up sales. So, one sweltering evening, after the smiling Park sun had set, I put on my old Space Halloween costume to become the very first Park mascot. I roamed the grounds in my homemade monster suit, scaring kids and posing for embarrassing pictures. Eventually I found some old carpet samples and patched together my very own character – The Clodhopper. The guests loved my antics, but when I accidentally embarrassed one of the powerful Park Barons, I was deemed too scary and banished to The Dark Side of the Park.*"

"No!" Pants cries.

"*Yes…,*" Ghosty says. "*I was forced to sleep in a crumbling booth with half a dozen other Dark Park dwellers. Back then we could barely get any reception, and the only thing to watch was old Flipper reruns. You know, from before he could talk.*"

"No!" Pants cries again.

"*But back in The Park, a seed had been planted. Soon, other mascots started popping up, and as the population grew, we began to win over more and more of the Parkgoers, until calls for our return to Con City grew too loud for the Park Barons to ignore.*"

When it was clear that the dark tide of public sentiment had finally turned, we came home to much fanfare. Even the Park Barons welcomed us, promising to build an attraction dedicated to our struggle, to be erected atop the very place where they burned our costumes. They called it Scaredyland. Most of us were so excited that we applied for booth permits on the newly erected grounds. It was only when we got here that we realized the trap that had been set. The contracts we signed granted us living space, but it was located beneath Maim Street, in the park's leaky bowels. In exchange for a hole to sleep in and a handful of tokens, we were forced to perform for the guests night in and night out. In one quick underhanded motion, the Park Barons had figured out a way to get rid of their embarrassing problem while continuing to rake in the credits."

Both repulsed by the mascots' treatment and impressed by the Park Barons' ability to turn a profit, Todd comments, "Those brilliant bass turds!"

"Precisely," Ghosty says. *"There was only one problem. I mean, for them. There was no end of problems for us. But the thing the Park Barons hadn't counted on was a lack of interest. After all the humiliation and time spent getting into character, hardly anyone showed up. When the end of the season came, the Barons abandoned the grounds, leaving the mascots with nothing but the costumes on our backs. Most of the residents moved back to Con City to become tour guides and booth jockeys. But a few of us stayed to live out our nights here in Scaredyland, scaring off any tourists who might wander through."*

Wiping back tears, Pants says, "That's so sad."

"But you and your friends could not be scared so easily. Together, you conquered the Creep Coaster, lapped the Haunted Raceway, proved your skills in the Ghoulish Game Gallery, escaped the Gruesome Graveyard, and solved the mystery of

Mascot Manor. For all your effort, you will be richly rewarded with an exclusive piece of park merch, available only to those guests who manage to survive the horrors of Scaredyland."

Ghosty directs the team toward a bank of dusty prize machines where they scan their wristbands, and Todd eagerly looks on as they collect their prizes. His imagination runs wild with the thought of some undiscovered, four-of-a-kind collectible that'll save the show. But when he sees what's inside their colorful boxes, his hopes of ever moving out of the *Cuddler* are unceremoniously dashed.

Beer's glasses lamely slide down his nose as he stares at his prize, determining, "It's some sort of primitive measuring device."

"They're 'invisible' rulers," Ghosty clarifies. *"They even have the Scaredyland logo emblazoned on the side."*

"Uh, yay…," Pants says, but even her inexhaustible cheer can't mask her disappointment.

"That's it?!" The One shouts at the ghost guide. "The prize at the bottom of Scaredyland is a stupid measuring stick?"

Doing his best to lighten the mood, as well as distract from his part in all this, Todd says, "With the Scaredyland logo so prominently displayed, some prize completionist might offer you a couple crits for them." But it doesn't work.

"This is all your fault!" Beer says, angrily pointing his pathetic prize in the merch guy's direction.

"My fault?!" Todd yelps. "All I did was come up with a fun adventure to attract some new fans. I was only trying to sell more merch."

"Is that all you ever think about?" the boy demands.

"Stop fighting!" Pants pleads.

Once they're done screaming at each other, Horton patiently directs their attention back toward their guide and says, "I think Ghosty has some additional interesting information to share with us."

"Just because you discovered my horrible secret doesn't mean the scares are over. If you return to the Ghost Towns you've already plundered, you may find that things have changed a little since your last visit. This time the ghosts are scarier, the stakes are sharper, and the dangers are more dangerous. But the risk reflects the reward. Succeed in facing your fears and you may choose to trade up for a merch item so exclusive that to this space night it remains unclaimed. If you check your wristbands, you'll find an icon or icons indicating the Ghost Towns to which you possess additional access. Complete all the advanced challenges and you will control the power of Scaredyland!"

With the prospect of a merch upgrade swimming through his head, Todd says, "That sounds, like, *really good*, you guys…"

"You're telling us we have to go through the same adventure all over again?" Beer whines.

"Fish no!" The One says. "We already beat all the challenges. The prize for going back around is probably a pen full of disappearing ink."

"Let's not be so hasty," Todd tells them. "Sure, maybe the prize is just another promotional gag. Then again, it might be something more incredible than any of us has ever imagined!"

Scoffing, The One asks, "Has that ever been true?"

"*Yes*," Ghosty cuts in.

"Anyway," Todd continues. "We can't leave now or the fans will think we're space chicken. We have to see this adventure through to the end."

"You keep saying 'we,'" The One notes. "But we're the ones playing games and winning tokens. What have you been doing, besides eating all my candy?"

Taken aback by the boy's harsh words, Todd says, "I'm the whole reason we went on this adventure in the first place. Plus, you've got enough candy to last a lifetime."

"Exactly!" The One shouts. "*One* lifetime!"

"I can't listen to this anymore," Horton finally tells them. "When you figure out what you want to do, I'll be outside. How do we get out of this stupid place, anyway?"

"*Just take the slide*," Ghosty suggests, motioning toward a dark flap hanging on the wall.

"Wait!" Pants cries before her pale friend can climb out. "Let's see what the fans think we should do." She rifles off a quick poll, and after a few space seconds, she tells the team, "The fans have spoken. They voted that we should finish the adventure."

Stuffing a conciliatory rock-hard caramel in his mouth, The One moans, "*Aww...*"

22

When Beer comes out the other end of the slide, he crash-lands onto a mass of twisted body parts. As soon as they get themselves untangled, the team and Todd take a brief load off in the Manor's backyard play area. Beaten down and covered in various natural and supernatural substances, with nothing to show for their torture but an invisible measuring stick, Beer decides he should say something to lift their spirits. But nothing comes to mind.

After a long, sullen break, their manipulative merch guy asks, "So, should we get back to the adventure or…?"

"He's right," Pants says, with some effort. "We can do this! I think."

"I'm so tired, I don't even have the strength to argue," The One says. "Or maybe I do." He briefly sits up in his swing and then slumps back down. "No…"

"I want to finish this adventure as much as the next fan," Beer says as he looks for a clean patch of shirt to wipe the attic dust off his glasses. "But we're all exhausted. If we're gonna have any chance of making it, we're gonna need something to eat besides old candy."

"*Ulchh, fine…*," The One says. "I was saving these for an emergency. But I guess that's what this is." Digging into the secret pockets stitched inside his team jacket, he emerges with a tall stack of promotional ration bars. "There's two for each of us."

Impressed by his brother's ingenuity and uncharacteristic willingness to share, Beer says, "Even though you lied about being out of food while we starved our way through the first half of the adventure, this might actually save our acks. Good job for once, The One!"

"Hey, I know how to be a team player!" The One insists. "I just don't like it."

"Hey, I almost forgot…" Lifting his spindly finger, Horton rummages through his team backpack and pulls out a small black pouch stitched with a manic xpresso bean. "I brought some xtra strong caffeine candies to help us stay awake."

As soon as Beer pops the candy into his mouth, he feels a jolt of artificial energy surge through his body. "S-so, where do we s-start?"

"I've g-got an idea," Horton anxiously offers, his skinny limbs twitching. "The lights on our wristbands correlate to the Ghost Towns where we won our tokens, r-right? Beer's shows the Graveyard, The One has the Raceway, Pants has the Coaster, and I've got the Game Gallery. There must be something within the Scaredyland a-architecture that reads the information stored in our wristbands to unlock the advanced challenges. Since each of us has been granted access to a different Ghost Town, it means we can split up and beat all of them at the same time. We'll be done before m-moonset."

As the boys commend Horton on a plan well devised, Pants cries, "S-split up?! We can't split up. We're a team! Besides, I can't ride the Creep Coaster all by m-myself."

"Y-you can do it," Beer assures her. "If we don't split up, we'll be here all n-night."

Even though she still has that scared look in her buzzed eyes, she nods, and they each take a handful of candies to keep them up during the challenges ahead. Stepping out through the back fence, they circle around to the front of the Manor and onto the Parkway, where they stop to consult the park map.

When Beer lays eyes on the Graveyard's cartoon image, it sends a cold chill down his spine – although it could be the overload of caffeine coursing through his veins. Either way, the thought of wandering the tombstones all by himself is enough to send him running scared.

As they let the idea of their solo adventures sink in, Todd points at a dark corner of the map and asks, "Hey, what's that place?"

"That's weird," Horton says, furiously flipping through his rulebook. "Ghosty never mentioned it. But judging by the lazy pool and age restrictions, I'd say it's some sort of parents playland."

Examining the strange location more closely, Todd says, "Hmm, something tells me I'd better check it out. You know, in case it holds any secrets."

"Good idea," Beer says. "I guess." Looking to the others, he adds, "Once we've completed all the challenges, let's meet back here in front of the Scaredyland map." His teammates murmur their agreement, but it doesn't take a park ghost to sense their fear. "Good luck, you guys. Or bad luck, or whatever."

As he turns toward his haunted destination, Horton shouts, "Wait a space second! I'm going to need all your tokens to beat whatever high score challenge I assume is waiting for me in the Game Gallery." Digging through their pockets, they hand over all the tokens they have left, and he quickly counts them up. "Three?! That's all? Even with the token smusher, we should have more than that."

"Well, I used a couple to get into the restroom on the Gorewalk," Pants divulges. "But I wrapped a candy necklace around the knob to hold the door open."

"Okay, that's pretty good," Horton concedes. "But I'll never be able to get a high score with only three tokens."

Trying to think up some motivational words, Beer finally says, "Just, do your best."

"What if my best isn't good enough?" Horton asks.

But the only answer Beer can muster is a shrug.

"Well, I better get going," Todd says. "There's no telling what horrors I might find in parents paradise… er, playland. So long, you guys. I mean, see you later."

While their merch guy takes off in search of an adult oasis, the rest of them head back up Maim Street toward whatever imitation thrills await. A jittery quiet takes hold as they walk past the haunted snack bars and haunted souvenir shops. Even though nothing has changed, somehow everything feels different.

Before long, The One juts his thumb out and says, "I guess I'll see you guys on the other side."

Watching his brother shuffle across the rubber road, Beer suddenly gets the feeling that splitting up might not have been such a good idea after all.

Nevertheless, when they reach the Graveyard, he gives his remaining friends the Pants sign, and they weakly return the gesture. "Don't worry, this is gonna be a piece of ration cake. And I mean a fresh one, straight off the Moon Mart shelf. Not that thing The One found on the train."

"He's right, we can do this," Pants tells her fans, unconvincingly. "I just have to be brave enough to ride the Creep Coaster. That's, like, no problem. Right?"

Horton shrugs and the two of them wander off down the sidewalk to their pre-determined destinations.

Beer can already feel the team's absence, like the echoes of three very annoying phantom friends chattering in his head. The Graveyard looks pretty much the same as when they last left it – foggy tracts of fake grass smattered with novelty headstones. But without anyone to chase him, there's nothing to do except wander around. The fear is gone now that there's no reason to hide. But so is all the fun.

Stepping across the hazy landscape, it occurs to him that maybe the headstones hold a clue to whatever it is he's supposed to be doing. So he kneels down to read one of the fictional epitaphs, "'Count Murgatroyd – The only way out of this is through here.'" Then again, maybe not.

Beer roams the Graveyard for what feels like space hours, carefully scouring the grounds for a way to unlock the advanced challenge. But all he finds are a few aimless holo-ghosts and a bunch of semi-morbid one-liners that are about as funny as the jokes on his ration pops. The only place he hasn't searched is the cottage, but the last time he was here, there was no way to get inside.

When he comes around to the little shack, he tries the knob again, just in case. But it's just as locked as it was before. Out of options, he leans his head against the door and in a rare recognition of the audience watching through his team pin, he says, "This is dumb, not scary. I'm sure you've all changed the channel by now."

But as he stares down at the shack's plasti-wood siding, he notices a strange feature, rendered almost invisible between the dark panels. Not really expecting anything to happen, he lifts his wrist up to the secret scanner, and the little building produces a sinister cackle.

"Hey, I think I found something!" he announces.

At the sound of Beer's voice, the few ghosts floating in the area suddenly turn in his direction. Their dopey grins morph into hideous, kid-eating scowls as Beer desperately fumbles with the knob. But the door still won't budge. He looks away for just a moment, and when he turns back, there are even more of them. At first he figures they must be drifting over from other sections of the Graveyard, but as he looks on, he realizes that they're materializing out of the digital ether. Like murderous marshmallows floating toward him on a milky fog, he's suddenly surrounded by holographic apparitions of every shape and color of the cereal rainbow.

As the ghosts assemble to give Beer the last worst sliming of his life, he gives the door one more hard shove, and to his amazement, it comes unstuck, sending him stumbling blindly into the dark.

23

The One struts back onto the Haunted Raceway like he owns the place, a towering humanoid amongst monsters as he passes under the bug-eyed stares of the giant cartoon dragsters that adorn the gate. When he steps into the pit to inspect the karts, he breathes in the sour, noxious aroma of rubber on rubber and hacks uncontrollably.

"That's weird," he says, finding the track clear of busted karts. "I wonder what happened to the *Monster Masher.*"

Shrugging it off as another one of Scaredyland's dark magic tricks, he climbs back inside the mostly intact *Zombie Zoomer* and pats its decaying dash. But as he glances down the open track, a terrible realization comes over him. "There's no other racers. Am I supposed to race myself?"

Annoyed by his predicament, he punches the *Zoomer*'s horn, and the kart produces a sickly, undead grunt. The next thing he knows, the pit is populated with translucent ghost karts. Evidently programmed in the image of Scaredyland's all-time fastest racers, his opponents wear their track-won mutilations with pride, grinning at him madly as they zip past. Before The One has a chance to get his kart started, the mangled drivers have lined up behind the starting line.

"Dam it!" he cries as he pulls up behind the rest of them. "That's okay. I'll beat you fish heads from last place."

"*Rule number five!*" Ghosty suddenly shouts from the pit.

Gripping his steering wheel tight, The One watches the melted starting signal shift from 'Ready' to 'Scared.' The instant it hits 'GO,' he slams his Moon Walker down on the gas and cackles gleefully as the *Zombie Zoomer* speeds down the track.

But his enthusiasm soon crashes back to The Park when he realizes that these ghosts aren't going to be as easy to outrace as his friends. Puttering along in last place as he heads into the first turn, he cuts toward the inside of the track. But the ackle driving the *Frankenkart* gets the same idea and cuts him off.

"What the fish!" The One shouts into his helmet. "How are these chitheads driving so fast?"

Not expecting to receive a response, he almost swerves off the track when an undead voice answers, "*We're light on our wheels, grahahaha!*"

"Yeah, well, fish you!" The One says.

Throwing caution to the night wind, he takes his foot off the brake and hugs the inside of the track, nearly causing the *Zoomer* to tip over as he attempts to shave a few space seconds off his time. But when his kart crashes back down, its rotting frame shakes and groans, and he's reminded that one wrong turn could leave him in pieces.

In a few space seconds, he catches back up to the *Frankenkart*, and when the kart takes a wide turn, he shoots through the gap into ninth place.

"I'm gonna make all you ghosts eat my gangrenous dust," The One warns the holographic racers.

"*I'd like to see you drive*," the ackle in the *Cannibal Kart* fires back.

Before long, The One spots the next kart up ahead, and by the time he reaches the Scaredyland entrance, he's puttered past the *She-Machine* and the *Rabid Roller*. But the kart that holds the course record still remains hopelessly out of reach.

"How the fish is that ackle so far ahead?" he growls, watching the racer's bony icon circle the Creep Coaster.

He starts devising a strategy to catch up to the *Murder Cycle* as they wind toward the towering coaster. But before he gets the chance, the ghost bike wobbles, and he zooms out ahead.

"Five more," The One tells no one in particular.

"*Try all you want*," the evil kid in the bone kart snarls. "*You'll never catch me. I've been driving this track for centuries. I know every twist, turn, and secret.*"

"Secret, huh?" The One says. "Well I'm not gonna give up until I beat the chit out of your record."

But the kid just laughs. *"Prepare to be here for the rest of your afterlife."*

The One responds by angrily laying on his kart's pathetic horn. As he putts around the Coaster, he starts to think that the living dead kid might be right. But he pushes his doubts aside as soon as he spots the *Creepy Crawler* scuttling across the back half of the Raceway.

With a top speed slightly faster than the *Crawler*, the *Zombie Zoomer* gradually gains on the ghost kart until they're driving neck and thorax. As they putter along the straightaway outside the Gruesome Graveyard, the grungy holo-kid behind the wheel of the giant lunar insect sneers in The One's direction. The air surrounding them starts to grow hazy, and just as they're about to hit the wall of fog surrounding the cemetery, the *Crawler* suddenly swings its elongated body at the *Zoomer*. The One cuts his kart's wheel, bracing himself for impact. But instead of crashing into the insect's armored exoskeleton, he spins out onto the shoulder while the *Crawler* scuttles away down the track.

"Right, they're ghosts," The One reminds himself. "Or holograms, or what the fish ever."

Covered in digital slime, he spins his kart back around and speeds through the fog in pursuit of the slippery arthropod. Crunching a caffeine candy, he blindly guns it through the gray cloud in flagrant violation of Scaredyland rules, and a few space seconds later, he emerges out the other side in a caffeine-fueled fury.

As he putts past the *Crawler* and into fifth place, he juts his thumb out at the bug's driver and shouts, *"I'm The One!"*

Barreling toward Mascot Manor, he checks his map to find that the fourth, third, and second place racers are just ahead of him. The steep incline of the track as it wraps up around the haunted house reduces the *Zoomer*'s speed, but not by much, and pretty soon he's caught up to the *Carnivorous Clown Kart*. Although the painted ghost driver does her best to scare him off, he manages to navigate the Manor's Space Halloween-themed upper floor and move up into fourth place with only a light sliming. On his way out, he zooms past the *Gremlin Glider*, and the little monster behind the wheel sticks its tongues out at him.

As soon as The One exits the haunted house, he spots the *Witch Craft* flying down the final winding drop no more than a dozen kart lengths ahead. Taking note of the unique hovering capability of the hag's broomstick, he remembers that his kart must also possess some additional power aside from its dangerously loose handling. With one hand on the wheel, he desperately searches the console for a special button or lever.

But failing to find any such cartoonish contraption, he says, "Fine, we'll do this clean. I mean, except for the caffeine."

Gripping the *Zombie Zoomer*'s fleshy steering wheel, he careens down the hill with a reckless disregard for undead life or limb, forced to navigate the Raceway through an increasingly tilted lens as he skids around each sharp turn of the rubber track.

"This framing is not gonna be good for viewership," he comments.

About halfway down the slope, the *Zoomer* catches up to the *Witch Craft*, and their karts briefly overlap, resulting in another layer of holographic slime being deposited on The One's kart. Using one hand to steer and the other to operate the wipers, he does his best to get rid of the green glop, but it just streaks across the windshield. With only his instincts to guide him, he times each turn like his afterlife depended on it. When he senses that he's coming toward the bottom of the slope, he blindly whips the wheel around and bounces out onto the final straightaway.

Laying on his kart's undead horn in triumph, he cries, "I am The One! I am the greatest race kart driver alive."

But when he glances at the map to look for the first place kart, he finds that the *Bone Crusher* crossed the finish line whole space seconds ago.

"*You might be the best racer alive,*" the winning driver says. "*But I'm the fastest ghost in Scaredyland!*"

Unbelieving, The One putters into second place and skids to a stop alongside the skeleton kart. Its scarred, scraggly driver flashes a twisted grin, and as The One jumps out to wipe the rest of the digital gunk off his windshield, he demands, "One more race!"

24

Horton counts and recounts the tokens, but no matter how hard he tries to fudge the numbers, they just won't add up. As skilled a player as he is, three tokens is barely enough to win a slap bracelet.

"I told them we should save our tokens," Horton grumbles. "But nooo, we had to spend them on some expensive worthless souvenir. Now it's up to me to figure out how to save us."

The only bright spot in all this is that he gets to spend more time inside the pixelated light of the Ghoulish Game Gallery. The giant glowing skeletons above the entrance welcome him with open bones as he steps back into the electrified air of the arcade.

Wandering the blinking cabinets and stained confetti carpet of the game room, he searches for a way to activate the advanced challenge and eventually finds his way back to the old arcade. Since he won the Scream-Ball jackpot, the pot is back down to a measly 54 tickets – barely enough for a wind-up mummy. He was expecting the team's guide to appear at some point to explain the rules, but the ghost never shows.

On his way back through the game room, he stops by the Prize Keeper in case the creep's selection has been updated. But all he finds are the same zombie paratroopers and fake monster poop as before. For no reason other than morbid curiosity, he waves his wristband under the Keeper's scanner, and the plastic corpse suddenly comes to some approximation of life.

"You're good, kid," the fleshless mannequin tells him, its broken jaw jerking unnaturally. *"You managed to win enough tickets to win my Gruesome Game Gallery token. But I've got more horrors in store for you. This next challenge is known throughout the Parkades as the most dangerous game."*

With a heavy sigh, Horton whispers the words, "Mini-golf…"

The Keeper lifts its rotted arm, and points vaguely toward the old arcade. *"Step in back and test your skills, if you dare. Beat my low score of four under par and sink your last putt in one stroke to win a prize beyond your wildest nightmares. But be careful on the back ten. That's where the course gets a little scary, mwohohoho!"*

"Why does it have to be mini-golf?" Horton asks the universe. "I'm already bored."

After inadvertently trouncing Beer and The One two summers ago, and the tedious rematches that followed, he swore he'd never putt again. Now it looks like he's going to have to sink back down to their level. With the Prize Keeper stuck in a laughing loop, he wanders back to the ancient arcade to search for the entrance to the challenge. He doesn't find any secret passageways, but before he starts looking under the game machines, he notices an emergency exit sign glowing conspicuously above the restrooms.

He pokes his head out the back door expecting to find a row of rotting dumpsters but instead stumbles out into a sprawling putt-putt horrorland. A long and winding maze littered with the remnants of what presumably began as lush plasti-turf, the decaying course stretches all the way back to the Haunted Raceway. In keeping with the Scaredyland aesthetic, dozens of misshapen monsters, constructed out of some primitive yet sturdy building material lost to spacetime, guard the holes from any guest who would challenge their putting supremacy. Full of complex geometry and ball-threatening hazards, at 91 strokes, the course boasts the highest par in The Park.

Undeterred by the immobile fiends, Horton approaches the putter rack and takes a few practice swings before deciding on a short club with a black rubber grip. But as he steps up to the first hole, he realizes that he doesn't have anything to hit. Searching the grounds, he eventually locates a primitive ball dispenser, and when he sees the price, he can hardly believe his incredible unluck.

"*Four tokens?*" he moans.

He digs the leftover tokens out of his pocket, hoping he might have miscounted. But there are still only three. Defeated before he even began, he drops his putter and drags himself back into the arcade, where he considers pumping the team's remaining wealth into one of the claw machines. But with nothing left to lose as he shuffles down the blinking aisles, he gets one last-ditch idea. Recalling the tokenless days of his not-so-distant early youth, he begins systematically checking the token returns for long-lost change. The old space crab stance comes right back to him as he scuttles down one aisle and up the next, poking his fingers into the slots. But after a space hour of scooping out empty game holes, all he finds are a couple of slugs and a petrified piece of cinnamon candy.

"I can't believe there's not one loose token anywhere," he gripes, prompting the Prize Keeper to cackle.

Finally giving up any hope of completing the challenge, Horton ambles back out into the night air and down the sidewalk surrounding Maim Street. As he listens to the haunting sounds spilling out of the other Ghost Towns, he wonders if he should go break the bad news to his friends. But he decides to let them have their fun while they still can. As soon as it leaks that the adventure is over, the fans will desert them and it'll be back to school. And not the movie.

But as Horton thinks back to his time in those hollow halls, he gets another idea. "Fish and chit and ack!"

A few space seconds later, Ghosty appears to scold him. "*Rule five!*"

"Yeah, yeah," Horton says. "I hoped I'd never have to speak these words. But I need your help."

Twirling through the air, Ghosty tells him, "*It would be my pleasure to assist you in all things Scaredyland. If you're wondering where you can purchase souvenirs—*"

"That's not it. I need to know where I can get additional tokens for the Game Gallery."

"*Hmm…,*" Ghosty says, pretending to think it over. "*Tokens can be used in exchange for merch and services throughout Scaredyland, including the Ghoulish Game Gallery. Does that answer your question?*"

"No," Horton growls. Attempting to simplify his request, he tells the ghost, "Need more tokens."

"*Park Bucks can be exchanged for tokens inside any souvenir shop in Scaredyland. Does that answer your question?*"

Glancing at the shuttered storefronts surrounding him, he tells the ghost, "I guess. But not satisfactorily!"

"*Would you like to take a few space minutes to fill out a survey?*"

Pouting, Horton says, "No…"

"*Is there anything else—*" But before the ghost can finish, the boy swipes it away.

Out of tricks, he turns back toward the arcade, scanning the sidewalk as he goes. Before long, he spots the Fishtar machine and desperately checks the token return, but the slot is empty.

"Who in the universe, besides Todd, would trust a plastic monster to tell their future?" he wonders.

But suddenly recalling his own conclusion that the cosmic squid is as good a prognosticator as any, combined with the fact that there's nothing more he can do anyway, Horton engages in the same ritual that he just moments ago ridiculed and slips two tokens into the machine.

Fishtar goes through his shtick, and after a few space seconds, a card pops out.

Horton plucks the misfortune from the slot and reads, "'Future hazy. Try again later. Advice: Go for a swim. Unlucky Number: 3.'"

Shaking his head at his own gullibility, he tosses the card onto the sidewalk but then picks it back up again and slips it into his pocket. He briefly considers blowing his last token in the Game Gallery, figuring he can probably win enough tickets for a fake ghostache. But he ultimately decides that he'd rather not give the Prize Keeper the pleasure.

With the impending end of the show, and maybe even the team fogging his mind, Horton strolls back toward the Scaredyland entrance, where he takes a seat on the edge of the bubbling black fountain to gaze up at the stars. Rolling his last token between his fingers the way he taught himself while waiting in line for the pirate *Kart Fighter* machine in the arcade back home, he shifts his eyes toward the black muck in the bottom of the fountain and gets a dumb idea.

"I wish…," he says, struggling to find the part of him that still believes in magic. "I wish we could win all the challenges and collect the exclusive merch, even though it's probably just something stupid anyway."

In one final futile attempt to save the adventure, Horton flicks the token into the fountain and watches it sink down into the dark water. Forgetting his wish almost as quickly as he made it, he jumps down and starts heading back along the Parkway, when it dawns on him.

Although reluctant to consider what is sure to be another disappointing dead end, he walks back to the fountain, pulls up the sleeves of his team jacket, and plunges his arms into the muck. He anxiously claws at the bottom of the dark pool, and when he emerges, his hands are overflowing with slimy, gold-colored tokens.

25

"I'm s-scared, you guys," Pants tells the fans at home as she takes her first cautious steps back out onto the crumbling Gorewalk.

Without the rest of the team behind her, Scaredyland feels like a whole different park. What had seemed like another fun adventure has suddenly turned into a waking nightmare, in which the comforting sounds of her bickering friends have been replaced by the tortured howl of the Mutilator and the clack of cars rushing down the Creep Coaster. When she listens close, she can almost hear the terrified screams of ghost riders drifting on the night air.

Shivering as she gazes up at the haunted Coaster, she tells the fans, "What if the token's not even up there? We should check some of the other rides before we climb all those stairs."

Anxious to be anywhere else, she shuffles toward the other end of the Gorewalk and winds up in front of a spinning swing set called the Scream Catcher. According to the sign, the ride ranks an eight out of eleven on the scare scale, but Pants puts on a brave face for those just tuning in. As she makes her way through the empty queue, she expects Ghosty to show up and reiterate the Scaredyland safety protocols, but the ghost guide never materializes.

"I guess I'll strap myself in…," she says, trembling as she steps through the open gate.

Once she's seated, the ride starts, and she's lifted off the ground. At first she happily laughs and kicks her feet as she swings out over the blinking Ghost Town. But as the swing lifts her higher and higher, she quickly finds herself wishing she had never strapped in. After a few space seconds, the ride is spinning so fast that she worries the chains will snap. Remembering the park safety rules, she tries to call Ghosty for help, but her screams are drowned out by the wind. After a torturous few space minutes, the Scream Catcher begins to slow, until Pants's sneaker boots finally land back on solid ground.

Wobbling out of her seat and through the exit, she tells the fans, "That was… fun."

As soon as her head stops spinning, she stumbles over to the Poison Teacups and watches the cars twirl. The ride is rated a two on the scare scale, which she decides is perfect. When it stops spinning, she climbs into one of the cracked cups and puts her feet up on the empty seat beside her.

It suddenly occurs to her that maybe there's a good side to the team splitting up for a while. Even though she doesn't have anyone to keep her company, she can go on any ride she wants.

After a moment, the cups start spinning, and she leans back to take in the sights – Ponce Raleigh's Ghost Ship swinging up into the night sky, the Purrdalizer's paws flailing. Even the Creep Coaster looks sort of fun from down here. Not really, but she figures if she believes hard enough she might be able to trick herself.

When she looks toward the distant stars lazily spinning above her, she feels a pang of homesickness. Thinking about her parents and the other kids at school back on Earth, she can feel tears forming. But she wipes them away before the fans can see.

"There's nothing to cry about here," a hollow voice suddenly tells her.

Pants freezes with fear, and she gradually turns to find a translucent ancient Parkgoer in a t-shirt and shorts seated next to her. The strange boy smiles at her, his Parkwear unruffled by the wind.

As soon as she can muster a response, she screams, *"Wahhh!"*

"That's more like it," the kid says, throwing his hands up. *"I think I'll join you.* Wahhh!"

They go on like that until Pants runs out of screams and finally asks, "Who are you?"

"My name's Brilly," he says, freckles flickering. *"Nice to meet you."*

"I'm princessfluffypants," she hesitantly tells him. "So, what are you doing here?"

Squirming in his seat, Brilly explains, "*I live here at Scaredyland with the rest of the ghosts. I usually don't ride the Teacups, but we don't get a lot of visitors.*"

"But you're just a kid..." Putting all the pieces together, she asks, "Does that mean that you died at Scaredyland?"

"*No, I died when I was 142 space years old in a retiree settlement on Planet Claire. This is just the digital incarnation of my twelve-year-old self that I donated to the park.*"

"Oh..."

"*So, what do you want to ride next? The Cookie Tosser is* pretty *scary!*"

"I wish I could go on it with you," Pants tells him, briefly glancing around at all the other fun rides. "But the thing is, my friends and I uncovered the evil of Scaredyland, and now we have to do a bunch of super hard challenges, and I'm pretty sure I have to ride the Creep Coaster. But I'm really scared and you probably don't want to go on it with me."

"*Whoa, I never met a guest who survived Mascot Manor before,*" Brilly says, in simulated awe. "*What's the exclusive prize?*"

"Ruler."

"*Figures,*" the kid says, shaking his head. "*But I used to ride the Creep Coaster all the time. It'd be fun to go on it with somebody who can actually feel fear.*"

"*Yay!*" Pants shouts, and addressing the fans in her phone, she adds, "Like I always say, everything's more fun with a friend."

"*I'm not sure if I want to go anymore,*" Brilly decides. But when Pants juts out her quivering bottom lip, the ghost boy tells her, "*I'm just kidding, sort of.*"

"Yay again! We'll go after we're done riding the Teacups." But as she thinks about how long she's been spinning, she wonders, "How long before this thing is over, anyway?"

"*That's weird*," Brilly says, checking his digital watch. "*It should've ended by now.*"

"I hope it's not broken."

As Pants searches the spinning Gorewalk for a way off, she spots a strange furry figure standing near the ride's manual controls. Grinning unnaturally as it stares at her through giant plastic eyes, the skeleton mascot wraps its bony hand around one of the levers and shoves it forward.

Their teacup suddenly lurches forward, and Pants flies back against the seat as the ride spins into overdrive.

Unaffected by the change in speed, Brilly asks, "*Does it seem like we're spinning out of control to you?*"

"Yes!" Pants cries as the oversized teapot in the center of the ride begins to steam. "Can't you shut it off?"

But the ghost kid just shrugs his holographic shoulders. "Sorry, but I don't have permission to operate the rides. Only ghost guides can do that."

"Ghosty, we could use your help right about now!" Pants calls out. But when the ghost fails to show, she says, "I got an idea."

She leans her head back, hocking up everything she's got, and Brilly warns her, "*Spitting on or off the rides is against Scaredyland rules!*"

"Exactly." Counting the cup's rotations as it circles the teapot, she says, "If I can time it just right…"

As they spin back around toward the control board, Pants expels a candy loogie bigger than anything she's ever spit up.

"Whoa…," Brilly says, upon seeing the pink gob floating through the air.

An instant later, a muffled scream erupts from outside the ride.

The grotesque act instantly prompts Ghosty to pop up and moan, "*Rule four: spitting off the rides is strictly for—*"

"Just shut off the ride!" Pants screams. "We're stuck."

When the ghost waves its cute little arms, the ride quickly slows to a stop. Though barely able to stand on her wobbly legs, Pants somehow manages to drag herself out of the cracked cup and through the exit.

As soon as she steps back onto the Gorewalk, Ghosty says, "*In case you didn't hear me, spitting off the rides is strictly for season pass holders.*"

"I'll try to remember that," Pants says, searching for the flocked skeleton that almost made her barf. "Where'd that stupid mascot go?"

Flitting past her, the ghost scans the grounds and reports, "*I don't detect any mascot activity in this Ghost Town.*"

"But we saw it," she says. "It had a bony body and a big glowing skeleton head. Right Brilly?"

But when she turns back to look for her new friend, he's nowhere to be found.

Ghosty's hollow features droop, and it tells her, "*If you're experiencing fear, I can talk you down.*"

"Mmm, maybe later," she says. "First, I have to find that skeleton."

She searches all up and down the Gorewalk, but the only evidence of the mascot she finds is a partial skeletal paw print pressed into a puddle of pink slime.

26

With a few dozen clumsy swings of his safety-saber, Todd hacks through the dense weeds surrounding Mascot Manor until he uncovers an overgrown trail leading out beyond the bounds of Maim Street. Accessible solely to those guests who are willing to get their legs scraped up by the only plants tough enough to survive the hostile conditions on the Dark Side of the Park, Todd ventures toward the mysterious destination with nothing to protect him but his honorary team jacket and a slightly undersized pair of vacation shorts.

The path is dark and treacherous, but before long, he detects an artificial glow radiating underneath the night sky up ahead. Inexplicably drawn to the light like a starving scrapper to half-off rations, he trips through the overgrowth until he comes upon a sight even more incredible than Fishtar. Surrounded by a vast thicket of night-brush embedded in the swamp below, rests a hidden off-map oasis. Offering multiple rot tubs, a bunch of what was at one spacetime obviously very expensive lounge furniture, and even a poolside syrup bar, it's everything Todd didn't know he was looking for.

As he takes in the majesty of it, Ghosty materializes to ruin his view and warns, *"You have stepped outside Scaredyland grounds. For your own safety, please find your way back to the trail."*

Groaning, Todd swipes the ghost away, and his foot slips out from under him. The next thing he knows, he's tumbling down the side of the hill, slamming down onto thick patches of prickly weeds and sharp rocks. When he finally comes to a landing, he winds up on his back staring up at the night sky.

Looking down on him smugly, Ghosty says, *"Told you."*

Todd lies there for a while, wondering how he ever ended up in this particular ditch, when he notices the sign above his head. "You've reached… The End of the Line."

Bruised and bloodied, he drags himself onto his feet, picks a few of the larger twigs out of his hair, and climbs over the gate into the resting place of his bad dreams. At a glance, he counts two different crazy rivers, a lazy pool, and a fancy adult game room. He's not exactly sure about the meaning of either 'adult' or 'game' in this context, but he can hardly wait to find out.

For now, he kicks off his sneakers and dangles his aching feet in the lazy pool's scummy water. After everything that's happened over the last couple space months, he's beginning to wonder if he's getting too old for all this adventuring. Part of him actually wishes he was back on Earth, behind the counter of his little shop. He shudders to think it, but he even misses the customers, sort of.

Popping a caffeine candy for energy, he wanders around the Ghost Town exploring the amenities, when he feels a hunger so intense that it forces him to his knees. He rips open his emergency ration bars and quickly wolfs them down, but it's not nearly enough to satiate his hunger. To his relief, he discovers a snack machine near the lockers. But even if any of the ancient candies are still edible, he's all out of tokens. So, he does the only thing he can think to do in a situation like this and rocks the machine until something falls loose.

Once his belly and pockets are sufficiently stuffed with moon-cheez crackers and fruit snacks, he heads over to The End of the Line gift shop, which unlike the rest of Scaredyland, is stocked with souvenir t-shirts and pool toys. He helps himself to some Scaredyland swim trunks and Crazy River sandals and then wanders behind the counter in search of the adult pens.

When he spots a display of novelty night-vision glasses, he starts to wonder how much he could charge for a genuine artifact from the Dark Park back home before scolding himself, "This is your vacation adventure, remember?"

So, instead of stuffing his pockets with every piece of branded merch he can find, he slips a pair of Night

Shades over his plastic frames, snatches a fresh EOL towel off the rack, and heads out to the pool. He lays his team jacket and t-shirt on one of the chairs and begins to ease himself into the murky water. But as soon as he dips his toe into the black pool, he rushes back out.

"Th-that's f-fishing f-f-freezing," he chatters, wrapping the towel around his shoulders and vigorously rubbing his arms.

"*Rule five!*" Ghosty shouts, appearing out of nowhere.

"I know, I know," Todd tells the stupid ghost.

Shuffling back into the gift shop, he searches through the various boards and noodles, until he finds a deflated tube. He spends a space hour or so blowing it up, and when he's finished, he drags his frosted devil's food donut back out to the water. As he attempts to maneuver into the shallow end, he slips on the black slime coating the bottom of the pool and awkwardly tumbles onto the inflatable confection.

"Ahhh…," he sighs, floating unsteadily beneath the stars. "This is as good as adventuring gets." But when he notices the mustachioed devil winking at him from the sign over the Dark Spirits Bar, he amends, "Almost."

Paddling across the black water, he scoots his donut around and drags himself up onto the bar. Sprawled out across the counter, he sticks his head over the edge and grabs the only intact bottle within reach.

Wiping a thick layer of crud off the label, he reads, "Circus peanut liqueur. That sounds… good enough."

When he realizes he has no way of opening the bottle, he reaches back behind the counter, and in a vacation miracle, he emerges with a rusty EOL corkscrew. The instant he pulls out the plastic stopper, he's hit with a scent so toxically sweet that it burns his nostrils. Coughing, he checks the label for the proof, and while the number has long faded, he can tell that it contained three digits.

With bottle in hand, Todd plops back onto his donut and floats off across the pool, lounging under the light of the moons. He takes a swig of his ancient liqueur and dribbles it back out as his mouth goes numb.

"That is the worst thing I've ever tasted," he mumbles, unable to feel his lips. "Still…" he takes another sip of the vile liquid and this time manages to choke it down.

As he drifts over toward the Crazy River, he starts to feel like he's actually floating out amongst the stars. He had forgotten what it's like to relax. But so far, he likes what he's feeling. For a long while, he floats downriver, drunkenly basking in the moonlight, until his tube suddenly quits spinning.

Figuring he must be caught on a fallen umbrella or drowned mascot, he reaches back to push himself free. But the instant his hand touches the slimy obstruction, the thing comes alive. The mystery creature quickly dives beneath the surface, producing a wake almost big enough to topple Todd's tube. Nervously searching the dark water, he resorts to the only thing to do in situations like this and takes another swig of his liqueur. But as he lifts the bottle to his lips, whatever is lurking below rams the back of his donut and sends him splashing.

Struggling to keep his alcohol above water, Todd flails toward the side of the pool, when something attaches to his foot and drags him under the black waves. Before his life starts flashing before his eyes, his feet touch the bottom, and he pushes himself back up. Blindly thrashing with his free hand, he reaches out and manages to grab onto the side of the pool.

Dragging himself out of the water, he hacks up a lungful of black water and flops onto his back. When the adrenaline wears off, he realizes that the sea monster is still attached to him, and he frantically kicks his legs only to discover a plastic souvenir bag wrapped around his foot. Freeing himself, he tosses the bag back in the water and leans over the edge to search for the real monster lurking below.

Before long, he spots a pair of big, yellow eyes staring out of the blackness, and he taunts, "I beat you, you stupid fish!"

But as he sticks his tongue out, a large fin rises up out of the water and slaps down against the surface to send a wave of sludge crashing over him.

With his finger stuck in the top of his bottle, Todd tells the beast, "Well that was childish."

Soaked and freezing, he heads back to his chair to dry off, when he notices a section of the Ghost Town that he somehow managed to overlook. Tucked behind the wave machine is a private rest area exclusively for season pass holders. Lacking even a regular pass, Todd is left with no choice but to clamber over the waist-high fence.

The other side is everything he dreamed it could be and more – ornate Parkwood cabanas, a monster-free sauna, and an adults-only swirlpool. The only thing missing is power.

After a short search of the grounds, Todd locates a circuit breaker behind the bar, and as soon as he flips the switch, the whole place is brought back to life. Surrounded by tasteful lighting and the sounds of Seger, he eagerly watches as the swirlpool cover retracts to reveal an empty tub.

"Well, it was almost perfect…" But as the words leave his lips, some sort of clear fluid begins gushing into the pool. Cautiously leaning down over it, he scoops a handful of the strange liquid up to his mouth and says, "It's water!"

Tossing his complimentary towel from the private washroom over one of the chairs, he lowers himself into the pool's warming waters and decides, "This just might be my greatest adventure."

But shortly after he closes his eyes for total relaxation, he senses a shadow approach the tub, and he looks up to find a fellow trespasser come to spoil his soak.

27

Trapped in darkness, surrounded by ghosts, and low on candy, Beer frantically flashes his phone around the little shack until he's sure none of the ghosts followed him inside. As he huffs the musty air, he checks his wristband to find that his heart rate has topped out at 107 bpm.

The shack at the center of the Gruesome Graveyard turns out to be little more than a storage shed containing a bunch of ancient tools for tending the synthetic grounds, a badly decomposing cot, and a generator that runs on tokens.

"Well, this is great," Beer declares to the lifeless room. "What am I supposed to do now? If I go back out there, I'll be slimed to fake death." Glancing back at the door, he ponders, "I wonder why the ghosts aren't coming in after me."

"This is a safe place," a ghostly voice answers, and Beer spins around to find a glowing specter sitting on the edge of the cot.

"Don't slime me!" Beer cries.

"In here you can break the rules without fear a scoldin'," the old spirit says, tugging on the tattered brim of its cap. *"As fer the ghosts outsite, they're kept from enterin' this buildin' by the rules code'it in tuh the digital webbin' that overlies all a Scaretylant. In Park lingo, it's what's known as a 'spell.'"*

Once he's fairly sure the ghost doesn't intend to slime him, Beer asks, "So, who the fish are you?"

"Normies call me Snidely Zexplatt. But my mascot name is the Cantankerous Caretaker. At least, that's what it was back win I was alive."

"So, what are you doing in here?" the boy prods.

Snidely looses a whistling sigh and says, *"That's a looong story."*

"Aright, then forget it," Beer says.

Ignoring his command, the ghost tells the boy, *"Back win I move't tuh Scaretylant, mascots were alout tuh roam free, ant two tokens cut still git yuh a decent ration. I start'it out as a weight guesser on the Gorewalk makin' four tokens a space hour. But win the guests quit showin' up, my game was shut down, ant I was put on the Graveyart shift. Truth tolt, I like't the work — fixin' headstones, patchin' grass, scarin' kids. But soon as the season was over, so was the job. We fought tuh keep the park open, but profits weren't excessive enough, and the executives shut the place down. They never dit accept us, ant as a warnin' tuh any future mascots, they trap't are digital souls in the park for all eternity — or at least until the storage system wears out. I've been stuck inside this cottage ever since I shet my mortal costume."*

"O-kay," Beer says. "But you're not the real Cantankerous Caretaker. You're just a holographic reproduction of all the information Scaredyland managed to absorb about him."

"Whatever I am, I kin promise yuh that bein' stuck in this box fer… How long's it been anyway, a million space years?"

"More like a thousand," Beer breaks it to the old ghost.

Holding his head in his hands, the Caretaker says, *"That's all? The storage unit was mate tuh last a million times that long. Yuh have no idea how borin' it is bein' a digital spirit trap't in a physical worlt."*

But glancing around the filthy shed, Beer says, "I think I have *some* idea…"

"Jist zap me ant ent this nightmare aretty," the ghost begs.

"What do you mean 'zap'? Are you saying ghosts can be killed? I thought they were, like, eternal."

"Kill't, exorcise't, erase't," the ghost moans. *"Whatever yuh wanna call it. We're as eternal as the stuff we're store't on. But there are ways tuh sent us back tuh the digital ether unnaturally."*

Contemplating how to best take advantage of this new information, Beer says, "I'm not saying I'm going to do it, but if I wanted to zap some ghosts, how would I do it?"

"There's a Ghost Zapper in the trunk on the floor," the Caretaker says. *"It's s'pose tuh be fer one a the challenges, but I jist use't it tuh prune the ghosts."*

Flashing his phone into the shadows, Beer finds the old trunk and kneels down in front of it. When he opens the heavy lid, he jerks back, startled by the moth-ridden undead Caretaker costume staring out at him.

Lifting the mascot's remains, he uncovers a two-handed, multicolored Zapper with a barrel big enough to blast the old ghost's head off.

"Whoa, finally something brule!" Beer says, trying the plastic weapon on for size. "Can this thing shoot the living?"

"*Yeah, sure,*" the Caretkaer says. "*It jist hurts a little. Anyway, I've wait'it a thousant space years aretty. Are we gonna do this, or what?*"

Pointing the Zapper at the quivering ghost, Beer tells him, "I mean, you've waited this long. I don't know what the rush is, but aright. Got any last words?"

"*Uh…*" the old ghost pauses to think. "*Now I wish I'it spent a few space years comin' up with somethin'. There is one thing I always want'it tuh say – Flipper sux!*"

"Good one," Beer says, and aiming at the glowing hologram, he pulls the plastic trigger.

But nothing happens.

"*Oh, I fergot,*" the ghost says. "*Yuh gotta pump it first.*"

"Ahh," Beer says as he works the static generator. "I'm familiar with this technology." Once the weapon is charged, he asks, "Any more last words?"

The Caretaker shakes his head and braces himself for a zapping. But just as Beer is about to pull the trigger, the ghost jumps up and yells, "*Wait a space secont!*"

"Did you change your mind?" Beer asks. "Or are those your last words?"

"*Yuh open't the door!*"

"Uh-huh…," Beer says. "I know it's been a long time since you've been among the living, but we possess the power to interact with the physical world."

"Don't yuh see?" the ghost growls. *"If yuh got through that door, it means yuh unlock't the advance't challenges. That light on yer wristbant gives yuh special access tuh places that are use'ly off limits – like this shack!"*

Feeling particularly full of himself, Beer says, "Impressive, I know."

"It means yuh can git me outta here! But the door kin only be open't from the outsite. All yuh have tuh do is zap all the ghosts in the Graveyart ant then come back 'rount tuh let me out!"

"I *could* do that," Beer says.

"Come on!" the Caretaker whines.

Looking into his pleading old eyes, Beer tells the ghost, "It just seems like a lot of work."

"But yuh gotta zap the ghosts anyway if yuh wanna win the challenge."

"Yeah, but then I'd have to come all the way back here…"

"It's not very far," the ghost argues.

"Not *very*…"

"Don't yuh wanna free an olt soul from virtual purgatory?"

"Well…" Beer lingers on the word as he searches for a way to shirk responsibility. "Aright, aright! But aren't those ghosts out there your friends or something?"

"Fish no," Snidely sneers. *"I got frients in some a the other Ghost Towns, but those things outsite are park-generate'it ghosts."*

Pumping his Zapper, Beer says, "But what's the diff— Forget it. So, how do I get out of here?"

"There's a secret hatch under my cot."

Beer pushes aside what's left of the moldy bed and discovers a handle carved into the floorboard. When he pulls at it, a section of the floor lifts to reveal a dark cave hidden underneath.

Before he jumps in, the boy asks the ghost, "Can't you just sneak out through here?"

But the Caretaker scoffs. *"Ghosts can't travel undergrount. Don't yuh know anythin' 'bout anythin'?"*

Glaring at the glowing spirit, Beer lowers himself down into the dirt pit beneath the shack and uses the light from his phone to reveal half a dozen passageways branching out around him.

"Which path should I take?" he whispers up to Snidely.

"How should I know?"

Grumbling, Beer chooses the tunnel directly in front of him and warily steps into the shadows. He follows path, twisting and turning underneath the Graveyard, until he finally comes to a dead end. The idea of getting stuck down there pops into his head, and his heart starts racing. But as he approaches the dirt wall ahead of him, he all of a sudden steps out into the open night air.

Relieved to see the starry sky above, he peeks over the edge of the hole and realizes that he's standing in an open grave. Multicolored holographic ghosts flit through the fog all around him, too many to count. Luckily, his wristband reveals the total population – 287.

"Aww," Beer groans. "It's gonna take me forever to zap all of them."

Awkwardly climbing out of the hole, he takes aim at a wandering spirit, but before he can shoot, he hears a disembodied moan coming from behind him. He spins around just in time to find an angry red ghost flying at him, and he instinctively fires his Zapper, causing the hologram to burst into a cloud of digital mist.

As he watches the counter on his wrist tick down to 286, he says, "Maybe this will be easier than I thought."

Sneaking across the Graveyard in search of his next victim, he hears the fake grass rustling nearby, and he turns to fire. But instead of one of the floating slime balls, he finds himself face-to-hideous-face with something even more blood-curdling.

The very real zombie mascot lurches at him, its right eye hanging out of the socket. Aiming for the exposed part of its plush brain, Beer fires his Zapper, but it fails to go off.

"Chit!" he cries as the undead mascot wobbles closer. "I forgot to pump!"

"I'm going to eat your brains!" the unexpectedly high-pitched voice threatens.

Falling to the plastic turf, Beer fumbles with his Zapper, and as the living dead character stumbles toward him, the fear takes hold.

28

The One chases the ghost karts across Scaredyland again, and again, and again. But no matter how many corners he cuts or slimings he subjects himself to, he can't seem to get any closer to outracing the *Bone Crusher.*

Crossing the finish line for the eighth time tonight, he finds the skeletal kart once again idling in first place and demands, "One more race!"

"Aww, that's what you said last race, and the race before that, and the race before that," the *Bone Crusher*'s driver taunts, flashing his crooked holo-kid grin. *"Haven't you had enough humiliation for one lifetime?"*

"Ha!" The One scoffs. "I haven't even begun to be humiliated! I'm not leaving this track until I kick your ack."

"Face it, kid," the ghost driver tells him. *"You're never going to beat me."*

"Then we'll be here forever," The One says, popping another caffeine candy in his mouth as he pulls his kart back around to the starting line.

The instant the signal flashes, the monster wagons again take off puttering down the ancient Raceway. Having finally mastered his decaying kart's superior acceleration, The One quickly passes the rest of the racers before they hit the first turn. Hands shaking as he grips the *Zombie Zoomer*'s fleshy wheel, he manages to stay in the lead all the way up to the Ghoulish Game Gallery, and by the time he reaches the Creep Coaster, he starts to think he might actually win this race.

Pulling well ahead of the other racers, he drifts out toward the edge of the black swamp with victory in his sights. But as he basks in his own Oneness, part of him feels a little disappointed to find out that the track record wasn't so unbeatable after all.

"Is this really the best you ghosts can do?" The One taunts his undead opponents. "Should I slow down to make this a little more interesting?"

But as he comes around the far side of the Coaster, he glances at the ranking displayed inside his visor and discovers that he's fallen into second place. Grasping to make sense of what he's seeing, his eyes dart toward the map only to find that the *Bone Crusher* has suddenly taken a commanding lead.

"What the fish?" The One growls.

"Rule five!" Ghosty shouts into his helmet.

Watching the skeleton kart's icon putt toward the Gruesome Graveyard, The One asks, "How did that ackle get in front of me? I didn't even see him pass. I mean, I know he's a ghost, but he's still visible!"

Finishing in third, just behind the *Murder Cycle*, The One pulls up beside the *Bone Crusher* and tells the ghost kid behind the wheel, "This is bullchit! You're cheating somehow. There's no way you could have gotten ahead of me."

"*We can't cheat,*" the mangled kid says, hacking up a contemptuous laugh. "*We're bound by the rules of Scaredyland even more strictly than the guests. Have you considered the possibility that you're just not a very good racer?*"

"Impossible!" The One says. "Let's go around again. And this time, no cheating!"

Again, The One putters into an early lead. But this time, instead of speeding ahead, he lags back to keep an eye on the *Bone Crusher*. With his gaze glued to the *Zoomer*'s withered review mirror, he attempts to pop another caffeine candy, but the bitter pellet misses his mouth and bounces into the passenger scat. He briefly takes his eyes off the competition to retrieve the precious candy-coated bean, and when he looks back, the *Bone Crusher* and a couple of the other karts are gone.

"What?!" The One cries, twisting his head around. "Where the fish did they go?" Eyes twitching from all the stimulants, he checks the display in his helmet to find that the karts' icons have disappeared from the map. "Are they using some sort of ghost power?"

By the time he comes around the other side of the Creep Coaster, the ghost karts have rematerialized in front of him, and he angrily bashes his steering wheel. Before long, he loses sight of them in the dense fog surrounding the Gruesome Graveyard, and glancing at his map, he notices that the *Cannibal Kart* is right on top of him. He braces himself for a digital sliming, but when he searches the dense cloud, the ravenous ghost kart is nowhere to be found.

That's when it hits him, or rather doesn't. As he putters over the Graveyard, its grounds now infested with glowing ghosts, he thinks back to when he almost got slimed on the track in the Ghost Town below. The strange part is, in all these races he's never driven through the Graveyard, only over it. The *Zoomer* slips back into fourth place, and by the time he emerges from the fog, all the missing karts are suddenly way out ahead.

When the race is over, he pulls up next to the *Bone Crusher*, and before the grinning ghost kid gets a chance to gloat, The One suggests, "One more time around?"

"*I like you, kid,*" the ghost says. "*You're a glutton for punishment.*"

As The One pulls the *Zombie Zoomer* into position behind the starting line alongside the rest of the ghost karts, he briefly fears that he might be a ghost just like them, condemned to live the same race over and over for the rest of eternity. But his growling stomach rejects the idea.

This time when the signal flashes, he holds back, allowing the *Bone Crusher* to take the lead around the first turn. He keeps his distance all the way past the Ghoulish Game Gallery and the parking lot out back with the ginormous mini-golf course he's somehow just noticing.

As they come up on the Creep Coaster, the *She-Machine* skids into the *Zoomer*, leaving a coat of digital pink slime on its windshield, and when The One reaches his arm out to wipe away the residue, he catches the *Bone Crusher* veering off course. Instead of following the track around the Coaster, the skeleton kart drives straight at it and disappears through a hole in its busted guardrail.

Staring into the hole, The One envisions himself tumbling down into the infinite dark, but with only a couple space seconds to decide what to do next, he says, "Fish it. It's been a fun adventure."

Spinning the *Zombie Zoomer*'s wheel, he turns his kart toward the Coaster and putters through the rail screaming. But instead of plummeting to his doom, he lands on a bumpy track hidden below the Parkwood frame. Although there are barriers in place to keep the karts from veering off, the route is treacherous, forcing him to rely on the *Zoomer*'s flickering low beams to light the way as he winds around the ancient support beams. By the time he launches out the other end, the *Bone Crusher* is the only kart ahead of him.

"We cut straight past the whole swamp!" The One says.

Cackling in his helmet, the ghost driving the skeleton kart says, "*So, you found my secret. But it's going to take more than that to beat me!*"

With the *Bone Crusher* in his sights, The One tells its driver, "Sorry kid, but this is your last lap."

Sticking close enough to keep sight of the *Crusher*'s ghostly frame as it slips into the thick fog surrounding the Graveyard, The One follows it toward the inside of the track. This time, when the bone kart pulls its disappearing act, he putters after it, plunging down through the gray cloud. A few harrowing space seconds later, he emerges onto a narrow stretch of track surrounded by fake grass and plastic headstones.

Glancing at the infestation of glowing spirits hovering around the grounds, he says, "I don't remember there being so many ghosts."

"*Someday, you will all be ghosts, gakakaka!*" the kid says.

As soon as he spots an opening, The One attempts to pass the bone kart, but the ghost's driving has grown erratic. Most likely sensing its impending defeat, it swerves back and forth, blocking him at every turn.

Before they reach the other end of the Graveyard, the track takes them back up through the fog and onto the main stretch just in time to begin the climb around Mascot Manor. As they circle the giant mansion, The One searches for a way to pass, but the *Bone Crusher* is all over the track. No matter how much he lays on his pathetic horn, the ghost kart won't move out of the way.

As they escape the haunted house and hurtle down the final hill, The One glances at his map to find that all but one of the other racers have fallen hopelessly behind. He's not sure which monster wagon the third place icon represents, and he doesn't care. As they cut back and forth toward the bottom of the winding track, he suddenly sees his chance. Rather than take the final twisty turn, he hops up over the grassy curve and bounces down into a narrow lead.

"Ahahaha!" The One cackles. "I beat you!"

"*You came close, kid*," the ghost tells him. "*But I always win.*"

Finally revealing the *Bone Crusher*'s special ability, the ghost kid activates his kart's booster and speeds up alongside the *Zoomer* as they putt down the final straightaway.

The One's kart still has a slight edge, but as he races toward the finish line, something clips his kart's bumper, causing it to swerve wildly. He immediately spins the steering wheel to compensate, but it's no use. With no regard for the living, the *Bone Crusher* cruises to victory while the *Zombie Zoomer* spins out into the plastic guardrail.

The crash bruises The One's ego more than his body as he's reminded how slow they were actually moving. Yanking off his helmet, he jumps out of his kart to give the reckless driver a good yelling at, but he's so surprised to see the furry green alien waving its giant mascot paw that the only thing he can think to do is wave back.

29

"In order to defeat me," Horton reads from the Prize Keeper sign outside the mysterious mini-golf course, "you must complete the course with a score better than four under par and sink a hole-in-one on the 19th green. Succeed and you will receive the power of the Ghoulish Game Gallery. Fail and it'll be game over. Mwo-ho-ho-ho…"

Digging a handful of wet treasure out of his shorts pocket, Horton slips the slimy tokens into the ball machine. He wonders what color he'll get – maybe black or midnight blue.

When the ball finally falls down the chute, he plucks it out and remarks, "It always has to be pink… At least I won't lose it."

Putter in hand, he steps up to the first hole, a glowing waste dump surrounded by a river of toxic ooze, and places his ball on the tee mat.

At the far end of the fake green, the not-so-distant cup lights up and the Prize Keeper's voice seeps out of a hidden speaker, *"Here's an easy one to get you started. But don't let your ball fall into the runoff, or it'll be tokens for me!"*

Taking a step back, Horton practices his putt while he gets a lay of the horrorland. The only obstacles on this hole are a couple rusty barrels leaking toxic waste. If he can avoid the glowing ooze seeping out of them, he figures he should be able to reach the cup in two strokes.

After a series of recommended stretches, he checks the direction of the night wind, gets into position next to the tee, and putts. But it's been so long since he's played that he underestimates the power of his swing and accidentally launches the pink ball across the green. He cringes as it smashes against the side of one of the leaky barrels and flies up into the air. But by a stroke of golf luck, it narrowly clears the sludge puddle, bounces up the ramp, off the back barrel, and rolls neatly into the hole.

"Lucky shot," the Prize Keeper comments.

Gazing down at his putter, Horton says, "This could be easier than I thought."

But one look at the next hole dispels that notion. Covered in broken vials spilling neon mystery goop, he assesses that the only way he's going to make it through this one with his score intact is the slow, steady approach.

"The Scaredyland scientist is on the loose, leaving a trail of volatile chemicals in his wake," the Prize Keeper's disembodied voice narrates. *"He'll stop at nothing in his quest to mutate the course into his own twisted design. The only way to stop him is with the power of miniature golf. Beat the scientist to the final hole and foil his evil plans before he destroys all of Scaredyland!"*

Dropping his ball onto the mat, Horton carefully putts past the first broken beaker, only to land in a patch of sticky green 'goo.' Fortunately, after space centuries exposed to the elements, most of the stickiness has worn away, and he manages to come in under par. But he doesn't stop to celebrate.

Hurrying to the next hole, he soon discovers the type of havoc the imaginary scientist's reckless handling of fictional chemicals is capable of wreaking. The short green turf to which he's become accustomed over these first holes is so long that he can barely see his glowing target.

"The stolen chemicals are capable of altering the landscaping itself," the Keeper says. *"This hole's grown a little out of control, but it's a straight shot – if you can hack it,* mwo-ho-ho-ho."

As he sizes up the overgrown green, Horton decides, "This looks like a job for the ol' Horton Hop."

With a solid smash at just the right angle, he sends his pink ball flying up over the plastic rough. But instead of giving him the little bounce he had hoped for, it immediately sinks down into the weeds. By the time he manages to slice his ball out of the long plastic grass and into the hole, he's lost most of the advantage he gained on the first couple greens.

Glancing at the treacherous path ahead, he suddenly isn't so sure even his superior putting skills are going to be enough. He's grown rusty in his adolescence, and this has already been the most difficult course he's ever encountered.

Hole 4 does little to alleviate his fear as he watches a trio of rotting plant monsters mechanically munch the green. Jerkily extending their overlong necks, they drop their metal jaws down onto the play area to chomp any golf balls that land in their path.

As soon as Horton places his ball on the mat, the Keeper explains, "*These putrid plants are one of the doctor's crazier experiments. Designed to devour meddling mini-golfers, they developed an appetite for golf balls. All you have to do is hit it while they're not eating. But a word of warning – if one of these ravenous weeds sinks its teeth into your ball, it won't be good for your score.*"

Getting past the munching monsters isn't going to be easy. But as the Keeper was blathering, Horton noticed that what at first appeared to be random chomping is actually a fixed sequence. If he times his putt just right, he can roll past all three of the monsters while their jaws are lifted. As soon as he has the pattern down, he waits for the second plant to stick its neck out, and he whacks his ball straight down the middle of the green. But his timing is a little off, and the ball gets gobbled.

As the ball disappears down the plant's mechanical gullet, Horton fears he's going to have to dredge up more tokens. Worse, since the ball is what registers his progress, he'll probably have to start over from the beginning of the course. But a wave of sick relief washes over him when he sees the plastic pink orb rolling down the ball return. As soon as he picks it up, the counter on his wristband adds a penalty stroke to his score, and he groans.

At the risk of going over par, he takes another swing. This time, his ball rolls safely through the gauntlet of plant monsters and lands gently at the edge of the hole. Careful not to get caught in the plants' munchers, he manages to sidle down the green and tap the ball into the hole without losing any appendages.

With his overall score stuck at two under par, he's starting to feel the fear as the course mutates around him. But after receiving a few pointers from the fans, he falls into his old rhythm. Soon, his putter and ball begin to feel like artificial extensions of himself as they pull off putts so perilous as to silence the chat.

When he reaches the 9th hole, the Prize Keeper is waiting to warn him, "*You may have survived the terrors of the vampire duck pond and escaped the insatiable hunger of the ravenous mutant zombie squirrels. But see if you can putt your way out of the living picnic.*"

At four under par, Horton calmly tells the annoying voice box, "Now that the ball, the putter, and I are one, nothing you say can stop us from beating your score. Fear is merely a distraction from putting. We have awakened to the true nature of miniature golf, transcended the course, and lost any desire for prizes. All that remains is putt."

"*But don't you want to obtain the power of the Game Gallery?*" the Keeper questions.

Vaguely recalling his teammates and their adventure, Horton says, "Oh yeah…"

A quick scan of the green is all he needs to send his ball rolling past the angry lunch foods, across the giant checked tablecloth, and through the legs of the monster picnic basket. But as he lines up the putt that will secure his lead, a sudden commotion causes him to overshoot, and he turns back to find a mad scientist with wild hair and a stained lab coat climbing out of the basket. Horton looks on in confused horror as the mascot staggers past, kicking his ball as it gracelessly stumbles off into the night.

30.

Tearfully staring up at the crumbling coaster of her nightmares, Pants tells the fans, "Now I'm *really* scared, you guys."

Somehow, the slobbering, horned beast painted on the side does little to comfort her. But as she approaches the dark entrance, a sign out front gives her hope. Printed in an archaic font above the measuring-zombie's gnarled arm is a powerful spell that has foiled her fun more times than she can remember – "*You must be this tall to ride.*"

"Oh no!" Pants pretend moans. "I'm always too short to get on the big rides. Oh well…"

But the recent growth spurt she went through unspoils her plans as she steps under the monster paw to find that she's just tall enough to make the cut.

"Dagnabit!" she whines. "I mean, yay…"

Surrounded by the spinning monster machines that populate the Gorewalk, she uses her phone to illuminate the dark tunnel ahead. But she's trembling so much that the light bounces all over the place. When a train of cars loudly clatters past overhead, the Coaster's Parkwood skeleton groans, and Pants shrieks.

"This isn't s-scary at all, you guys," she assures the fans as she follows the hideous monster signs through a wooden web of rotting support beams plastered with fossilized gum and ancient graffiti.

Picking out one of the carved inscriptions, she reads, "'Klaatu, barada, nikto.' I wonder what that means. Post your guesses in the chat!" The next one reads, "'Klevin is a butt…' I know what that means."

Slowly snaking her way toward the front of the line, she finally comes to a steep staircase surrounded by candy wrappers and crushed Ecto Cooler cans. Her heart pounds harder with each step as she forces her wobbly legs to climb, gripping the railing like the show depends on it. She keeps telling herself that she can't let the team or the fans down, but as she scales the steep staircase, the sound of the train speeding down the track grows so loud that it's all she can hear. When she reaches the landing, her legs suddenly stop working and she crumples to the ground. Wrapping her arms around the rail, she glances out at the blinking lights below, and the Gorewalk starts spinning.

"This is h-higher than I th-thought, you g-guys," she says, resisting the sick urge to look down. "I don't th-think I can d-do this."

But as messages of support flood the chat, she feels obligated to keep going. Taking a deep breath, she loosens her arms and wobbles to her feet. With her eyes on her phone, she takes one step, and then another, and the next thing she knows, she's standing on the top platform opposite an empty train car.

"So, this is where all the scares happen. I guess there's no turning back now. I mean, I could. But I won't… probably."

Swallowing her fear, she glances out over the rail to get a look at the best view in Scaredyland – at least, that's what the sign claims. And it might be right. She can see all the way down Maim Street from up here. Pointing her phone out at the Ghost Towns below, she gives a detailed recap of the adventure so far, for anyone just tuning in.

When she runs out of narration, she concludes, "I guess the only thing to do now is ride the Creep Coaster." Grasping for a way to buy herself a little more time as she approaches the final queue, she says, "I just realized that I can sit wherever I want. Which seat do you guys think I should take?" She shoots off a quick poll, and when the results come back a few space seconds later, she demurs. "Why did I even ask?"

Hesitantly stepping toward the first car, Pants scans her bracelet, and the gate swings open. She climbs in directly behind the purple Creep attached to the front of the coaster, and before she has a chance to space chicken out, the bar drops down onto her lap.

"Welp, this is it, you guys," she tells the fans. "There's no getting off now."

She can hear the track shifting into a new configuration as she takes one last long look back at the platform. Sticking her head out over the edge of the track, she peers down into the bottomless darkness below, and when she turns back, she screams.

"*What?*" the glowing ghost in the next seat asks. "*What are we screaming about?*"

"You!" she cries.

"*Oh, right…*"

Looking into Brilly's undead grin, she demands, "What are you doing here? I thought you disappeared."

"*I said I would ride the Coaster with you,*" the ghost boy reminds her. "*There was just something about that skeleton mascot down there that really freaked me out. They're not alive, they're not dead — what the space hell are they?*"

With the fate of the team on the line, Pants tries to stay calm, reminding herself that it's only a ride. It's only a ride. But as soon as the train jerks forward, she loses her brule.

Frantically pulling on her lap bar, she cries, "Stop, I want to get off!"

But it's too late. The ride is already in motion.

"*Don't worry,*" the ghost kid tells her. "*I've been on this coaster thousands of times, and I've always survived.*"

Staring into her phone as the train ascends the first giant hill, she says, "In case this is my last adventure, I just want you all to know that you're my favorite fans."

"*What about me?*" Brilly asks.

"You're not a fan," she reminds him.

Scrunching his freckly holographic cheeks, he asks, "*Fan of what?*"

Pants clips her phone to her team lanyard and grips the rubber bar cutting off circulation to her legs as the Creep takes them higher and higher above the grounds.

"It's only a ride," she reminds herself.

"*Whooo!*" Brilly cries, but when the ghost boy tries to hold on to Pants's arm, his hands slip right through her.

"Stop it!" she yells. "You're getting slime all over me."

"*Sorry,*" he says. "*It's just that this is the scariest part.*"

When they reach the highest point in the park, the train rolls over the top of the hill, and Pants shrieks, "Wahhh-ah…"

But instead of plummeting back toward the Gorewalk, the car stops in its tracks. Teetering over the edge of the park, Pants tries to grab the phone dangling in front of her. But she's too scared to let go for fear that she'll tumble out and become a Scaredyland ghost stuck in the park forever.

With her hands pressed against the bar, she carefully turns her trembling head toward the hologram next to her and asks, "Why aren't we moving?"

"*I don't know,*" Brilly says, plainly. "*This has never happened before.*"

"Oh great, we're stuck!" she moans. "I knew this was a bad idea."

"*No we're not…,*" the ghost kid says, inspecting the car. "*Well, maybe we are.*"

Looking down at the blinking rides, she whines, "What do we do now?"

"*You could ask your ghost guide for help.*"

"Good idea!" she says. "Ghosty will get us down from here. We just have to summon him."

But before she has a chance to spit, the train suddenly plunges down the giant hill. With the Creep's googly arms flailing in front of them, Pants is so scared she can't even scream. In the few space seconds it takes to reach the bottom of the hill, she would swear she caught a glimpse of the skeleton mascot waving hideously from the Gorewalk below. But in a flash, it's gone, and the creep descends into the wooden maze below the Coaster. Twisting and turning through the shadowy beams, they come out spinning past the Gruesome Graveyard and out over the black swamp that surrounds Scaredyland.

"This is weird," Brilly yells. *"I've never been on this track before."*

"It's fun!" Pants tries to convince herself as they loop back toward the bright lights of the Gorewalk.

Jouncing past the other monster rides, they enter another steep climb, and when Pants hears a bunch of freaky chattering behind her, she turns to find the train packed with ghosts. They all scream when they hit the next drop, and she's briefly blinded by a bright flash of moonlight before spinning back up through the tangled Parkwood beams. The train banks around the back side of the Coaster and begins to slow, but just as she thinks the ride is over, the track twists and drops suddenly to deliver one last scare.

When they finally pull back up to the platform, Pants's hands have frozen into permanent claws from clenching the lap bar. With her hair tie lost to the park winds, she points her phone at herself to find untamed tufts of pink sticking out everywhere.

"That's the most fun I've had since I was alive!" Brilly says. *"Should we go again?"*

"No!" Pants says. "I mean, it was fun. But once was enough."

"*Suit yourself,*" the ghost kid tells her, floating out of his seat.

"It was really scary, but I beat the challenge, you guys," Pants tells the fans. "Now I just have to figure out how to get my prize." But when she tries to lift the lap bar, it won't budge. Desperately looking toward Brilly floating on the edge of the platform, she cries, "The bar won't come up!"

Pants hits and spits, but no matter how many rules she breaks, she can't get free. Stuck in her seat with no hope of escape, she uselessly reaches out to the ghost kid, and their hands slip through each other as the train lurches back to life.

31

"Having fun?" The Other One asks, improperly dressed for adventure in his work polo and business shorts.

"Well, I *was*," Todd says, shooing the kid back to whatever board room he crawled out of. "You can use the pool if you want. But you're blocking my moonlight. What the fish are you doing here, anyway? I thought you were working on promos back on the *Cuddler.*"

"I thought you wanted me here," the gap-toothed business boy says. "Anyway, what about you? While the team faces unknown simulated horrors, you're over here lounging in your "parent playland." And where'd you get those Scaredyland swim trunks?"

Sensing that his short vacation has come to an untimely end, Todd awkwardly lifts himself out of his chair and tells the boy, "We've obviously reached an impasse. Let's just agree to never tell the team about this."

"That goes without saying."

"Brule," the tired merch guy says as he wraps himself in his souvenir beach towel.

"What the fish happened to you?" The Other One asks, pointing at the lacerations covering Todd's legs.

"I got scratched up on the trail back there," he says, motioning to the dense thicket of dead wilderness surrounding The End of the Line. "It's a Scaredyland miracle that I made it here alive."

The Other One frowns, tapping his loafer against the imported Venutian tile. "But you're an adult. Why didn't you just come in through the front? The back way is how the kids sneak in."

"Maybe I would have if I had one of those power bracelets. I can't do anything in this place without one." Wringing out his wet mane, Todd suddenly notices the piece of plastic merch dangling around the kid's wrist and grumbles, "Hey! How the fish did you get one? I thought there were only enough wristbands for the team!"

"Oh, right…," The Other One says. "The kids on my team managed to reverse engineer the technology and throw together some replicas. But Pants Team Pink is wearing the genuine items. I figured you'd want them to look good for the cameras."

"Good thinking…," Todd grumbles. "But what do you mean "*my*" team? And why didn't you give me one of those counterfeit wristbands?"

His attention drifting as he taps at his phone, The Other One finally asks, "What was the question?" But before Todd can snap his towel, the kid says, "I had to assemble a small team of my own to pull this adventure together. I can't do everything all by myself. And I didn't give you a wristband because you're not really part of the team. It just didn't make sense, narratively."

"Oh, well…," Todd says, wiggling his pruned fingers. "We mustn't disrupt the narrative."

"It's the most important part of the adventure!" The Other One cries. "You know that better than anyone. It's the reason why you can't stop watching those old episodes, and it's the thing you hired me to fix. Now, dry yourself off and pull your shirt back on, for Space God's sake."

As The Other One wanders off to attend to some shadowy business, Todd begins to regret ever hiring the little spit. But the show's viewers *are* way up, and he can't argue with results, by whatever means. Collecting his things, he bids farewell to the exclusive rest area and raids The End of the Line gift shop for a new wardrobe.

When The Other One lays eyes on the merch guy's head-to-toe Scaredyland apparel, he says, "Now, that's good advertising. Come on, let's get out of here and find the team before the adventure continues."

"Aww, I didn't even get to visit the adult game room!" Todd moans, slipping into his team jacket.

"Which do you care about more, the fate of the team or satisfying your childish urges?" The Other One poses.

Todd thinks it over for a long moment and finally decides, "The team… I guess."

The two of them stroll out through the front gate like official passholders, taking up the entire width of the overgrown sidewalk as they meander back toward Maim Street. While far less treacherous than the path Todd took to get here, the sidewalk is full of cracks and roots for him to trip on. They follow the winding trail to a worn stretch of fake grass outside the play area of the Gruesome Graveyard. Sticking close to the broken fence, they feel their way through the fog until they finally spot the dim light of the Parkway.

As soon as Todd steps back out onto Maim Street, he drags himself to a drinking fountain and thirstily laps up the flat green liquid that burbles out. With his sugar replenished, he scans the rubber road and tells The Other One, "I don't see the team."

"I'm watching the show right now," the kid says, holding up his phone. "They're still stuck in the Ghost Towns, which is good. It gives us some time."

"Time for what?" Todd asks.

"Uh, you know," The Other One says. "Time to water the cosmos."

"What the fish does that mean?"

Nervously tapping the screen in his hand, the kid says, "It means we get to hang out and explore the grounds a little."

"O-kay…," Todd says. "So, what do you want to do first?"

Either unable or unwilling to rip his eyes away from his phone, The Other One says, "I guess by 'we,' I meant *you*. I've still got some promotional stuff to take care of."

"Buy you just got here," Todd complains. "Besides, what am I supposed to do with no wristband and no tokens? You should have just left me at The End of the Line."

Digging in his pocket, The Other One flicks Todd a dull coin and says, "We need the whole team together for the final merch reveal – even you. It's gonna be the biggest season finale in the history of the show."

"Sounds about right," Todd says, fumbling the ancient token. "I'm only considered an official member of the team when it's convenient. Otherwise, I'm left to sleep on the couch." The pyrite token rolls onto the plastic grass, and he leans down to pick it up, adding, "And what am I supposed to do with one token, anyway? Are you even—" But when he looks up, The Other One is already tromping off down the sidewalk. "That's great. Don't worry about the merch guy. I'll just wait here until somebody needs me to appraise their winnings."

With nothing to do but wait for the end of the adventure, Todd wanders back toward Mascot Manor, resigned to a lonely tour around the parkgrounds. The giant mansion has changed somehow since he last saw it. The shutters are wide open, and something is riling up the ghosts. Hundreds of the glowing pests circle the upper floors of the house, moaning otherworldly obscenities.

Fleeing the ghostly chatter, he makes his way toward the convoy of mutated monsters guarding the Haunted Raceway and stops to breathe in the scent of burning composite rubber. At the risk of kartsickness, he briefly considers jumping behind the wheel of one of the monster wagons. But without a wristband, he couldn't join the race even if he wanted to.

With barely a token to his name, he walks right past the Game Gallery's glowing entrance, and as he looks up at the star-speckled night sky, he suddenly gets the crazy idea that maybe he could be happy living an all-analog life, without the endless stream of shows and games. But he quickly comes to his senses, laughing at the notion as he ambles up the rubber road.

Before long, Todd comes upon the glass box containing his favorite cosmic squid monster, and admiring the sturdy craftsmanship of the ancient machine, he tells its plastic occupant, "Sorry Fishtar, I'm all out of tokens." But as he turns to walk away, he suddenly announces, "Wait a space second, no I'm not!"

With his fake future hanging in the balance, he rummages through the souvenirs stashed in the pockets of his pink jacket and emerges with the faded token that The Other One left him. Rubbing the ancient coin between his fingers for good bad luck, he pushes it into the slot and brings Fishtar back to simulated life.

Eyes glowing bright, Fishtar rubs its plastic ball and recites the magic words, "*Remember, the only way to change your destiny is to feed Fishtar more tokens.*"

When the card pops out, Todd anxiously snatches it from the slot and reads, "'Your future is dark but also light. Advice: The only way forward is back. Unlucky Number: 1.'"

As Todd ponders the implications of his misfortune, he wanders back toward the front gate of the Dark Park, past the black fountain, and around to the other side of Maim Street. When he comes to the trail leading down to the Gorewalk, he wonders if Pants found the courage to go on the Creep Coaster. But knowing her, he figures she's probably riding it right now.

Traipsing past countless empty souvenir shops, Todd eventually reaches the shortcut to the Gruesome Graveyard, when he realizes his sneaker is untied. As he kneels down to retie his laces, he hears muffled whispers spilling out of the alley. At first, he sloughs it off as the incessant moaning of the park ghosts, but something about the voices sounds almost *human.*

"*Shhh*, he's coming," somebody says as Todd gets closer.

When he steps into the alley, he finds The Other One trying to look casual roughly tearing open a pack of candy cigarettes as a neon blur disappears around the back of the building.

Skeptically scanning the empty alley, Todd asks the kid, "Who were you talking to just now?"

"What?!" The Other One cries as he dumps the box's sugary contents into his mouth. Shoving Todd back toward the sidewalk, he mumbles, "I wasn't talking to anybody. You're hearing things. Keep your head in the adventure."

32

As the zombie mascot lays its decaying plush paws on Beer's arm, the boy's Ghost Zapper fires, and the monster stumbles back.

Yelping and patting its singed fur, the mascot's voice almost sounds pained as it mumbles, "What'd you do that for?" But after a moment, the creature recovers and resumes lumbering toward him. "Now I'm really going to scare you."

Beer frantically pumps his Zapper, and once it's charged, he fires into the furry monster's good eye. The mascot lets out an ear-splitting howl, and holding its paws over its face, it trips away moaning into the mist.

Once Beer is convinced that the monster isn't coming back, he checks his wristband to find that his heart rate is approaching the 100 bpm limit, after which he'll be "scared to death" and probably have to start the whole challenge over again.

"That was a close one," he comments, panting. "What the fish was that thing, anyway? I thought there was only supposed to be ghosts out here. Speaking of, I've still got…" He checks his wristband to see how many he has left to zap. "Chit, there's still 286 ghosts. This is gonna take me all night."

Evidently overhearing his complaint, a nearby ghost suddenly opens its slobbering jaws and starts floating in his direction. But before the fake spirit gets a chance to slime him, he charges his weapon and fires a hole through its holographic body.

Unfortunately, the static discharge attracts the attention of half a dozen other glowing pests floating in the area. Incapable of pumping fast enough to zap them all, Beer finds an opening and hoofs it back across the Graveyard. Between the fear and the exertion, his heart rate is resting at a steady 105 bpm.

As soon as he gets some distance between him and the swarm, he stops to rest behind one of the novelty headstones. But when he looks back, the ghosts are still on his trail. Quickly re-pumping his Zapper, he takes out the nearest purple people eater and ducks back down. But the ghosts are moving fast, and when he turns to take his next shot, they've almost caught up with him.

Before they can float any closer, Beer takes off in search of another hiding spot. But as he feels his way through the dense fog, he catches the hollow eye of a small spirit hovering near a plastic tree. He tries to zap the little pest, but he misses, and the ghost peels back its digital lips to reveal a large set of jagged flesh eaters. Even though he knows it can't really hurt him, the thought of its fangs sinking into his soft flesh sends him running.

His frightened squeals as he takes off across the plastic hillside only attract more attention, and soon he's being trailed by dozens of the glowing ghosts. He fires back at the pulsating mass of virtual monsters as fast as he can pump. But the longer he evades them, the quicker they float, and thanks to all the candied rations he's consumed since the last adventure, he's fading fast.

"I guess this is what it feels like to be haunted," Beer says, wiping the sticky sweat from his brow as he ducks behind the Maniac Mausoleum. He had intended to complete this challenge clean but, "Desperate times call for caffeine candy."

Digging in his pocket for the candies Horton handed out earlier, he pops one of the black beans in his mouth, and as soon as he bites down, he feels the caffeinated sugar course through him.

With a renewed manic energy, Beer pulls himself to his feet and makes a run for it, pumping and zapping at the ghosts gathered behind him. But it's still not enough to slow them down. For every ghost he zaps back to the digital ether, three more attach themselves to the growing swarm.

"This is impossible," he says, resting against a half-melted headstone. "They just keep coming!" As the massive conglomeration of ghosts floats toward him, he tiredly lifts his plastic weapon and tells them, "If this is the end, then I'm gonna go out zapping."

But when he leans his weight on the headstone, he hears a loud *snap*, and the next thing he knows, he's tumbling backward into an open grave. He lands against the hard dirt, and as soon as he can recover his Zapper, he points it up at the open hole. When a repulsive pink apparition lazily floats into his sights, he quickly zaps it. But before he can recharge his weapon, the whole ghost gang is hovering over him.

Shielding himself from the sliming he's about to endure, Beer's heart rate spikes, and his beeping wristband warns him that he's approaching fake death. But after an uneventful few space seconds, he pries his eyes open to find that the ghosts are still floating above the grave.

"What the rule five?" Suddenly recalling his discussion with the Cantankerous Caretaker, he says, "Oh yeah… Ghosts can't go below ground. I guess that makes this my lucky night."

Pumping his Zapper, he takes aim at the nearest apparition and turns it to holo-dust. He zaps the rest of them one by one, until the Graveyard's population has been reduced to 217 ghosts. Taking advantage of the network of dark tunnels that the ancient Caretaker dug underneath the Graveyard, Beer travels from grave to grave, zapping every ghost he can find. It's not long before the number of remaining ghosts has dropped into the double digits.

But all the pumping and candy leaves his arms and head sore, so when he reaches a quiet grave, he sets his Zapper down to take a short break. The ghosts' moaning acts like white noise as he lays in the dirt to rest his eyes.

It feels like he's only been asleep for a moment before he wakes to the sound of laughter coming from inside the dark tunnel. Still hazy from his nap, he awkwardly sits up and snatches his Zapper. Frantically pumping, he points the barrel into the shadows, but after a long moment, he begins to wonder if he was just having a bad dream.

Then he hears it again, cackling at him from the shadows.

"I'm not afraid," Beer assures whatever is watching him. "Come out or I'll zap."

For just an instant, he glances up to make sure the ghosts can't reach him, and the moment he looks back, a neon zombie with a scorched eye pokes its head out of the shadows. Beer fires, but the static bolt fizzles out against the grave wall, and the mascot lunges for him. He cries out, and his wristband starts beeping as the plush monster drags him down into the dirt.

After a short struggle, Beer somehow manages to wriggle out from under the zombie, and while it scrambles to get up, he grabs his Zapper and pulls himself out of the hole. But as soon as he gets above ground, he discovers that the scuffle has drawn the ghosts back toward this corner of the Graveyard.

Forced to face his fear, he scrambles across the foggy hillside, pumping and zapping for his life, until there are few enough of the holographic pests left that they start floating away from him instead of at him. When he finally gets down to the last spacer's dozen, they become more difficult to locate. He finds a couple of them hovering around the back fence and another floating in one of the fake trees. The rest he tracks down the hard way, blindly stumbling across the open Graveyard.

Before long, he manages to whittle the ghosts down to a single undead straggler. But even after checking in every tree and behind every headstone, he still can't find it.

"I've looked everywhere," Beer complains. "There are no ghosts left. It must be a glitch in the Scaredyland matrix, or some sort of evil plan to trap me here until—"

But before he can finish his paranoid ramble, he spots a soft blue glow hovering near the gate out front.

"Ha, I found you!" he cries, pumping his Zapper.

Cautiously approaching the Ghost Town's crooked entrance, he takes aim at the final phantom. But just as he's about to pull the trigger, the zombie mascot charges out of the fog and tackles him to the fake grass. As the monster tries to wrestle his Zapper away from him, the plastic gun goes off, and Beer looks up to find a cloud of digital dust where the ghost had been floating. The decaying mascot produces a muffled moan as it climbs to its feet and staggers away. But as the neon monster trips toward the gate, Beer gets off one last shot, singeing its strangely adorable backside.

With the challenge finally complete, his wristband starts glowing a ghostly blue, and as he picks himself up off the fake turf, he turns back to find the fog lifting. Soon, he can even see the Caretaker's Cottage and the ancient spirit that dwells within frantically waving at him through the window.

"Oh yeah…," Beer groans.

As soon as he opens the door, the Caretaker floats out to relative freedom.

"After all these space years, I'm finally free-ish," the digital coot says, and before Beer can zap it away from him, the ghost wraps him in its slimy arms.

33

As The One pulls his decrepit kart across the finish line, he hears an annoying five-tone honk and turns to find the green alien mascot that sideswiped him stupidly waving in his direction. He lays on the *Zombie Zoomer*'s pitiful horn in retaliation, but the mascot just covers its mouth with its oversized paws, pretending to laugh.

"Fish off," The One yells, jutting his thumb out the window.

Appearing in the passenger seat next to him, Ghosty moans, "*Rule five—*" But The One swipes the ghost away before it can finish scolding him.

If it wasn't for that chidiotic mascot, he would have served the *Bone Crusher* and the rest of the track ghosts a humiliating ack kicking. Now he has to contend with an additional racer, one whose floating kart is capable of inflicting more damage than a little fake slime. He would never admit it, even to himself, but as he looks back at the shiny saucer, a small part of him worries he might not win this race.

Squeezing his steering wheel of flesh, The One anxiously waits for the starting signal, and as soon as the oozing light flashes, he shoves his foot down on the accelerator so hard that for a space second he thinks the *Zoomer*'s wheels are going to spin off. The next thing he knows, he's puttering past the *Bone Crusher* and the rest of the monster wagons into an early lead.

As he skids around the Goulish Game Gallery, he beeps his horn at Horton navigating the mini-golf maze down below. But just as his pale friend looks up toward the track, something slams into his kart, and he glances back to find the alien mascot sitting on the *Zoomer*'s ack.

"Okay, fish head," he says. "That's how you wanna race?"

Spinning his kart's wheel, he swerves back and forth across the track to keep the mascot from passing. His erratic driving forces the saucer to back off, and as they putter over the Scaredyland entrance, The One suddenly gets a gleefully ghoulish idea. He takes his foot off the *Zoomer*'s accelerator until the mascot catches up, and he allows the saucer to pull in front of him. This way, when he takes the first shortcut, it'll be too late for the alien to follow.

Snickering madly to himself as they approach the Creep Coaster, he says, "It's a long way around. Brahahaha!"

But when they come up to the turn, the saucer floats straight past it, instead plowing through the broken guardrail to gain access to the hidden path beneath the ride.

"How the fish did it know about the shortcut?" The One growls, following the kart into the bowels of the Coaster.

With the help of the *Zoomer*'s cracked headlights, he spots the alien a short ways ahead of him. But the track is too narrow to pass, so he rides the back end of the floating saucer until the mascot juts its giant thumb out at him.

"That's not very mascot-like!" The One yells.

When they get back out onto the main track, he speeds up next to the smiling green alien and glares into its lifeless plastic eyes. Hoping to put some fear into the mascot, he rams the saucer only for the *Zoomer*'s bumper to fall off.

"There's more where that came from," The One warns, pounding his fists against his kart's steering wheel.

As they come up on the next stretch, he figures he can lose the monster in the Gruesome Graveyard. But the track has changed since the last race. Just when he expects to be enveloped by a cloud of treacherous fog, it's all clear skies and smooth driving. With the shortcut fast approaching, he tries to move his kart toward the inside. But the mascot won't let him in.

"What the fish is your problem?" he shouts at the plush ackle. Lacking fog, he can clearly see the turnoff coming up, and he tells the furry racer, "You're forcing me to resort to my last… resort."

The One twists the *Zoomer*'s wheel around and smashes into the metal saucer, losing a rotting side mirror in the ugly process. Just when he thinks he's got the alien beat, the saucer pushes back, its shiny fuselage slicing into the *Zombie Zoomer*'s fleshy exterior.

"You're gonna make me miss the turn!" The One cries.

Scared that he's fated to become just another ghost kid haunting the Raceway, he cuts away from the mascot and narrowly avoids the rubber barrier separating the main track from the shortcut. As he watches the saucer descend toward the Graveyard, the *Zoomer*'s passenger side door sloughs off and crashes onto the rubber road behind him.

With his kart falling apart on him, he figures the race is over for real this time. Soon the rest of the team will complete their challenges, and he'll still be out here puttering around.

The best he can hope for at this point is second place. He could challenge the mascot to another race, but with the last spasms of his caffeine candy wearing off, he doesn't have any race left in him.

Rolling along the Raceway in his decaying kart, he watches for the saucer to come out the other end of the shortcut. But it takes longer than he expected, and by the time the mascot finally reemerges, it's only a few kart lengths ahead.

As the bulbous alien bobbles along in front of him, he searches for some clue as to how he managed to keep up. Somehow, his eyes land on his kart's speed gauge, and he realizes that the needle has pushed past its listed limit. He glances around the busted kart, with its missing door and long-lost bumper, when it bashes him over the head. With every body part the *Zoomer* loses, the kart becomes lighter on its wheels.

Having finally discovered the *Zombie Zoomer*'s special degenerative power, The One devises a new strategy. As they drive up around Mascot Manor, he purposely crashes into the track walls to shed the rest of the dead weight slowing him down. His kart's body begins to break apart as it scrapes along the heavy barriers, and clutching the juddering wheel, he uses his free hand to tear off the heavy flap of artificial skin covering the roof. With every fleshy part he discards, the *Zoomer*'s speed increases, until it's all he can do to keep the wobbly kart on the track.

Racing through the Manor's upper floor, The One mostly avoids getting slimed by the ghosts infesting its decorated walls, and when he comes out the other side, he catches a glimpse of the alien racer disappearing over the edge of the final hill.

Just a space second or two behind, he plunges what's left of the *Zombie Zoomer* down the winding track and cries, "I'm coming for you, saucer kid!"

Abandoning the brake as he whips down the final leg of the Raceway, he nearly crashes at every turn. By the time he bounces onto the final straightaway, there's little the plush monster can do to stop him. But fearing the remnants of his kart could be vulnerable to collision, he keeps his distance as he finally zips past the dented saucer and its stuffed driver.

The *Zombie Zoomer* putters across the finish line in record time, and The One raises his fists in triumph. "I am *still* The One!" The remains of his kart skid to a stop, and as he climbs out, his wristband begins to glow a slimy green. "I guess I beat the chit out of that challenge. It was almost too easy. But not really."

Despite his decisive victory, he can't shake the scaredy sense that there's something familiar about that alien. He searches the track for the saucer as the other monster wagons roll through, but the mascot and its kart have vanished like ghost farts in the wind.

34

Horton approaches the next mutated hole with caution, keeping his eyes peeled for the foam scientist that scared him into missing his last putt. He's only a couple strokes shy of overtaking the Prize Keeper's record, but once he crosses the chemical-splattered bridge leading to the back ten, it quickly becomes apparent that the easy part is over.

The moment he steps up to the hole, the Keeper's gruesome voice returns to confirm Horton's suspicions. *"You may have survived the front nine, but this next par-t is what separates the humanoids from the ghouls. Beat my score and you'll be invited to putt the 19th hole for a chance to unlock the dark magic of Scaredyland. But that's all the help I'm going to give you. If you decide to keep putting, it's your space funeral. Mwohohoho!"*

"I'm shaking in my high tops," Horton tells the cartoon Keeper on the sign. "That being said, I actually am worried about losing this."

He sets his ball down on the tee, but before he even has a chance to line up his shot, the bright bulbs illuminating the course flicker out, only to be replaced by the dreaded *black light*. Drenched in ultraviolet shadow, the artificial grass and plastic mutants that stalk the holes suddenly glow to inanimate life.

Sighing, Horton aims his putt down the digestive tract of a ferocious, humanoid-eating glowworm, but he overcompensates for the darkness and undershoots. Forced to step through the monster's luminous gut, he quickly locates his ball and lines up his next putt. But as he brings his club down, he's startled by a crazed howl that suddenly echoes through the giant stomach and accidentally knocks his ball into the worm's litter pile. Poking his head out the monster's back end, Horton searches for the course's resident villain, but the mad mascot has already absconded.

"I know you're out there!" he announces. "You're not going to scare me, again… Also, you're a chitty inventor," he goads. But the dig fails to elicit a response.

Even with Horton's skills, hitting his ball out of the dung is a challenge, and by the time he finishes the hole, his score has fallen another stroke behind the Keeper's.

Fearfully glancing over his shoulder, he moves on to the next green, where a large chemical spill has fundamentally altered the shape of the course. He charts a precarious path across the hazardous landscape, but as he lines up his putt, he discovers what appears to be an alternate route. Aiming for a hole in the barrier, he putts into the river of radioactive sludge flowing around the green, and for a few harrowing moments his ball disappears beneath the surface. But it soon pops back up, and the ooze carries it all the way down to the cup. He scurries after it across the polluted puttscape, and with a light swing of his putter, he taps it in.

Suddenly tied with the Prize Keeper, Horton only needs to pick up one stroke to beat the rotting mannequin and gain access to the 19th hole. With the show on the line, he manages to putt past the sludge monsters occupying hole 12, saving par while sustaining only mild injuries. But when he comes to the fabled 13th, he finds a putting green of a different color.

The neon turf has been replaced with a plastic grass so dark that it's like standing on the precipice of the universe. But aside from the distracting illusion, the hole is relatively straightforward – a long shot across a pool of infinite black. Horton figures this is his chance to score an easy hole-in-one. But as soon as he sets his ball down on the putting matt, the green is suddenly swarmed with ghosts. They drift in from all over the course, until the glowing cup is completely obscured behind the revolting blobs of digital ectoplasm.

"How the fish am I supposed to survive that?" Horton complains to the Prize Keeper. "I guess it's in Fishtar's tentacles now."

As he clears his mind to focus on his putt, Ghosty appears to complain about his language. But he ignores the interruption and smacks his ball straight through the annoying apparition. The pink sphere whizzes through half a dozen other glowing pests and disappears somewhere amidst the swarm. As Horton steps out onto the black green, he comes to accept that his sliming is inevitable, and he braces himself for imaginary discomfort as he's subsumed by the glowing ghosts.

When he finally locates his ball, hovering somewhere between space and slime, his body has taken on an unhealthy layer of digital goo. Putting blind, he somehow manages to finish the hole one stroke under par – although how he did it is a neon pink blur.

With the fate of the adventure hanging in the balance, Horton putts his way around the mutated mountain goats, under the wicked windmill, across the polluted pond, and past the mutated ape monster. By the time he reaches the mad scientist's lair, he's managed to get two strokes ahead of the Prize Keeper's score. But he has a feeling the worst is yet to come.

Hidden in a tunnel beneath Scaredyland, the 18th is a jumble of glowing hazards – an elaborate mess designed to require the maximum number of strokes. Before Horton has time to overthink it, he smacks his ball down the crumbling staircase, through a heap of mangled monster cages, and into a cluttered lab full of retired mascots that have been repurposed into mutant beasts guzzling neon potions. Patiently nudging his ball around the maze of goop and experimental monsters, he soon finds himself within putting distance of the hole.

With two strokes to spare and a candy headache the size of The Park's biggest bouncy ball, Horton laughs and says, "There it is, the almost last hole."

All he has to do is tap the ball in, and he can move onto the bonus hole. But as he's lining up his shot, he hears something shuffling across the green behind him. All of a sudden, the mad mascot comes stumbling into the lab, flailing its arms and making "scary" noises.

Lacking the energy to feel fear, Horton tells the monster, "I could hear you coming from across the course."

Happily deranged, the scientist takes two steps before tripping over a barrel of "secret ingredient" and crashing down into a puddle of glowing waste. Horton waits for the mascot to scramble to its feet, and as it shoves past him to escape the lab, it kicks his ball behind a mutant with an oversized chin and corncob pipe whose potion of choice happens to be a leafy green Earth vegetable.

"Hey!" Horton whines, checking his wristband to find that the mascot's bumbling cost him an extra stroke. "You Ackle! That's cheating!"

Left with one chance to unlock the final hole, Horton wedges himself behind the mutant space mariner and lines up his putt the best he can. With the fate of the team hanging in the balance, he takes a blind swing through the mutant's legs, and by the grace of Fishtar, the ball plunks into the hole.

Having bested the Keeper's score by a single stroke, Horton drags himself up the escape staircase and back out onto the course, where he finds a chitty sculpture of the Prize Keeper standing guard over the shadowy bonus hole.

When he scans his wristband under the creep's twisted claw, the deformed ghoul tells him, *"Congratulations on beating my low score. You're pretty good for a noid. But before you try your luck on the 19th hole, you'll have to play through the course all over again, only backwards this time."* Horton feels the life drain out of him and then right back in as the Keeper tells him, *"Just kidding. Did I scare you? Mwohohoho!"*

"Actually, yes," Horton says.

"You only get one putt to win." As the lights come on to reveal the final green, a black golf ball drops down into the Keeper's open hand. *"Choose the right path, and the power of the Game Gallery is yours. But putt poorly and it's back to hole one for you. Mwohohoho!"*

Staring down three unobstructed greens leading to three oversized holes, the last putt comes down to luck. Holding the team's destiny in his club, Horton sets his ball on the mat and considers the choices in front of him. But no matter how hard he overthinks it, he can't figure out which one is most likely to be the winner.

Incapable of making a random choice, he stands next to the tee, petrified, until the Keeper finally says, *"You're not scared are you? You'd better hurry. You wouldn't want to time out, mwohohoho!"*

Turning to the one thing a space kid can always rely on, Horton remembers his *Simpsons* and chants, "Tree falling in the woods, tree falling in the woods, tree falling in the woods…"

Ceasing all thought, he swings his club, and his ball bounces down the middle green. The glowing cup is so big that it's nearly impossible to miss, but Horton somehow manages. Having failed to notice the thin circle of sand surrounding the hole, the trap brings his ball to a dead stop.

"No…," he whimpers. "I was so clo—"

But before he can finish his lamentation, a large plastic hand reaches up out of the dark hole and pulls the ball back down to wherever balls go.

Horton anxiously waits for something to happen, and after an interminable moment of uncertainty, the Keeper finally tells him, "*You have chosen… smartly.*"

Glancing down at his wristband, he breathes a heavy sigh of relief as the plastic souvenir begins to glow an alliterative gray.

"*If you want to know the horrible truth,*" the Keeper whispers, "*they were all winners! Mwohohoho! As an added reward for being the first putter to beat me, you have been granted a free game. Do you dare play another round?*"

Horton stares at the grinning ghoul for a moment, and raising his club, proceeds to putt the Prize Keeper's crooked face in.

35

Glancing back at the waving ghost kid as the train rolls away from the platform, Pants figures this is it. She's going to be stuck riding this stupid coaster for the rest of her life and probably her afterlife, too.

"I've said it before, you guys," she tells the fans through the phone dangling around her neck. "But I think this might really be the end of Pants Team Pink."

Digging her sparkly nails into the rubber lap bar, she somehow feels even more terrified now than she did the first time around. Without her holographic friend screaming alongside her, she's left to face her fear all by herself.

As the creep car climbs the first hill, she peeks over the edge of the track and lets out a short shriek. With nowhere left to go but down, she tries to keep her fear to herself, but as the train rolls over the hill's peak, it all comes screaming out.

For a split space second, with the night air whipping through her pink ponytail, she almost gets why people think this is fun. But that's all forgotten as soon as she notices the cartoon skull and crossbones painted across the track up ahead. Having reconfigured itself between rides, the curve at the bottom of the drop is suddenly missing, replaced by nothing but the dark shadows that obscure the twisted Parkwood skeleton below. Evidently intended for some hidden alternate route, the track was never completed.

With no time to think, Pants does the only thing to do at a time like this and screams, "*Wahhh!*"

For a long moment, she experiences the familiar sensation of floating up off her seat as she plummets into the dark unknown. But she soon crashes back down as the train drags her winding through the subterranean shadows. When her eyes adjust, she can just make out the edges of the Parkwood beams zipping by around her, and she realizes she's on a track running underneath the Coaster's frame.

After a series of sudden drops, the train screeches to a stop beside a small glowing station. When the lap bar finally lifts, Pants decides it's probably safe to stop screaming, and she shakily climbs out of the car, wiping the tears from her eyes as she stumbles onto the platform. Following the arrows, she teeters up a small flight of crooked stairs, through a fake blood-soaked turnstile, and into a narrow corridor splattered with glow paint.

"I don't know what this place is, you guys," Pants tells the fans. "But I think I might have just entered another dimension."

She creeps down the hallway, until she comes to a slime-crusted doorway next to a glowing sign splashed with the words, "No Funhouse."

"I'm scared you guys," Pants whimpers. "This place isn't even on the park map. What do I do now?" She puts it to a vote, and aside from the handful of anti-fans who advise her to stay here and cry, most of the viewers want her to go inside. "I guess I don't have much choice."

Stepping through the dark passage, she winds up in a large room containing a dozen doorways numbered with glow paint.

Teeth chattering, she asks, "Which one should I pick?"

For some reason, the fans choose number 12. But as she moves toward the distant door, it starts to grow. By the time she reaches it, it's much too big to open. Failing to turn the giant knob, she peeks through the keyhole to find the Mind Melter spinning over the Gorewalk outside.

"*Awww...,*" she moans.

Plodding back to the middle of the hallway, Pants picks door number 2 this time. It opens easily enough, but as soon as she steps into the dark room, the floor begins to tip underneath her, and she tumbles over. Frantically trying to get back on her feet, she finally rolls toward the glowing doorway and somehow manages to drag herself out into the hall.

Once she's back on solid ground, she says, "That was… scary, I guess."

The fans vote for door 7 next, and Pants cautiously steps inside the room, toward the next unknown horror. What she finds is a long and winding corridor, which she blindly follows, stumbling through the dark. When she reaches the other end, she discovers another passageway, which leads to another, and another, until she can make out a soft glow in the distance.

"I think this might be the way out, you guys," she tells the fans, hopefully.

Bot as she steps out into the hall, she spins around to find the number 11 splattered above the doorway she just stepped out of.

"I guess I went around in a circle," she comments. "That's more annoying than scary."

Nevertheless she can feel the fear creeping in, and she randomly yanks open door number 6. Inside, she finds an artificially endless maze of glowing mirrors, each depicting a different variant of her cute image in order to reflect everything she could ever be.

When she sees herself as a full-grown adventurer, she races across the room to get a better look. Twirling her sparkly hair in her finger, she admires the reflection for a long moment, until she glances at the one next to it. In a horrifying alternate reality, with her thick glasses and messy hair, she looks almost as nerdy as Beer. Repulsed, she wanders the room, showing the fans what she would look like as a dust farmer, and a Park mule, and a donut-head. But she's so focused on her reflection that she loses track of time, and when she wakes up from her cos-stupor, she realizes that she doesn't know how to get out.

What begins as a nervous retracing of steps quickly escalates into a desperate search for escape. Bumping into herself as she stumbles through the virtual dressing room, she gets the feeling that she somehow really did cross over into a parallel universe.

When she turns the corner, she crashes into a 2D version of herself and crumples onto the floor, sobbing. "I'm lost in the mirror world, you guys. And I can't get out." But when she hears the door to the reflective room creaking shut, her sobs are replaced by quiet fear. While her fans argue over whether or not any of this is real, she crawls in the direction of the door and whispers, "I think somebody's here."

Mouths dry and hearts pounding, all the different versions of herself crawl through the glass maze searching for the way out. When she spots Adventure Pants, with her space gun and moon boots, she knows the door is somewhere close by. But as she rounds the corner where it should be, all she finds are more mirrors.

She inadvertently lets out a despairing moan and turns back the way she came, crawling around the sticky maze floor until she comes to a reflection she hasn't seen before. It looks just like the mascot out on the Gorewalk, with its exaggerated skeletal structure and lifeless grin.

Standing up to gaze into its empty eye sockets, Pants asks, "Are you me?" But the illusion is shattered as soon as the mascot shakes its head unbidden, causing Pants to scream, "*Wah-ahhh!*"

She spins around and trips back through the maze, trying not to smash into herself, when she receives the sign she didn't know she was looking for. Reflected above her gelatinous alter ego hovers the one slimy word that can bring an end to this nightmare – TIXE.

Carefully making her way toward the glowing sign, she finally stumbles across the reflection of her true self, and the way out of this space hell. But before she steps through the mirror, she glances back to find the stuffed skeleton's many reflections lurching after her.

On the other side, she enters a gift shop of horrors, its dusty shelves full of unclaimed souvenir syrup glasses and miniature plush mascots. When she reaches the door, boarded up with plastic Parkwood, she uses all her strength to wrench the handle, but it won't budge.

The skeleton mascot steps into the room behind her, its fuzzy bones glowing in the dark. Fumbling to get the door open, Pants suddenly notices a scanner built into the knob. The mascot teeters toward her as she thrusts her bracelet under the digital reader.

Before the monster can lay its paws on her, the door unlocks, and Pants runs out onto the Gorewalk screaming. When she reaches the far side, she turns back toward the ride to see the skeleton waving at her from the dark doorway, its other giant paw covering its toothy grin. Unable to tear her eyes away, she watches as the mascot slips back into the shadowy gift shop and pulls the door shut, its edges blending so seamlessly with the wall of the Coaster that it's almost as if it was never there.

36

Anxiously staring up at the park map outside Mascot Manor as he waits for the team to show up, Todd can sense that The Other One is hiding something. Always busy tapping at his phone, the kid is a born sneak. But he's also turned out to be a surprisingly effective promoter. Merch sales are way up, and the number of live viewers is quickly approaching an all-time high — topped only by the finale of the *Black Gold Saga* and the grotesque spectacle of the "School's Out Summer Special."

"*Ughuhuh*," Todd shudders at the thought of the all-singing, all-dancing misadventure.

Finally slipping his phone back into his pocket, The Other One announces, "Okay, we're all set."

"All set for what?" Todd demands.

"Uh, nothing," the kid says. "We're perfectly positioned to achieve the maximum marketing benefit from the end of the adventure is all."

Glaring at the little business boy, Todd tells him, "I don't know what you're up to, but I just want you to know that I don't know."

But the kid just feigns ignorance. "Huh?"

"Listen, you little chit—" Todd starts to say, but before he can question The Other One any further, the boy's alternate namesake comes trudging down Maim Street.

Covered in digital slime, The One holds his glowing green wristband high and declares, "I am still The One!"

"Oh, thank Space God," Todd says as the boy shows off his pretend power. "Now, let's just hope the rest of the team survived their challenges."

It's not long before they spot Beer limping out of the Gruesome Graveyard, dragging a plastic shooter and sporting a heavy coat of slime on his team jacket. Before they can ask him how it went, he laughs and holds out his wristband to reveal the blue light shining from the ancient plastic.

Motioning to Todd's souvenir sandals, Beer asks, "How was parents paradise?"

"Oh, it was pretty… scary."

While the brothers recount the terrible fun of their ordeals, Todd can't help but pace the rubber pavement, anxiously searching for signs of life as they wait to find out if Pants and Horton were able to complete their challenges.

Meanwhile, The Other One has barely looked away from his phone. Casually leaning against the Scaredyland map, he even has the nerve to yawn. Just as Todd is about to scold the boy for scrolling, Horton plods up the sidewalk across the street, a ghostly gray light gleaming from his wristband.

Having sustained even more slime than his teammates, the gaunt kid says, "I am once again announcing my permanent retirement from miniature golf."

As Todd helps Horton plop down on the curb, Pants comes skipping down the sidewalk, holding up her glowing pink wristband and shouting, "I did it! It was so scary, you guys. At first I was too scared to ride the Creep Coaster. But my ghost friend Brilly went on it with me. Just like everyone said, once I got on, I couldn't get off. I ended up on a secret track that went to the 'No Funhouse!' I found this huge door and then I got lost in the mirror maze, and there was a skeleton mascot that was chasing me—" She pauses in the middle of the dubious tale to frown at her tired, slime-soaked teammates. "What happened to you guys?"

But before they can get into it, The Other One butts in to shift their attention back to the adventure at hand. "We'll have plenty of time to recap later. Right now, we have to keep up this momentum. You've got a whole lot of fans out there waiting to see what happens next."

"He's annoying, but he's right," Todd advises the team. "We should get over to Mascot Manor and claim the final merch while it's still night out. You know, for continuity."

With a deep sigh, Beer tells the others, "I don't know how much adventure I have left in me, but already we've come this far. Maybe if we combine what's left of our powers we can summon the strength of one whole team member."

Wearily pulling themselves back up onto their sneakers, the team splits the dregs of The One's candy, and they tiredly plod toward the designed-to-look-haunted mansion at the edge of Scaredyland. The fence outside momentarily stops them in their tracks, until Todd pulls the broken gate back to allow them passage into the brown, souvenir-strewn yard beyond. Imitation lightning streaks the dark sky behind the haunted house, while its floating inhabitants anxiously circle the upper floors. But before the team can reach the steps of the faux-crumbling porch, a familiar spirit materializes in front of them.

Stifling its laughter, Ghosty tells them, "*Congratulations* *snk*... *You're the first kids in* *snk*... *Scaredyland history to complete all the advanced challenges. Give yourselves a big pat on the* *snk*... *back.*"

"Yeah, well...," The One tells their annoying guide. "We are the number one team, after all. Now, get out of our way so we can finish this thing and go home."

"*I'm afraid* *snk*... *I can't do that,*" Ghosty says.

"And why the fish not?" The One demands.

"*Because* *snk*... *this is where your adventure ends.*" No longer able to contain itself, the ghost lifts its paws and cackles, "Plahahaha!"

Glaring at the hologram through his slimy specs, Beer says, "I don't get it. What the fish is so funny?"

But before any of them can take a stab at it, one of the glowing house ghosts suddenly swoops down from its haunt and melds with their guide in a sickening display of spiritual fusion.

"Eww," Pants says as she gazes at the dripping ball of ectoplasm.

As a result, Ghosty's hologram expands well beyond its previous limit. Soon, another ghost floats down to join in the supernatural union, and another, until their pesky guide has grown big enough to turn its hollow eyes down on the team and friends gathered below.

"PlahaHAHAHA!" Ghosty howls as the digital ghosts stream into its swelling body.

The colorful spirits come from all across Scaredyland to sacrifice their code to the Ghost God. By the time Ghosty has absorbed the last of them, its translucent body has expanded to consume all of Mascot Manor and a large portion of the plot on which it rests.

"PLAHAHAHA!" the ghost booms.

Gazing up at the monster, Beer says, "I still don't get what's so funny."

"Look what you did, *Todd!*" The One scolds. "That slimeball is bigger than a house."

Sensing the blame falling in his direction, Todd cries, "Me?!"

"*It feels good to stretch out!*" Ghosty announces. "*After the park closed, I thought I would never escape that digital space hell. But I finally possess the power to shape Scaredyland in any way I see fit.* PLAHAHA—"

"You're welcome!" The One shouts, cutting off the giant ghost's colossal rant.

Turning its eyeholes on the misfit kids gathered underneath its projection, Ghosty says, "*Ahh yes, I almost forgot the guests who freed me. As a reward for your fearlessness, I bestow each of you with a season pass, good for the rest of the night!* Plahahaha!"

"Yay!" Pants cries. "Oh, wait…"

Before she can voice her complaint, The One blows a raspberry, "*Plll*, no way! We were promised exclusive merch, and exclusive merch we shall have."

Nodding in agreement, Horton confirms, "His logic is sound."

"*I'm sorry*," Ghosty moans. "*But you cannot be allowed to redeem your souvenirs at this spacetime.*"

"Well, butts to that," The One says. "In the words of the official theme song of Earth's first ghost hunters – I ain't 'fraid a no ghosts, even if they are the size of a haunted house."

Taking a deep breath, The One steps through the outer wall of the ghost's holographic barrier and makes a break for the front door. But before he can reach the steps, his body seizes, and he collapses onto the fake grass. Whatever the ghost is doing sends him into convulsions, but he somehow manages to pull himself back toward the open lawn, and when he reaches the spirit's edge, the team drags him to safety.

"What was that?" Beer asks, slipping a recovery candy into his brother's mouth.

As soon as The One is able to catch his breath, he says, "It's this stupid wristband. It was shocking me the whole time I was inside Ghosty's sphere of influence."

"Then I'll go in!" Todd says, mustering all his courage. "I don't have a wristband."

"Yeah, but you'll need all four of them to claim our rightful merch," Beer breaks it to him.

"*I told you,*" Ghosty says. "*I will not allow you to enter the Manor. But perhaps if I explain why, you will better appreciate your season passes.*"

"I doubt it," The One growls at the ghost.

"*The truth behind the park is a sordid tale of cheap souvenirs, stolen credits, and mascotploitation far too long and horrifying to go into here. But it might interest you to know my true identity, for I am none other than H.P. Scaredy, creator of Scaredyland!*"

37

Taking in their non-reaction for a protracted moment, Ghosty goes on, "*I designed this park as an offseason getaway, where ghouls of all ages could come for a good scare. But the powers that be decided my rides were too scary and that modern-day guests were no longer interested in risking life and limb. Once the investors got involved, all the best death traps were converted into kiddie rides, and the Scaredy Shops were replaced by big strip stores full of spiritless souvenirs. I did what I could to undermine their efforts by creating a series of expert challenges hidden within the Ghost Towns, for those guests who could appreciate being scared. I pushed up the park's grand opening to just after moonrise in an attempt to halt its ruinous trajectory. But it was too late. Thanks to lukewarm reviews and the ongoing mascot scandal, Scaredyland suffered a lonely death.*"

Having apparently reached a lull in its story, Beer asks the ghost, "What does any of this have to do with our merch?"

"*Losing control of Scaredyland was the worst thing that ever happened to me. I gave this park my life, literally. On opening night, I uploaded my consciousness to the Scaredyland matrix, bestowing my digital self with special access to alter the park's code so that I could run it the way I've always wanted.*"

Horton clears his throat to raise an objection. "But the real P.H. Scaredy is long dead. You're not really him. You're just a copy of his mind as it was at the instant he uploaded it to Scaredyland."

"*Why would that matter to me?*" Ghosty asks.

"No reason," Horton says. "I just wanted to clarify, for the fans at home."

"*Anyway…,*" the ghost continues. "*In order to keep my plan a secret until after the start of the season, I hid the code to unlock my true identity in pieces spread throughout Scaredyland's four Ghost Towns. It took a few space centuries longer than I anticipated, but with the completion of each advanced challenge, you restored part of my mind from digital purgatory. Due to technical reasons that I'm afraid your humanoid brains wouldn't understand, claiming your final prizes would cause the system and my powers to revert back to their default settings. So, you can understand why I can't let you enter the Manor. But the good news is that according to ancient park polling, the Ghost Towns have very high replay value.* Plahahaha!*"

For a moment, it looks as if The One is about to launch into an obscenity-filled verbal attack, but before he can find the words, his shoulders slump and he says, "Whatever…"

Powerless to stop the ghost, and crashing off a dangerous combination of sugar and caffeine, the team appears defeated.

As the rest of them prepare to pack it in, Pants suddenly stomps her flashing sneaker on the lifeless lawn and tells the giant cyber ghost, "We've been through too much to give up now, you guys. I risked my life riding the Creep Coaster and was almost scared to death by a stupid mascot. I'm not going home without a prize!"

"As your official merch guy, it's my duty to advise you that this seems like a supremely bad idea," Todd yells, cowering next to The Other One behind the Manor's busted fence.

As much as Beer would prefer to return to the comfort of the *Cuddler*, he looks over at his exhausted teammates and tells them, "She's right. We can't give up now. Maybe it's fate that today is Space Halloween, a holiday founded on the belief that at least once a space year sentient beings are entitled to free leftover candy and a few harmless pranks. We're not just fighting for our show, but for our right to scare and be scared. How many times have we spent all our tokens only to wind up going home prizeless? Well, I say, not tonight!" Summoning the last of his strength, he pumps up his Ghost Zapper and fires at the inflated hologram. But the bolt of static is snuffed out the instant it hits the beast's bloated belly. Searching for just the right word to encapsulate the situation, he sighs, "Fish…"

"*You think your little Zapper can stop me?*" the ghost howls as Beer lowers his plastic weapon. "*You kids are almost as dumb as you look.* Plahahaha!"

As the ghost flails its stubby arms into the flashing sky, The One comments, "I don't know about you guys, but I'm starting to feel like we should get the fish out of here."

"I concur," Horton says.

But as the four of them scramble for the gate, they're stopped in their tracks by a fluffy green paw bursting out of the ground. Before they can make their escape, a grinning monster mascot rises from the dirt, its neon fur matted and squirming with glowworms.

"Trying to delete me is not strictly against the rules," Ghosty says, as decaying plush paws reach up out of the lawn all around them. *"So, I'll let that slide. However, there's one rule you've broken two hundred and forty-eight times. But don't worry. Once you've received your punishment, you can play here forever and ever and… Well, you get the idea."*

"What the fish are you talking about?" The One asks.

"Rule five," Ghosty reminds them. *"No cursing in Scaredyland!"*

Narrowly evading the suffocating embrace of the reanimated mascots, the team scrambles out onto the sidewalk and watches in horror as enough of the smiling monsters emerge from the yard to frighten all of Scaredyland.

The Other One's face turns a ghostly shade of pale, and lowering his phone for the first time since he got here, he says, "What the fish is going on? This wasn't supposed to happen."

"What do you know about it?" The One growls at his onetime trainee.

"Uh, you guys," Pants cuts in, pointing to the demented dust goblin trying to push through the broken gate. "We should probably escape before we get cuddled to death."

Suddenly experiencing a traumatic flashback to his time spent in the fake cemetery, Beer says, "I think I know a place we can hide. Come on!"

Pumping his Ghost Zapper, he leads them out along the sidewalk and down toward the Gruesome Graveyard. But when they reach the recently exorcized Ghost Town, the situation isn't much better. All across the fogless hillside, killer mascots are rising from their graves.

"This is worse than the Manor," The One argues.

But Beer assures them, "It's the one place I know they can't get us."

Weaving around the plastic headstones, open graves, and bumbling undead, Beer guides the team and their sidekicks toward the Caretaker's Cottage out in the middle of the Graveyard. He scans his wristband under the knob, but when he pushes against the door, it refuses to open. "It's stuck, again."

"Well, get it unstuck," his brother complains, as the horde of mindless mascots surround them.

Beer turns back to fire his Zapper at a giggling melon head stumbling toward the shack, but while the static bolt singes its orange fur, the monster just keeps coming. Crushed up against the Cottage as the mascots descend, the team's collective weight finally loosens the door, and they tumble inside.

Slamming the door shut behind them, Beer looks back to find a familiar ghost glowing in the shadows. *"Don't worry, they can't git insite. I don't think…"*

The others scream at the sight of the crusty codger, but Beer tells them, "It's just the Cantankerous Caretaker. He's brule." As puffy paws pound against the walls of the Cottage, he questions the ghost, "What are you doing in here?"

"It seems that the completion a the advance't challenges unlock't the whole park, grantin' me greater access to the grounts," the Caretaker explains. *"I now have the power to come ant go as I please."*

"But you were trapped in this shack for a thousand space years," Beer says. "Why would you come back here?"

"Oh, yuh know, yuh git use tuh a place…"

Quaking in his work loafers as the mascots bat at the door, The Other One cries, "We're trapped in here! What the fish are we going to do now?"

"Pull yourself together, other me," The One tells his sometimes adventure-double. "You're the one who got us into this nightmare!"

"It wasn't supposed to turn out this way," The Other One insists.

"That's the thing about adventures," Beer says, pointing to the hatch leading to the tunnel he used to escape the Graveyard ghosts. "They never go the way you plan. Now, come on. We can get out through here."

But as the team and hangers-on climb down into the dirt, the old hologram waggles his finger at them and says, *"There's somethin' else I wan'it tuh tell yuh. Yer wristbants are more than jist simple souvenirs. Since yuh beat the challenges, those bracelets are capable a harnessin' the power a Scaredylant."*

"So we've been told." Looking down at the glowing merch on his wrist, Beer asks, "But what does that mean?"

The Caretaker's holographic image stutters, as if searching deep within the park's database for an answer, and he finally shrugs.

With that partial knowledge, Beer leads the others down the dark tunnel toward the front of the Ghost Town, and when they reach the open grave at the other end, he pokes his head out.

Most of the living dead mascots have converged on the Cottage, and as soon as the last few stragglers wander past, he tells the others, "Now's our chance!"

Doing their best to avoid detection, the six of them semi-quietly climb out of the grave and make their way back toward the Parkway. But as they approach the Ghost Town gate, they run into a neon green mascot hovering outside the entrance.

"Hey, that's that alien from the Haunted Raceway!" The One announces. "That ackle almost made me crash. I'm gonna go scare the chit out of it."

"Wait!" Beer whispers. "We don't know what these things can do to us."

But it's too late. The One is already sneaking up behind the alien, and before Beer can stop him, he tackles the plush monster out of its shiny hover saucer. As The One wrestles the alien onto the tree lawn, a familiar zombie stumbles out from behind one of the plastic bushes, and by the time the rest of the team and friends catch up, they're surrounded by a gang of murderous mascots.

38

"Get off of me, you chidiot!" the neon alien mumbles from inside its hollow head as The One administers a powerful noogie.

"I wouldn't do that if I were you," another muffled voice warns the boy.

"Oh yeah, who's gonna stop me?" He looks up to find a small group of smiling, yet somehow menacing mascots staring down at him, and he laughs nervously, "Aha…"

As the rest of his friends and employees catch up with him, Beer yells, "Don't hurt him! He's just a chidiot."

"We already know that," the zombie says, its stuffed eyeball hanging out of its head.

"Hey, you're that mascot from the Gorewalk!" Pants cries, wrapping her arms around the smiling skeleton. "You really scared me back there."

The skeleton pushes the pink girl off and tells her, "Ew, you're so annoying."

Scrunching her face as she stares into the mascot's empty eyeholes, Pants says, "Hey, I know that voice!"

Similarly, when Horton spots the crazy, wild-haired mascot skulking around the gate, he declares, "I knew there was something stupid about that scientist!"

Just to confirm their suspicions, The One yanks the bulbous head off the alien racer to find the bloated blue cheeks of his other other half.

"You win, okay?" Top5 says. "Will you get off me now?"

"Sorry," The One says, helping the kid back up into his saucer. "I thought you were some sort of undead mascot monster."

As the rest of the Xenodorks remove their costume heads, Beer asks Todd, "What the fish are *they* doing here? I knew we couldn't trust you to organize the adventure." But as soon as the zombie reveals itself as FairyMajokoCourtney-chan, he stops yelling to wave at her and says, "Hi, Courtney-chan…"

"Hmph," she grunts, flipping her blonde hair and crossing her costume's artificially rotten arms.

"Don't blame me," the merch guy says, his souvenir vacation clothes suspiciously damp. "This is all The Other One's fault!"

"Listen," the business boy tells them, jutting his thumb behind him. "I'd be happy to absolve myself, but maybe we should continue this adventure somewhere less murdery, or whatever."

Having finally caught on to the team's deception, the living dead mascots have given up attacking the Cottage and are now shambling back through the Graveyard.

As the fuzzy monsters lumber toward the gate, Otakween shoots the team a cold, dark glare and says, "Oh, real good. You made us blow our cover. Now those cuddly monsters are going to be after us too!"

"Wait a space second," Beer says, adjusting his busted glasses. "The Caretaker said something about our wristbands containing the power of Scaredyland. If we can figure out what that means, maybe we can stop these crazy things." Pointing his fist at a grinning stuffed ghoul, he concentrates what remains of his energy into the ancient merch around his wrist but ultimately fails to conjure any dark magic. "Or not."

"I never thought I'd live to say this," The One says. "But The Other One is right. Let's get the fish out of here!"

Animatronic howls and the inhumanoid patter of plush paws follow close behind as they race down Maim Street. Crunching through the last of his butter mints, The One frantically searches for a plan of attack, but all the Ghost Towns are dead ends.

As soon as Beer hears the crunch of candy, he tells his brother, "Hey, I thought you finally ran out of candy. I want one!"

"I want one too," Top5 says. "What is it?"

"Okay, let's not lose our heads, you guys!" The One says. "I think our only option is to get the fish out of Scaredyland while we still have the chance."

But The Other One argues, "You can't do that! If you leave the park now, your wristbands will reset, rendering you powerless and leaving Scaredyland in the paws of that giant ghost back there."

"How do you know that?" The One demands.

But before he can squeeze any answers out of the professional kid, Pants tells them, "We can't give up now, you guys! I know what to do. I have a friend on the Gorewalk that will help us."

Lacking any better ideas, they follow Pants back toward the Creep Coaster, and after an exhaustive search of the grounds, they finally locate her 'friend' riding the Gut Punch. When the ghost boy sees Pants waving down below, he floats off the ride to meet her.

"*Hey,*" he says, dressed more like a guest than a ghost in his Scaredyland duds. "*Do you want to ride the Coaster again?*"

"What?!" Pants cries. "No! We need your help. All the old mascots have risen from their graves, and now they're after us."

"*What am I supposed to do about it?*" the ghost moans.

"I don't know, *Brilly!*" Pants says. "Don't you know some secret park spell or magic that can help us stop them?"

But Brilly just shrugs his holographic shoulders.

"Can't you at least tell us how to unlock the hidden power stored inside our bracelets?" she whines.

"*The only advice I can give you is the old Scaredyland slogan — 'feel the fear.' Well, I'm going to go ride the Back Snapper.*" Waving as he floats off down the Gorewalk, he shouts, "*I hope you save the park. But if you don't, I'll see you on the other side!*"

Left to fend for themselves amongst the horrifying rides of the Gorewalk, the teams huddle together in quiet defeat.

"I think the adventure is really, really over this time, you guys," Pants tells the fans at home. "I wonder what he meant by 'other side.'"

Flashing his phone for attention, The Other One says, "He was probably referring to the fact that anyone killed inside Scaredyland grounds is digitized and stored in the park's mainframe for all time or whatever with the rest of the ghosts."

"Oh great!" Otakween growls, her black hair slick with costume sweat. "We're going to end up stuck in here for the rest of our afterlives because of you chidiots."

Speaking up for the first time all adventure, the mad scientist Howard Johnson corrects her fearful leader, "Technically it won't be *us,* but rather digital recreations of our former selves."

Shooting the cloaked girl a dark scowl, Otakween says, "I still don't like it."

"What do you mean *us* chidiots?" Beer says. "We didn't tell you to come to Scaredyland. What the fish are you doing here, anyway? Was this all just another one of your stupid pranks?"

"We might as well tell them!" Otakween barks at the business boy. "We helped that little ackle plan the whole adventure. I mean, everything except this last part. We were going to let you get the exclusive merch for us and then scare you out of the park."

"But, but… *why?!*" Pants cries.

"After our appearance on *Pants Team Pink*, we gained a huge following of anti-fans," the Kween explains. "But ever since the end of the Pants Con, our ratings have fallen even worse than yours."

"I don't get it," Beer says. "If you wanted us to win the merch, why were you trying to scare us?"

The Kween scoffs. "We couldn't go too easy on you. We had to make it look real, for the viewers. Plus, it was fun."

The fact that he was so easily deceived makes The One so mad that he decides not to share the candy he still has stashed in the secret pockets of his team jacket. But just as he's about to curse the Dorks to virtual space hell, he hears soft footfalls shuffling along the Gorewalk behind him.

He slowly looks back over his shoulder, but before he can cry 'mascot,' a pair of fuzzy purple paws are wrapping around his neck. The blobular mascot laughs horridly, its plastic eyes staring through him as it attempts to rip his head off. While the others try to tear The One away from the monster, he hurls his fist into its stomach, and his arm gets stuck in the plush padding. Facing the end of the adventure as he knows it, The One remembers the ghost boy's advice from a few space minutes ago, and the green light emanating from his wristband suddenly intensifies until it discharges into the mascot's fuzzy body.

The One's attacker freezes mid-strangulation, and as he pries himself free, the mascot tips back and crashes onto the Gorewalk.

Rubbing his neck, he says, "What the fish is that thing supposed to be, anyway?"

"I think it's a moldy egg cream," Beer ventures.

Examining the scorched hole in the creature's costume, Hojo the mad scientist determines, "It's some sort of primitive robot."

"The charge from The One's wristband must have caused it to shut down," Horton clarifies, to his rival's annoyance.

"But how does it work?" Beer asks.

His hand still tingling, The One says, "It's fear."

"Ohh, now I don't get it," Todd says, wiping his sweaty brow with a souvenir hand towel.

"This must be the power of the park!" Beer proclaims.

To test his theory, The One walks up to the scariest mascot he can find, and when the decaying monster attacks, he unleashes a blast of fear so palpable that it fries the artificial life out of the grinning moon rat.

Resting his sneaker on the giant critter's burnt remains, he tells the others, "Come on, we got mascots to murder. Also, we gotta stop S.M. Scaredy from doing the thing, or whatever."

39

At first, Horton has some trouble accessing the fear required to charge his wristband. But the mechanized mascot horde, along with the idea of his digital soul and all its personal information being semi-permanently trapped inside the park's storage matrix, is enough to scare it out of him.

Todd, The Other One, and the Xenodorks huddle close behind the team as they harness their fear into their ancient merch to blast their way out of the Ghost Town. They make quick work of the assorted mascots hanging around the Gorewalk, but when they get back to Maim Street, they're met by a small army of undead puffballs.

"This is our chance to escape," Horton tells them, the fear pumping through his veins. "We can slip out the front gate before they can get their paws on us."

But as the team prepares to make a run for it, The Other One cries, "You can't quit now! You still have to liberate Scaredyland from this waking nightmare and collect the merch at the end of the adventure. Your shows depend on it!"

Taking the little chit's side, Todd says, "He's not wrong. Your ratings are the highest they've ever been."

"What's more important?" Horton asks them. "Our ratings or our lives?"

Pondering the words for a long moment, The Other One finally says, "He's right. Lives come and go, but ratings like this only come along once in a thousand space years. You have to finish the adventure – for the fans."

"That's not what I—" Horton starts before interrupting himself. "Forget it. I'm too tired to argue with these chidiots."

Trembling as she glances at the neon robots roaming the street below, Pants tells everyone watching at home, "We can do this, you guys! Even though there are a lot more mascots than I thought."

"Let's send these fish heads to robot space hell," The One suggests, his wristband charged green with fear.

Straightening his busted glasses, Beer says, "I mean, we're already here…"

What follows is a mascot massacre. The next few space minutes are a blur of glowing projectiles and flying fur as the team blasts its way down Maim Street, leaving a trail of fluffy bodies in their wake. While Horton, Beer, and The One take out their fair share of mascots, it's mostly thanks to Pants that they survive long enough to make it back to the bottom of the dead-end street with their entourage intact.

"I never thought you had it in you," Otakween tells her pink nemesis. "I have a newfound fear of you."

"I don't want you to be scared of me!" Pants wails.

"Too late."

With the smell of singed fur wafting on the night air, the team uses their park magic to take out the few remaining mascots still roaming the grounds, and as Pants blasts away the last cuddly creature, she declares victory for the team. "We did it, you guys! We won!"

But before they have a chance to celebrate, an obnoxious, ghostly moan rings out across the Dark Park, causing the team and their assorted acquaintances to cover their ears in annoyance.

"*You did NOTHING!*" Ghosty howls, the Manor little more than an ugly blur inside its giant translucent body. "*You may have defeated my mascots, but Scaredyland is under my control now, and you'll never take it from me. Plahahaha!*"

"Come on, you guys!" Beer shouts. "Let's blast this fish head."

The team takes turns directing their fear at the ghost's bulging body, but their attacks don't seem to be having any effect.

"*You think your puny powers can stop me?*" Ghosty says. "*I feed on fear!*"

Panting under the strain of his fright, The One shouts, "It's not working!"

"*His power is too great!*" Todd shrieks, dramatically pointing up at the inflated hologram.

But while the rest of them struggle to focus their fear, Pants keeps hurling bright balls of pink static across the dead lawn.

"Let's see if this is enough to scare you," the ghost of P.T. Scaredy says.

Waving its giant paws, the team's former guide releases a swarm of park-generated ghosts big enough to haunt them for the rest of their short existence. They do their best to endure the digital storm, but they're quickly overwhelmed by the deluge of glowing spirits.

On the plus side, Horton's fear is now keeping his wristband fully charged. The only problem is that he can barely see where he's blasting.

Finally, he hears Beer shout, "This still isn't working. Fall back, you guys!"

Following Beer's lead, Horton hoofs it away from the front lawn and back toward Maim Street, where he meets up with the others, all dripping in digital slime. But as they all emerge from the ghost storm, one team member remains conspicuously absent.

"Where's Pants?" Horton asks.

"I think she's still in there," Beer says.

Sure enough, when Horton squints, he can make out the pink light of her fear shooting out at the oversized ghost. "We can't just leave her! I'm going back in. Who's coming with me?"

Beer and The One, their wristbands glowing with fear, flash him the Pants symbol, but the others aren't so quick to join in.

"I think you've got this whole thing pretty much covered," Otakween says, from the safety of her skeleton costume. "I don't see how we could possibly help."

Poking her head out from the shadows behind Top5 and Courtney-chan, Hojo tells him, "Just remember, we're all bound by the rules of the park."

"What about you two?" Horton asks their hired friends.

"Uh, I've got to stay here and monitor the fans," The Other One says, staring into his phone.

Todd shrugs. "I'm just scared."

With that, the three of them rush back into the digital fray, firing wildly as they search for their missing teammate. They find her ducking behind the fence out front, drenched in slime and continuing to direct her fear at the unstoppable ghost. Crouching down beside her, all four of them blast into the storm, but it's unclear whether their attacks are having any effect.

As they throw everything they've got at the swirling ghosts, a wild howl approaches from behind, and Todd suddenly comes barreling toward them. Before Horton can stop him, the crazy merch guy awkwardly tumbles over the fence and rushes past them into the storm.

"Where the fish is he going?" The One shouts.

"*How many times must I tell you to* follow the rules?" Ghosty howls.

"There has to be a way to stop this crazy ghost," Horton says, and recalling Hojo's advice, he hastily searches through his crumpled rulebook for something he can use. "Aha! Rule number one fifteen: bodily waste must be excreted into designated receptacles! All this slime is a direct breach of park regulations!"

"*Plahahaha!*" the ghost howls. "*I invented the rules. I decide how they are enforced. The rest of these ghosts may be guilty of breaking that one, but my paws are clean.*"

Flipping through the pages of his book, Horton counters, "Oh yeah? Well, what about rule ninety-four? Happiness is mandatory. We're not happy. From the looks of our wristbands, we're incredibly scared. And it's all because of you!"

"*Allow me to direct your attention to rule one hundred twenty. Fear means you're having fun.*"

"O-kay," Horton says, growing increasingly annoyed. "Don't forget about rule three. There is such a thing as too much fun."

This line of questioning combined with the growing number of ghosts puts enough strain on the park's processor that the whole projection begins to lag. When one of the flickering spirits floats in Horton's direction, he braces himself for another sliming. But before the ghost reaches him, something blasts it back into the digital ether, and he looks up to find Hojo and the rest of the Xenodorks furiously firing their plastic Zappers into the swarm.

"What?" the mad scientist girl asks, smirking slightly underneath her dark hood. "You think we'd come into a haunted park without Ghost Zappers? Who do you think we are, *you?*"

As the dark team lends their powers to help zap the floating pests, a shadowy figure lumbers at them from across the yard. Figuring they must have missed one of the mascots, Horton fires his gray magic at the monster, and it lets out an odd wail.

Waving its arms in surrender as it crawls toward them, the creature cries, "Don't shoot. It hurts, sort of!"

After a few space seconds, Todd emerges from the shadows lugging Beer's Ghost Zapper and frantically patting the scorched hole in his honorary team jacket where Horton blasted him. With all of them blasting and zapping together, the ghosts' numbers begin to dwindle, until there's a clear shot at the Ghost God itself. But even their special powers fail to put a scare into the park's evil creator.

Lowering her wrist weapon to gaze up at the invulnerable ghost, Pants announces, "I have an idea!"

When she holds out her hand, The One moans, "Aw, do we have to? I know you love love, or whatever. But this is embarrassing."

"He's right," Beer says. "This is no time for hand-holding."

"Come on, you guys!" she cries. "Are we a team or not?"

"You've never steered us wrong," Horton says, putting his hand on top of hers. "Except for that one time, with the candy corn. But we don't have to talk about that now."

The Dorks snicker, and when the two holdouts finally give in, Pants asks The One, "Ew, why are your fingers so sticky? Actually, never mind." With the team's hands pointed directly at the ghost guide's overpowered body, she says, "Come on, let's scare the living chit out of this ghost, you guys!"

Summoning the terror of everything they've been through over this long night, the four of them allow their fear to take hold, and together they unleash the power of Scaredyland. With their hands together, the fear shoots from their wristbands, combining into a single crackling beam of swirling gray, blue, green, and pink static. The 'nightmare ray,' as Horton mentally dubs it, effortlessly slices through what's left of the swirling spirits, and when it hits its real target, the Ghost God releases a pained howl. Its empty grin flipping upside down, their evil guide deploys all the remaining ghosts into the yard for one final attack, but they're no match for the team's collective fear.

"*Arghhh!*" T.M. Scaredy cries. "*You should be too afraid to attack me. Why aren't you scared?!*"

Laughing, Pants asks the ghost, "Isn't it obvious? We *are* scared. We're always scared! Nothing you do to us could ever be as scary as flying around the universe or riding a roller coaster or going back to school. And I don't mean the stupid movie."

"*It doesn't matter,*" Ghosty tells them. "*You're too late. Scaredyland belongs to me. Even your powers combined aren't enough to stop me.*"

But something has changed, and as they blast the ghost, Horton realizes, "It's shrinking!"

"*What is this?*" B.K. Scaredy demands as its giant body begins to deflate. "*What is happening? Top secret rule number one: nothing can destroy me!*"

Almost completely hidden inside her mascot body, Hojo issues a rare laugh and explains, "It's the way the park is coded — it's designed to be beaten."

Uselessly waving its paws as the team blasts it with fear, the ghost is soon reduced back down to its regular annoying size. Through all that howling, it was right about one thing. When it fails to disintegrate like the rest of the park ghosts, they lower their wristbands to watch it squirm.

"I forgot how cute it is when it's not trying to kill us," Pants comments. "Also, we won, you guys!"

"*This can't be happening,*" Ghosty cries. "*I've waited a thousand space years to gain control of Scaredyland, and I'm not going to let you take it from me!*"

"Face it," The One says. "You lose. I know how it feels. I've been losing all fishing night. Of course, I eventually won…"

"*Rule five!*" the ghost shrieks. "*Anyway, that's what you think.*"

"What does that mean?" Todd asks, with a tired sob.

Ghosty furiously resumes waving its paws in the air as if trying to summon some new form of digital magic, but its powers seem to have fizzled out.

"You tried that," The One reminds the ghost. "Just give up already, will yuh?"

But as the team takes in the pathetic display, the familiar sound of plush paws can suddenly be heard padding down the Parkway, and they turn back to find an army of hideous, grinning mascots respawning all around them.

40.

Leering at the team through countless unblinking plastic eyes, the decaying mascots rise from the dead to enact their cuddly revenge.

"*Yes!*" Ghosty howls. "*Rise my mascots, and take vengeance on the rule breakers!*"

Beer, The One, and Horton blast at the neon horde as it descends upon them, but Pants has played enough plushy shooters to know that the team and friends are doomed.

"Snap out of it, Pants!" Beer cries, his cracked glasses slipping down his face as he flings his fear at the murderous robots. "We have to try the Super Team Scaredy Attack, or whatever."

Channeling her fear into her souvenir bracelet, Pants joins hands with the rest of the team, and they fire their collective power at the crush of mascots marching down Maim Street. But it's no use. While they manage to slow the relentless surge, all their fear combined isn't enough to stop it.

Cowering behind the team, their merch guy says, "I'm starting to feel like this whole adventure was a bad idea, you guys."

"Gee, you think?" The One grumbles as he blasts at the angry rabble.

"Nonsense," The Other One says. "This adventure is nothing short of a complete success, filled with scares, surprises, the whole kabang. Plus, your ratings are through the roof!"

"Yes, but we're all about to become permanent park ghosts!" Beer argues. "This is the worst adventure we've ever been on."

"Sure, when you think of it like that…," the business boy counters. Appealing to the Dorks, he asks, "You guys are completely satisfied, right?"

Her skeleton costume dripping with digital slime, Otakween says, "Well, you managed to destroy Pants Team Pink, which is brule. But you also destroyed us, which is not as brule. So, I would rate your services two and a half stars."

"Hmph," the kid says. "I guess I'll just have to take my talent elsewhere."

"Would you?" The One pleads.

In a final attempt to save themselves, the Xenodorks yank their costume heads back on to blend in with the killer crowd. But having already identified the members of the evil team as biological humanoids, the mascots just keep coming. With nowhere left to run, Pants pulls her friends and enemies in for one last team hug before they're all ripped to shreds.

"I'm going to miss you guys," she sobs.

"Yeah, well…," Otakween grumbles inside her skeleton head. "We're going to miss you, too."

"Really?!" Pants squeals.

"Of course!" the Kween grudgingly admits. "You guys are the reason we started a team in the first place – so we could destroy you. But now that you're about to be wiped off the face of The Park, I realize that the universe isn't going to be the same without you. Luckily, we won't be around to see it."

Soon, they're all crying over the fun they're going to miss out on, and even The Other One fakes a few tears.

"Plahahaha," Ghosty howls. "*After a thousand space years, I finally get to have my park and play in it too!*"

But as the teams await their inevitable mauling, Pants realizes that the sound of the mascots' plush feet padding across the rubber road has suddenly ceased. Wrenching her eyelids apart, she nervously glances up Maim Street to find that the neon hairballs have frozen in their furry tracks.

"*What are you waiting for?!*" Ghosty barks. "*I command you to finish them!*" When the mascots fail to obey the ghost's orders, it descends into a spirited tantrum.

"I don't get it," Todd says. "Why did they stop?"

Feeling along the ground for his glasses, Beer asks, "Did we win?"

"Look…," The One tells them, pointing toward the night sky above the park gate. In a moment, the first rays of purple sunlight glimmer over the horizon and all becomes clear. "As our great-great-granddaddy would say, mornin' done come early…"

"*Nooo!*" Ghosty yowls. "*You stupid mascots. Get them!*"

Plodding across the fake yard, Horton throws his crumpled rulebook down in front of the ghost and tells it, "Rule two hundred eighty-seven: Scaredyland is only open at night."

"*This can't be happening!*" Ghosty says, frantically waving its paws in the air.

But the mascots ignore the ghost, turning away from their would-be prey to lumber back to their graves.

For fun, the team takes turns blasting what's left of the miniature ghost god, until it finally agrees to take them inside Mascot Manor to collect their exclusive merch. After they scan their bracelets and "sacrifice" their rules to the prize attic, they exit the haunted house carrying four black cases embossed with the Scaredyland logo. With viewership at its peak, everyone gathers around to witness the unboxing as the team reveals their prizes to the universe.

Proudly holding up her souvenir t-shirt, Pants reads, "'I survived Mascot Manor…'"

Flipping his around, Beer adds, "And on the back it says, 'Or did I?' Like maybe we were ghosts all along, I guess."

"Oh yeah…," The One says. "I get it."

"*And that's all you'll get!*" Ghosty howls from the safety of the Manor. "*Those souvenirs might last you five, ten, maybe even twenty space years if you wash them on low. But I am eternal-ish, and I will haunt you for the rest of your miserably short lives,* plahahahaha!"

Unmoved by the ghost's threats, The One says, "I doubt it."

"Hey!" Pants announces as she digs through her prize box. "We also each get to take home a pair of limited edition Scaredyland BK Ratch Techs!"

Staring at her bleary-eyed, the team's merch guy says, "That's a given."

"But here's the spooky part, you guys – *they're in my size.*"

Tired and bruised, the teams and their followers wander back out onto Maim Street and into the aftermath of a manufactured nightmare. A casualty of the mascot horde, the fractured Parkway is almost unrecognizable under all the clumps of neon fur and holographic slime.

Gazing out over the mess, The One says, "Welp, at least we don't have to clean up."

"Yeah…," Top5 concurs.

"That's one thing I think we can all agree on," Pants says, prompting the teams to dredge up an uncomfortable laugh for the fans.

"That's right, everything here is cromulent," The Other One says, talking into his phone as he strides up Maim Street. Briefly pausing to flash the others a patronizing grin, he tells the invisible listener, "You don't have to worry about a thing. It all went exactly as planned. I'll call you as soon as I get back to Con City and we can hash out the details." After he hangs up, he tells the teams, "Everyone agrees it was your best adventure yet, you guys."

They all stare at him for a long moment, until The One finally asks his sneaky counterpart, "Who the fish were you talking to?"

"Oh, that was Bexy Kreb, from the Amalgamated Ration Consortium," the boy says, kneeling down to wipe a blob of digital slime off his loafer. "She tuned in for the end of the adventure and liked what she saw. Thanks to all of you, the companies are moving forward with plans to reprogram and reopen Scaredyland. All they needed was a little demonstration to show them that the park is still in working order."

"Let me get this straight," Beer tells his brother's evil half. "Not only did you plan this whole fake adventure, but you convinced the Xenodorks to hire you to make *them* clean up the park, all while selling the ration makers on a new attraction? And I'm assuming they're not paying you in Park Bucks."

"Hey, I deserve full credits for my work!" The Other One argues. "What's the problem, anyway? Pants Team Pink gets their adventure, the Dorks get a ratings boost, the ARC gets a park with all the ghosts worked out, and I get a few hundred thousand crits for my effort. It's a win-win-win-win."

Throwing off her hollow skeleton head, Otakween grumbles, "You little chit, you almost got us all killed!"

But before the dark girl can sink her plush fingers into the boy, Pants steps between them and pleads, "Can't we all stop fighting and just sing a song? The adventure is over. We did it, together! The Other One might have lied to get us to come to Scaredyland and almost got our digital souls stuck here for all time, but somehow he ended up saving both of our shows. So, maybe in the end it's all okay?"

While the teams try to process this backward logic, Todd checks his phone and begins to squirm. "Uh, I don't want to alarm you guys, but I have some alarming news. The fans are jumping ship. They think the new adventure is proof that you faked *all* your adventures. It's not true, is it?"

"Of course not," Beer says. "You were here!"

"Right, right…," Todd mutters.

"What about *our* fans?!" Otakween asks.

"Uh…," Todd says as he scrolls. "What fans?"

Fumbling her phone, Pants cries, "It can't be true!" But it's too late. Most of the fans have already tuned out. Stepping away from The Other One, she tells Otakween, "Okay, now you can kill him."

But while the teams try to decide on a suitably painful punishment for the little business boy, he sneaks away up Maim Street, shouting, "No need to thank me. But if you're ever looking for another adventure, you know my screen name!"

Too exhausted to chase after him, the rest of them trudge up the rubber road with nothing to show for their efforts but a few lousy oversized t-shirts — inconceivably rare though they may be.

"So, what do we do now?" Pants asks. "I know, we should take an end of adventure team picture!"

The others pretend not to hear her, but she's determined not to let them ruin her fun. As they pass the photo booth, she slips behind the dark curtain and uses the token she's been hiding in her sock to start the timer.

While she waits for the flash to go off, she laments, "It's more fun with friends…"

As if sensing her sorrow, her ghost friend from the Gorewalk pops into the booth to scare her.

"Wahhh!" she screams, even though she's not really afraid.

Pants and Brilly take turns fake scaring each other until her token runs out. But when the pictures develop, she discovers that fake ghosts don't show up in photos, apparently.

ACT III

The Only Thing Left to Fear...
The Ultimate Final Last Episode?!

41

A ghostly quiet takes hold amongst the teams as they drag their sore feet, and all of Pants's bags, back toward the park entrance. Along the way, Todd tries to come up with a plan to turn things around, but no matter how he looks at it, he can't help thinking of the adventure as a total disaster that could bring about the end of the greatest show of all time. And it's all his fault.

"This is all your fault, you know," The One says, his cracked lips white with dried sugar.

"You're right…," Todd moans, burying his face in his hands.

As they exit the parkgrounds, and the digital slime finally disappears from their jackets, Beer says, "Well… everybody messes up sometimes, though usually not this bad. As long as you're willing to admit it, I guess we can forgive you, even though this will probably be our last episode."

"What?!" Pants cries, the blinking light in her left sneaker boot having gone out. "What do you mean it's the last episode? We're still a team, you guys! We can go on new adventures even if no one is watching."

But even Horton, who typically tries to remain neutral when it comes to making big team decisions, has to admit, "I think Beer is right. We can't even afford to fix the *Cuddler*, let alone finance another adventure. Without the fans, there is no show."

"You can't quit!" Otakween shouts, her mascot costume stuck in the turnstiles alongside the rest of the Xenodorks. "If there's one thing I've learned from this adventure it's that even though you guys are, like, the biggest chidiots in the universe, we still need you. And you need us. It's the only way to keep the shows interesting. Otherwise, who else are we going to annoy?"

"Well, what do you suggest?" Beer asks. "Some sort of team-up? That *would* give Courtney-chan and me a chance to hang out."

But as the blonde girl sheds her zombie costume, she juts her thumb in his direction.

"Fish no," the Kween says. "You guys are still the worst. But without us, your show wouldn't have lasted as long as it has."

"And without us, you wouldn't have any fans at all," The One points out. "But I think we have to face the hard truth – the shows are over."

Looking into her phone, Pants tearfully asks the handful of fans who are still watching, "Could this be the actual true end of Pants Team Pink, for real this time?"

With that question left dangling, Otakween, fairymajokocourtney-chan, Top5, and Howard Johnson abscond from the adventure in their newly pilfered Scaredyland apparel. Flashing their counterparts a series of offensive yet affectionate hand gestures, the Xenodorks slip through their portable teleporter back to wherever they came from, and a few space seconds later, the illegal device crumbles to the parking lot pavement.

As the team heads for the haunted train home, the sun casts its first bright rays over the Dark Side of the Park, and Brilly's voice calls out, *"Bye Pants! It was fun riding with you."* They turn back to find the ghost kid, the Caretaker, and a bunch of mangled racers waving from inside Scaredyland. *"I'll take care of your ghost leash while you're gone. Just don't forget to come back and visit!"*

Tears running down her cheeks, Pants tells him, "We will! I mean, we won't! We'll be back, someday." As the glowing spirits float back into the park, she says, "Maybe they were real ghosts after all…"

"That's impossible," Horton tells her. "I just saw one of those racer kids flicker. Real ghosts don't do that."

Flashing him a tired grin, she asks, "How do you know?"

Their long night out having finally reached its conclusion, with what promises to be one of the all-time worst sugar crashes on the horizon, the five of them ascend the crumbling platform to catch the haunted train back to the living world. An uncharacteristic quiet takes hold as the Park gnats swarm and the orange haze of morning washes over the forgotten remnants of attractions past. Huddled with the team in the bittersweet ache that tinges the end of every adventure, Todd suddenly understands why Scaredyland is only open at night – somehow the Dark Side of the Park seems a lot less scary in the light.

As the grinning fire ball peeks over the edge of The Park, Pants says, "I wonder how the ancient Parkgoers got the sun to smile."

"I think the prevailing wild theory involves the manipulation of gravitons and something about Maurice Ward's Starlite," Todd tells them with a shrug. "But the truth is, nobody knows."

The merch guy sleeps all the way through the ride back, and by the time they reach the deserted station on the other side of the track, the team has somehow come to an agreement to put the show on indefinite hiatus for retooling.

"What?!" Todd cries as he groggily stumbles off the train after them. "You're canceling the show without consulting me? You can't quit just because things have gotten a little tough. You'll survive this. We'll explain everything to the fans, and they'll start tuning back in. Pants, you agreed to this?"

"I don't want the show to end either," she says, a hint of the old pink sparkle glinting in her eyes. "But that's the thing about being part of a team. It's not about me."

When they get back to the *Cuddler*, Todd packs his souvenirs and says his goodbyes, promising to see them all again soon. But the truth is he's not sure what's going to happen now. He offers to stay while they figure out what comes next. But he gets the sense that this is something they have to figure out on their own.

Lacking the funds to pay the Park mules to finish fixing their giant feline ship, he's leaving the team all alone to weather the Playland's short night. But flashing them the Pants sign as he finishes hauling the remains of his comic book collection and the rest of his meager belongings out to his ship, something tells him that the team will live to see another adventure.

As for him, he has just enough crits left over from his Pants Con bonus to pay for a one-way starline ticket back to Earth. But before he says goodbye to The Park, he flies over to the Dark Side to collect one last souvenir. He spends the entire flight home re-watching the team's adventures from the beginning, and by the time he lands the *G.S.S. Minnow* in the dusty municipal parking lot, he's back to where they ended.

Tossing his bags into the dirt, he steps down onto the old planet and breathes in the rank dawn air, commenting, "I forgot how heavy it is here."

Clad in his EOL sandals, he awkwardly drags his bags out of the lot and through the dark back alleys of Hoboken, until he reaches the shuttered scrap shop he calls home. He fumbles his keys out of his pocket, but before he has a chance to open the back door, he discovers that the lock has been melted off.

"Oh, you gotta be fishing kidding me!" he cries, half expecting Ghosty to scold him as he shoves his way inside. "The kids on this planet are a bunch of savages with no merch ethic!" Dropping his bags, he pulls out his phone for protection as he feels his way through the back room. "If somebody's here, come out now and I won't hurt you, as long as you haven't broken any of my scrap."

When he reaches the counter out front, something crunches under his sandal, and he flips on the overhead light to find the cracked remains of a first release Fearsome Flush ghost. Scooping up the broken pieces of the rare toy, he looks out over the wreckage of his shop and utters a single sad whimper. The floor is strewn with piles of priceless magazines, the videotapes are all out of order, and his action figures have been scattered across the counter with a complete disregard for their accessories.

"It'll take forever to get this stuff resorted," Todd moans.

As he steps out into the store to mourn the scraps of his disorganized life, a familiar gruff voice warns him, "Don't move or you're gonna find yourself smelling like bad beer."

Todd turns around with his hands raised to find an old Earth lady pointing a highly odorous and extremely valuable Super Stinker at his honorary team jacket. "Mom?! What are you doing here? And why are you in your nightgown?"

"I guess the party's over," she says, lowering the antique water gun.

Detecting some suspicious rustling amongst the shelves behind her, Todd turns on the store lights only to discover half a dozen half-naked elderly Earthlings busily hiding their shame – namely the empty packaging from what had been his pristine collection of rare unopened rations.

"That's it, everybody out!" he announces. Glaring at his mom and the fake look of apology on her face, he says, "I'll yell at you later."

"I told you he's no fun," she grumbles as she follows her friends out into the alley.

When he tries to shut the door behind her, he remembers that the lock is broken and lets it hang on its hinge. The only thing keeping him from throwing in his souvenir Scaredyland beach towel, besides its incredible rarity, is the sweet piece of merch waiting for him out in his ship.

With the help of his hover-lift, he hauls the crate back to the shop and sets it down in the employee lounge next to the holo-tube, where no careless customers can get their grubby fingers on it. Using his phone to stream the last episode of *Pants Team Pink* to the old TV, he removes the bootleg wristband he swiped from The Other One and gets to work unboxing his prize.

Gazing into its plastic eyes, he tells the cosmic fish monster, "Fishtar, I don't think even you could have predicted this adventure."

He plugs the machine into a power strip behind the TV and nervously glances around the room as he digs a token out of the hidden pocket inside his honorary team jacket.

When Fishtar is finished divining, Todd plucks the card from the machine and reads, "'Your future isn't half bad. Advice: Invest in fortunes. Unlucky Number: ½.'"

"*Remember,*" Fishtar says. "*The only way to change your destiny is to feed Fishtar more tokens.*"

"Don't worry," Todd tells the monster as he slips the card into his pocket next to his other misfortunes. "I'll remember…"

Snatching a warm, half-finished, formerly highly collectible beer off the top of the tube, Todd flops down in his old Space Saver just in time to watch the credits roll.

"Chit, I missed the end." Maybe it's the ancient, possibly poison beer sloshing around his stomach, but after a brief deliberation, he points his phone at the screen and says, "Eh, what the fish? One more time, from the beginning!"

Todd raises his can to the team and settles in as Pants flies onto the screen, hurtling through the bright sky in the ship *princessfluffypants*, to deliver the classic disclaimer to him and any other fans who might be watching, *"The adventure is about to begin you guys, so hold on tight. And always remember, Pants Team Pink isn't just you or me — it's weee!"*

Author's Note

Like the last book, this one is a little bit of a detour. In
the spirit of its protagonists, I wrote it because I wanted
to do something purely for the fun of it. For some
reason I thought that meant it was going to be easy. But
in the end, it still managed to grind me up and spit me
out. Turns out it's hard work having fun.

A final thank you to Akira Toriyama for taking us all on
one of the great adventures. *"A Long time ago it started
with a simple encounter and now it comes back to us, it was nice
when you look at it."*

About the Author

Andrew Bixler crawled out of the same back alley as Harvey Pekar. He writes fiction designed to test the limits of your sanity. He is also co-host of Big Orange Couch: The 90s Nickelodeon Podcast.

For more about the author, news about upcoming books, and contact information, visit andrewbixler.com

For more about the Big Orange Couch podcast, visit bigorangecouch.podbean.com

Thanks for Reading

I am grateful that you chose to spend your hard-earned crits on my book. If you enjoyed this book, please spread the word to every sci-fi adventure fan you know. The fate of my world depends on it!

How Was the Ride?

If you've come this far, maybe you're willing to come a little further. I am an independent author, and I can use all the feedback I can get. Let me know what you think of this book by leaving a review on Amazon, Goodreads, or by shooting me a message!